THE PROMISE OF FOREVER

BROOKE HARRIS

Ebook ISBN: 978-1-80508-092-3
Paperback ISBN: 978-1-80508-093-0

Cover design: Emma Rogers
Cover images: Shutterstock

Published by Storm Publishing.
For further information, visit:
www.stormpublishing.co

ALSO BY BROOKE HARRIS

Memories of You

When You're Gone

My Daughter's Choice

For Coláiste Árainn Mhóir class of 2000
Thank you for the memories (and the fáinne óir) xx

'I loved her against reason,
against promise,
against peace,
against hope,
against happiness,
against all discouragement that could be.'
Charles Dickens, *Great Expectations*

PART ONE

ONE

DEE

March 2000

My ear is hot. The phone pressed against it is irritating. I switch to the other ear as Lainey, my best friend, goes on and on about Irish College. Or the Gaeltacht, as she calls it. As if she has any interest in improving her Irish.

'And there'll be lots of guys there. Not like bloody Saint Mary's. The Gaeltacht is nothing like school, I swear.'

I twirl the phone cord around my finger and stare at the double-sided brochure that our Irish teacher gave out in school today. It's not much bigger than a bookmark and it boasts a picture of a turquoise sea and some fishing boats on the front.

The slogan promises a fun summer of learning and making friends on *Inis Cloch Bheag*.

'Little rock island,' Lainey says, translating. 'Doesn't that sound cool?'

'Little stone island,' I correct her, and I can't think of anything that sounds less cool.

'Whatever, I was close,' Lainey says. 'Anyway, who cares about stupid Irish, this summer is all about getting out of this shithole for three weeks.'

I shift my gaze from a generic seaside picture and stare at the circular pattern in the hall carpet that I always think looks like a small alien face.

'Anyway, I better go,' Lainey says. 'My mam will kill me if I go over an hour again. She'll go on about the bill for a week.'

'Doesn't your mam want to talk to my mam? Something about lifts to camogie this weekend?'

'She can call her back.'

'Yeah, okay.'

'Right. Bye so. See you in school tomorrow.'

'Yeah.'

Lainey's end goes dead, and before I have time to hang up, the kitchen door creaks open and my mother appears in a floral apron with a wooden spoon in her hand.

'Off,' she says, pointing the round end of the spoon at me.

'She called me.'

Mam retracts the spoon and her expression softens. 'Tell Lainey I'll call her mother later. We're playing in Kilkenny this weekend. I'll drive. Will call into your Aunty Kitty while we're there.'

I stare at Mam's apron. There's a splash of red sauce. We're having spaghetti Bolognese. My favourite. I know for sure Irish College is no longer up for negotiation. It is already booked. I decide not to do tonight's maths homework. Lainey can't copy what I don't have. Lainey is one more forgotten copy away from detention. Maybe an hour with Mrs Livingston and her salmon breath will give her time to reflect. Her mam can tell my mam that Irish College is the best thing since sliced bread all she wants, but I'm never going to forgive any of them for ruining my summer.

TWO

DEE

June 2000

Four buses are parked outside Trinity. There's a bus bay, but two don't fit and block traffic. Car horns honk but the noise becomes a background sound after a while.

Dad turns up the nearest side street and pulls over.

'We're fine here,' he says. 'Everyone is parked arse-ways.'

Mam rolls down the window and sticks her head out.

'There's double yellow lines, Dessie. We'll get a ticket.'

Dad looks at me and rolls his eyes. He gets out of the car and opens the boot.

There's a squeal behind me and I turn round to find Lainey with her arms stretched out as wide as they go, as if I hadn't hugged the shit out of her last week when we finished school for the summer.

Her arms are round my neck as Dad slams my case down on the footpath and Mam gets out of the car, glancing up and down the road for the guards.

'Jaysus, Dee, how long are you goin' for?' Dad says.

'She needs layers, Dessie,' Mam says. 'It can be very cold up there.'

'It's Donegal,' Dad says. 'It's not the bleedin' Antarctic.'

'Bus B,' someone calls.

'That's us,' Lainey says, releasing my neck to link my arm instead.

'What? Already?'

'Yeah, c'mon. They wanna hit the road. Takes five hours. And then the ferry.'

'How d'ya know which bus we're on?'

Lainey puts her excitement on pause to stare at me.

'It's in your welcoming letter. Didn't you read it?'

I shrug. 'Course. Just forgot is all.'

My mind rewinds to sometime around Easter. Mam knocked three times, as always, on my bedroom door and entered before I answered.

'Here you are, love,' she said, passing me an envelope with my name and address handwritten on the front. Inside was a letter. *Cloch Bheag* was stamped at the top in large, swirly font. The rest was in Irish. I didn't read it.

'It says that you'll need to pack swimming togs. That's exciting. You love swimming.'

'In a pool. Not the Atlantic.'

Mam's excitement visibly deflated, like someone letting the air out of a balloon. We didn't speak of sea swimming again and I didn't read the English version on the back to find out what other activities there were to endure.

Mam wraps her arms round me and I take a deep breath. She smells of fabric softener and the musty perfume Dad bought her for Christmas.

'What will I do without you for the next three weeks, eh?'

You'll play golf with Lainey's mam and bitch about our camogie coach.

'I'll miss you too,' I say.

I mean it. I untangle myself from my mother and watch Dad slide my case into the bowel of the bus.

'Ah love.' Dad returns and dots a kiss on the top of my head with his voice cracking as if I might never come back.

Lainey's grip on my arm grows firmer. 'Bye, Mr and Mrs McKenna.'

Mam's suddenly panicky.

'Right. Right,' she says. 'You'll call, love. Won't you?'

I'll call.

'Where's your mam?' Mam asks Lainey.

Lainey glides her free arm through the air and points at the woman managing the cases hold as if she's getting paid for it.

'They're off, Mags. The girls are leaving,' Mam calls out.

Mrs Burke abandons a man trying to stuff a weathered bottle-green case on and hurries towards us.

'Have your togs?'

Lainey nods.

'Have your hurl?'

Lainey nods.

'Have your—'

'Have it all. We have to go. All the good seats will be gone.'

Lainey doesn't let me go as her mam hugs her and my parents hug me again. Then, linked, we ascend bus steps, shuffle down the aisle, take a seat close to the back and wave goodbye as the engine comes to life and we follow bus A and lead bus C.

Lainey unlinks me, plonks her knees on the seat and faces the back of the bus before we turn the first corner.

'Anyone got a cigarette?' she says, as if she smokes.

I hear laughter but I don't turn round. This is going to be a long summer.

. . .

The bus stops at some point in the north so we can pee and restock on sweets and crisps. Everyone uses the loo. And almost everyone buys more junk food. Lainey disappears and I queue alone to pay for popcorn and a bottle of 7up that's big enough to share. The lady behind the counter is telling me that my fiver is no good and I need to pay in sterling when Lainey returns with a pale patch around her lips where her heavy make-up has rubbed off.

'Shifted a really hot guy outside the boys' toilets,' she says.

Then she passes the lady English money and shoves the change in her pocket.

'He's on one of the other buses. Bus A, I think. All the hot guys are on bus A. Pity.'

I cradle the 7up in my arm like a baby and pass Lainey the popcorn.

'Should we switch?' she says

'Buses? What? No.'

'Okay. Fine. But we're sitting with them on the ferry.'

The bus smells of armpits, lollipops and salt and vinegar crisps. Lainey junked up on sugar is more entertaining than pissed Lainey. I can only imagine the brick Mrs Burke would shit if she saw her precious Elaine either way. Or my mam. My mam's face would be bloody hilarious.

Lainey makes do with the boys on bus B and spends the next two and a half hours playing some sort of card game that involves the losers kissing. Lainey loses a lot. I don't play and by the time we reach the port the boys have labelled Lainey great craic. They've also asked more than once if I'm frigid or gay.

'You're going to have to shift at least one of them,' Lainey tells me.

'I'm saving myself for bus A.'

Lainey rolls her eyes and we get off the bus. Hundreds of kids litter the small port car park and stare into the holds of buses waiting for the driver to pull out their case. Mine is one of the first off. But Lainey's is buried and we stand, shivering, for ages. The weather is entirely different up here than when we left in Dublin and I'm sorry I gave Mam such a hard time about packing jumpers and my warm coat now.

'Is it always this cold?' I say, my teeth chattering.

'Well, yeah. It's the Atlantic coast.'

'But it's June.'

'And?'

Lainey's case finally lands at her feet and we drag them behind us like boulders as we file onto the ferry. The boat is much smaller, older and wetter than the one in the brochure. The indoor, seated area is tiny and already full of other kids dressed for a much warmer day. Lainey leads the way and finds us a free spot next to the edge of the boat. I roll my case through a puddle as I follow.

'Do we get life jackets?' I ask.

Lainey laughs and turns away. No doubt to scan the boat for the bus A boys. I hold on to the edge with both hands. The engine groans and everyone cheers. I close my eyes. We're moving. Slowly at first. But soon excited chatter and giggles are replaced with the distinctive sound of a boat slicing through waves. The wind claws at my cheeks, and yet nonetheless the sea air brings with it a warming sense of tranquillity.

The island comes into view suddenly. As if someone is drawing a line on the horizon that grows bigger and bigger. Tucking the ferry neatly at the port is tedious and my hands are stiff and numb when I finally unwrap them from the edge and reach for my case. We shuffle off in reverse order as a small group of locals sitting on the wall stare and point.

'Islanders,' Lainey says, shaking her head. 'They come down to meet the ferry every year. S'pose they're curious who's coming.'

'Oh.'

'Don't know why they bother. It's not as if we're allowed anywhere near them.'

'Oh.'

'Yeah, just wait. You'll get the lecture tonight from your Bean an Tí. *'Only mix with the children from your course,'* Lainey mimics. 'Shauna Monroe from the year above said so.'

'Oh come on. You don't believe anything Shauna "the gossip" Monroe says, do you?'

Lainey's eyes narrow as if she's disgusted that I would question her source.

'Eh, Shauna has been to the Gaeltacht four times.'

'And I thought going once was bad.'

Lainey's eyes close a fraction more and I'm questioning if she can see at all now.

'Anywaaay,' she says, long and exaggerated. 'Apparently one of the island boys got a girl off the course pregnant a few years ago and her parents went apeshit. She was our age so...'

'A baby at sixteen. Wow.'

'I know, right. Like how shit would that be?'

There's a mix of boys and girls on the wall. Two girls and three boys, I count. All teenagers except one. Who can't be much more than six. He reminds me of a cartoon character, with dark hair that sticks up and out at odd angles, and he has huge, round brown eyes like milk chocolate buttons. One of the teenage boys is looking out for him. Keeping an arm round his waist and making sure he doesn't fall off the wall. Brothers, I suspect. The older boy has the same eyes, but his hair is combed. I panic when he catches me staring and dart my eyes to the ground. I stumble and almost trip over my case but Lainey manages to steady me before I hit the ground. My face is on fire as the group on the wall snigger.

'Oh Dee, no,' Lainey says. 'Even I wouldn't go near the

islanders. It's not worth it. You'll get sent home if they catch you. And that would leave me stuck here on my own. So don't you bloody dare.'

Their laughter seems to echo around the port. Lainey has nothing to worry about. I won't be going near them.

THREE

FIONN

'Oh Christ, here we go,' Dad says, as he makes a big song and dance of pointing at the calendar hanging on the kitchen wall.

'Oh Christ, here we go,' Seány echoes.

My little brother sits with his back to the window and butters some toast. The majority of the butter is going on the table.

'Language, Seány,' Dad says.

Mam sighs but she's smiling as she takes over the toast-buttering.

Dad makes a paper boat out of the gold foil from the inside of his cigarette box and points out the window towards a grumpy sea that tosses and turns as if it doesn't like mornings either. 'I hope none of them are pukers this year.'

He passes the small, delicate boat to Seány, whose face lights up. He immediately begins sailing it across his toast.

'The ferry gets in at five,' Mam says. 'After that don't you dare set foot back in this house.' She points the buttery knife towards me. 'Do you hear me, Fionn? Not a foot.'

'What are you looking at me for?'

'Ah love. Three weeks without the telly. It's not easy on them,' Dad says.

'As if you or I had television at their age. They'll live. Seány can pop in to watch *Rugrats* and *Pokémon* for an hour or two when the girls are in class. Other than that you're all to stay put in the shed.'

'Doesn't help that you keep calling it the shed, love.'

'I've ten teenage girls arriving this evening. I don't care what you call it, Seán. So long as you're all out there by the time they get here.'

Dad converted the garage into a pretty decent summer house a few years ago. We've a bedroom each since my older brother, Oisín, moved to London, and there's soft carpet that feels like cotton wool under bare feet. There's no heating, mind. Dad says starting the day with a cold shower will make men out of us. I'm pretty sure Seány would go the whole summer without a wash if Mam forgot about him. Mam never forgets about anything though.

I've a pretty good memory too. I remember when Mam first started keeping students. Dad slipped on the boat and did his back in. He couldn't fish for months. That was the first summer our house was not our own. It belonged to teenage girls with accents like the people on telly. They smelt like flowers and they were loud. Mam slept in the house with the girls. But anyone male was banished.

The garage was full of lobster traps and fishing nets. It smelt funny. We slept in sleeping bags, anywhere there was space. They were the best summers. Oisín and I slept outside some- times. Dad said we had to promise not to tell our mother. We would lie on the grass in our sleeping bags, and stare up at the night sky. Oisín could see shapes among the stars. Heroes from old legends. I could never see them, but I said I could. One night I woke when the wind pinched my cheeks. Clouds hid the moon and stars. I wasn't frightened at first, but when I couldn't find Oisín I began to panic. I was running towards the garage to find Dad when I tripped. A rusty fishing hook caught in my knee. I screamed and screamed. I woke Dad. And Mam. And all the girls.

Mam brought me into the house. Washed my knee and patched me up. The girls were nice. One who smelt like strawberries gave me a lollipop and another told me I was brave. Mam said I was brave too. But I could tell she was mad. As mad as the sea during a storm. Dad too. At first, I thought they were angry with me. But it was Oisín. He was nowhere to be found and one of the girls was missing too.

When the girls were long gone and the house was our home again and Dad had just come back from the mainland with a Christmas tree, people from Dublin arrived at our door. Mam made tea but that didn't stop the shouting and arguing. The people from Dublin said their daughter was having a baby and Oisín was the father.

The following summer was different. Seány was a baby and we didn't move out of the house. I saw the Gaeltacht kids around the island like every summer but Mam said if she caught Oisín or me talking to them she'd redden our arses with the wooden spoon. Oisín barely spoke to anyone any more so I didn't think Mam had anything to worry about. We didn't leave our house the summer after that either. Oisín sat his leaving cert that year and three days after his final exam he moved to London. Mam cried for the next three days. And on the fourth day we moved into the newly converted garage as ten teenage girls filled our house with accents, and perfume and noise. That was five years ago. I'll sit my leaving cert next summer. And I think about moving to London too. I won't. It would break Mam's heart.

'Right, best get out of your hair, then,' Dad says, swiping a slice of toast from Seány's plate and demolishing half with a single bite.

Seány protests with a scowl and his hands on his hips. Dad puts the other half back.

'Are you ready?' Dad says, looking at me.

I'm still in my boxers and a greyish-beige t-shirt that used to be white.

'And where do you think the two of you are going?' Mam says.

The look on Dad's face is priceless. The question seems rhetorical, but Mam's eyes are wide and look like two giant marbles that might fall to the ground if she shakes her head. She wants an answer and Dad knows it. But he knows better than to say anything that might ruffle her feathers on the day the Gaeltacht kids arrive.

'Aren't you forgetting someone?' Mam points to Seány.

There's butter all over his face.

Dad steps back. 'Oh, not a chance, love. The boat is nowhere for a boy Seány's age. I can't keep an eye on him and fish at the same time.'

'I'm not asking.'

'Right, you two. You heard your mother. We're leaving in five minutes.'

'Thanks,' Mam says, kissing Dad. He gathers her into his arms and kisses her back. Hard.

'They're kissing,' Seány says, as if I don't have eyes of my own. 'Gross.'

Outside Dad adjusts his woolly hat and puts one on Seány's head too. Seány pulls it off straight away.

'June m'arse,' Dad says, zipping up his coat. 'That wind would blow the balls off a brass monkey.'

I'm more worried about trying to keep warm tonight but I don't say anything. Dad seems to have enough on his mind today.

He shoves a fiver into my hand and my fingers curl instinctively round it. 'Keep an eye on this little man, okay?' He ruffles

Seány's hair. 'Buy him a few sweeties and stay out of trouble. And whatever you do, stay away from the house. My life won't be worth living if your mother sets eyes on you.'

'You're going out on the boat on your own?'

The sea is grey and yawning. I can hear the swish-wallop of frothy waves slapping the shore.

'Don't look so worried. It's just a few hours to collect the crab cages. I'll be back before it gets too rough.'

I take Seány by the hand. It'll take us an hour to walk across the island to the shop and by then it should be opening. It's going to be a long day.

FOUR

FIONN

I sit on the port wall with my friends. I keep an arm round Seány's waist as he sucks on his fifth lollipop of the day, and watch wobbly sea legs stumble off the ferry. The mainland kids are distinctively different to me and my friends. They wear brightly coloured jumpers with the manufactures advertising on the front. *Adidas. Nike. L.A. Gear.* My navy jumper is hand-knitted and used to belong to Oisín. It suddenly feels more scratchy than usual. I count the pukers. Six, I think. With faces as stony grey as the wall. I can't wait to tell Dad later. His money was on at least ten in this weather.

'Look, Look! Do you see your one in the red jumper?' John Paul, my best friend, says.

His elbow in my ribs is redundant. I've already seen her. In fact, I can't take my eyes off her. She's not a puker. But she doesn't like the water. I can see it on her face. She doesn't want to be here and who could blame her?

'The size of her case.' John Paul is pointing. I want to tell him to stop. 'Where the hell does she think she's going?'

Katie and Aisling begin to laugh.

Seány pulls the lollipop out of his mouth and squirms and

turns. My arm round him tightens instinctively and he presses down on it, trying to free himself.

'Who? Who?' he says. 'I want to see.'

'She's hot though. I'll give her that,' John Paul says.

I try not to think about it.

Katie tucks a strand of hair behind her ear and tilts her head. 'Do you think she's hotter than us?'

'No. No way.' John Paul's answer is quick and almost believable. Almost. 'What age do you think she is?' he says. 'I'm going to say the same as us.'

I nod.

'God, I hope she's staying in your house.'

Aisling's expression is wholly unimpressed. 'Why are we still talking about her? Everyone knows Fionn is afraid of mainland girls.'

I inhale until salty sea air fills my lungs so full I think I might burst. Holding it, I stare at Aisling O'Brien. I don't like her, I decide. Actually, I've known for a while Aisling isn't my type of person. Every time I shift her, I swear it'll be the last. She bit my lip once. Probably saw it on *Home and Away* or read about it in a magazine, and thought it was sexy. It wasn't. It was just weird. I still shifted her a couple of times after that. Once when I was bored and another time when I was drunk. But I promise myself definitively right here and now, I will never again kiss her. Never.

'She *is* very pretty,' Katie says, placing a hand above her eyes and squinting as she stares.

'From here, sure.' Aisling shrugs. 'But up close, who knows?'

'I plan to get up close to find out.' John Paul thrusts his hips.

'Ugh. You're disgusting,' Katie says.

He does it again. And again.

'Seriously, JP,' I say when Seány begins to copy.

John Paul laughs. 'He's a chip off the aul block. Your big

brother knew how to show a mainland girl a good time, didn't he?'

If Seány wasn't here I'd punch him, I think.

'I know you're afraid mainland girls bite,' John Paul says.

'Aisling bites,' Katie says with a snorty giggle.

Aisling drills her fist into Katie's arm. 'Shut up. Shut up.'

'But take it from me they don't. Unless you want them to,' John Paul says.

'Have you met my mother?' I say.

John Paul is my next-door neighbour and we've been best friends for as long as I can remember. His mam and my mam are equally close.

'Who do you think I'm afraid of? The mainland girls or my mam?'

'I love your mam,' Katie says.

'Everyone does. But trust me... she tells you to do some-thing, you best just do it. Same goes for not doing something.'

'But just look at her...' John Paul says, and he points at the girl in the red jumper again and this time I know for sure she notices. Her eyes meet mine for a split second and then she stumbles. I jump off the wall, as if I could catch her from here. I scare the shit out of Seány and he begins to cry.

'Sorry, buddy,' I say.

'Why d'you do that?' He stomps his foot.

'I don't know,' I say, feeling almost as scared as Seány. Scared that, no matter what Mam says, I'm not sure I can stay away from this girl.

I hope so hard that she's staying in a different house. A house on the far side of the island. As far away from me as possible.

FIVE

DEE

A blonde lady in a multicoloured tracksuit and a clipboard in her hand calls my name. And Lainey's. And several other girls. Every single word after that floats in the air like clouds that I can't reach.

'Oh my God, what is she saying?' I whisper to Lainey, who is listening and nodding.

'Shh.' Lainey places a finger against her lips. 'We have to speak Irish now. If they catch you speaking English they'll send you home.'

Not for the first time, I wonder if that would be such a bad thing.

Soon after, a minibus arrives to gather groups of us and deposit us at our accommodation. Thick black smoke blows from the exhaust. The sliding door is blue, the bonnet is yellow; the rest is white and rusting as if it's pieced together from LEGO.

We are last to be collected. The kids from the wall left a while ago. I don't admit it out loud but I'm curious about where they go. I wonder what they do to occupy their time living here. From what I can see, there's a small beach adjacent to the port.

A corner shop, a post office and a pub. A phone box. Walls made from round grey stones stacked on top of each other that look like they might roll away at any moment.

The rest of the island is a grid of narrow, winding back roads and grassy hills that stretch on for miles. Houses, a church and a school are dotted haphazardly among the hills, like a life-size game of Monopoly.

The bus stops at the top of the steepest hill where a burgundy bungalow observes the ocean.

'We're here,' someone announces as we get off.

There's a sheep in the front garden. Chilling out the way family dogs usually do. At the side of the house are several rusty fishing cages. I crane my neck to get a better look but I pull it back quickly when the little boy from the port comes into view. I'd recognise his cartoon-like hair anywhere. Seeing me, he tucks between the cages. His bright blue jacket isn't easy to disguise. I wave. He stands up and waves back. His older brother appears suddenly. Closer than before, I can see how alike they are. Their tanned faces, dark hair, square shoulders.

'Seány,' he says, sounding like an angry parent as he tugs the little boy by the hood of his jacket. 'You know you're not supposed to be out here.'

Seány wriggles free and runs round the back of the house. His brother stares at me. His eyes are narrow and seem to search my face for something. It's the same way he looked at me at the port. I wave awkwardly. He doesn't wave back. Instead, he turns and disappears round the back of the house too.

The Bean an Tí, a tiny woman with dark brown hair that she piles on her head in a neat bun, meets us at the front door and introduces herself as Lorna O'Connell. She lets us choose our own rooms. Lainey and I take the smallest room. A box bedroom with bunk beds pushed up against the window that overlooks the ocean. Four friends from Tipperary take the largest room. And four other girls who travelled alone share a third and final room. Once we've unpacked, Lorna calls us to the kitchen and ten teenage girls sit round a large table and tuck into oven-warm scones and raspberry jam. By the time we finish eating you could be convinced we've all been friends for years.

Lorna runs through the house rules quickly. We will have three meals a day and we will take turns washing up and cleaning the kitchen after each meal. No boys. No bitching or bullying. Five minutes in the shower each, max. And lights out at eleven p.m. She says it in Irish first, but recaps in English to be sure we understand.

Lainey and I volunteer to clean the kitchen first and the others are more than happy to leave us to it.

'No boys,' Lainey says as she ducks a plate into sudsy water. 'What does she think this is? Prison?'

'I think she means in the house,' I say, taking the plate from her and wiping it all over with the tea towel.

'She better. Boys are the best part of coming here.'

Lainey has talked about the Gaeltacht since we were in primary school. Her older siblings all came here before her and she counted down the years until it was her turn, as if three weeks stuck on an island off the coast of Donegal is some sort of teenage rite of passage. It's a passage I'd rather not write.

SIX

DEE

In bed, with the lights off by eleven, Lainey recalls all the boys she shifted on the bus. Then she tells me about all the boys she plans to shift from the other buses.

I lie on the top bunk with my eyes closed and wait for her to stop talking so I can fall asleep.

'You're going to have to kiss someone up here, you know.'

It sounds like a direct order and I've no doubt that's how she means it.

I pretend to be asleep.

'Dee? Dee, are you listening to me?'

After a while gentle snoring fills the room. I turn towards the window and I'm about to place my pillow over my head when I hear a noise outside. I recognise the distinctive bleating of a sheep, but something is wrong. The poor thing is in distress. I hope it's not trapped or caught in something. The fishing cages spring to mind. I hold my breath and listen but all I can hear is Lainey's damn snoring. Another bleat wails and I'm on my knees in bed and draw back the curtains.

A near full moon lights up the garden and I muffle a laugh

as Seány tries to wrestle a runner out of the sheep's mouth. I crack the window open just a smidge and listen.

'Give it back,' Seány commands.

The sheep is winning, hands down.

Seány tugs harder. 'Give it back. Oh, please give it back. Mam will kill me.'

The sheep ignores the little boy; his grip on the black and gold runner is holding fast. The same can't be said for the air bubble on the back of the old runner. It won't withstand much more of this tug-of-war.

'I said give. It. Back. You big, fluffy eejit.'

Seány's face twists, his shoulders shake and he begins to cry. 'Mam is going to kill me,' he repeats, as if trying to plead with the sheep's conscience to show mercy.

I don't want Lorna to kill this sweet boy and, before I have time to think it through, I find myself whispering, 'Don't let go.'

Seány searches the moonlit garden for a person to go with my voice. He finds me inside the window and a toothy smile creeps across his face.

'Don't let go. Hang on. I'm coming to help.'

I open the window as wide as it goes and pop my head through. But I've completely misjudged the size of the gap. My shoulders make it out, but I run into difficulty somewhere around my waist and hips.

'Jump,' Seány tells me with enthusiasm and confidence.

'I can't. I'll land on my head.'

He laughs at the idea of it.

'I can fit.' He giggles.

I try to edge back the way I came but my feet have lost contact with the bed and I'm afraid I'll fall backwards and crash onto the chest of drawers, or worse still crush Lainey in her sleep.

'Lainey. Lainey, wake up,' I whisper.

'You're stuck,' Seány tells me, laughing so hard I think he'll lose his grip on the runner.

'Lainey, wake up,' I try again somewhere between a raspy whisper and actual shouting. It's hopeless. Our sleepovers throughout the years have taught me that Lainey is a deep sleeper. I can't wake her without rousing the rest of the house too. I'm contemplating full-scale shouting for help when I hear his voice.

'What the—'

'She's stuck,' Seány tells his older brother, who has appeared from round the corner of the house.

He looks at me. Then at the sheep. Then at Seány. He grabs a fistful of wool from the back of the sheep's neck and shakes. The shoe falls to the ground and Seány snatches it and clutches it to his chest. His brother lets the sheep go and it runs away. Seány wraps his arms round his brother's thigh and I feel a familiar pang inside. I wonder what it's like to have a sibling. I decide it must be marvellous.

He turns his attention towards me. My stomach aches, trapped see-sawing between the garden and the bedroom, but not so much that I can't feel my face glow and sting with mortification.

'What happened here?' he asks.

His lips twitch and he's stifling a laugh, I can tell.

'She was helping,' Seány explains.

'Helping?'

My face is on fire as he walks towards the window, stopping when we're face-to-face.

'I'll pull you out,' he says.

I shake my head. 'I'll fall.'

'You won't.'

'I—'

'I'll catch you.'

I take a deep breath and resign to let this boy rescue me. He places his finger over his lip and I nod, promising not to make a sound. He reaches his arms up and hooks them under mine. His skin is warm and my breath catches.

'Three. Two. One,' he whispers.

He shimmies backwards and I edge forwards. It's unbearably awkward and a little painful.

'Wait, wait,' I say, panicking.

In a blink we're on the ground. Me on top of him. I scamper to my feet. 'Are you hurt? Did I hurt you?'

He lies in silence for a moment and I'm certain I've caused him an injury. I can only imagine the trouble we will both be in when Lorna finds out. Slowly, he gets to his feet and dusts himself off. I sweep my eyes over him, searching for possible cuts or a sprain.

'I'm not hurt,' he says, as if my gaze makes him uncomfortable.

I am more embarrassed than ever.

'Please don't tell anybody about this?' His accent is thick and fits him like a glove.

'Trust me. I won't.'

The sense that we're not supposed to be talking is strong. And strange. Even Seány seems button-lipped as he stands clinging to his runner as if it's a cuddly toy.

'Not even your friend,' he says, rolling onto his tiptoes in an attempt to better see into our room and catch a glimpse of the snoring body on the bottom bunk.

'Not even Lainey. I promise.'

'Lainey,' he says, as if he's trying her name on for size.

'Well, Elaine.'

'And what's your name?'

'Deirdre. But everyone calls me Dee.'

'Dee-Dee,' Seány whispers.

I don't correct him. I quite like it.

'I'm Seány.' He taps his chest, then points to his brother. 'And this is Fionn.'

Fionn. I repeat his name silently in my head, trying to make it fit him. Fionn means fair-haired and shy one in Irish folklore; we learned a poem about it in school last month. But the boy in front of me has hair so dark it's almost black and eyes that match.

'Nice to meet you both,' I say. 'So this is your house, then?'

'Not for the next three weeks,' Fionn says, and I detect a hint of resentment. I'm not sure if it's directed at me or the situation in general.

'Lorna's your mam.'

They both nod.

'So do students stay in your house every summer?'

'Yup,' Seány says. 'And we sleep in the shed. Or under the stars sometimes.'

'It's a converted garage,' Fionn explains.

'Under the stars sounds amazing. I've never slept outside.'

Fionn's eyes widen but he doesn't say anything.

'Do you usually talk to the girls through the window?' The question seems to hit the ground and I wish I could shovel the words back into my mouth.

'Fionn never, ever, ever talks to the girls. Mam says we're not s'posed to.'

'Oh.'

'It's just easier that way,' Fionn says.

I think about the rumour Lainey shared at the port. About an island boy getting a student pregnant. I'm starting to wonder if there might be some truth to it.

'Fionn and JP said you're the prettiest girl they've ever seen in their whole entire lives. That's JP's house there.' Seány points to a bungalow in the distance. 'JP said he wants to know if you bite?'

Even in the moonlight I can see Fionn blush.

'What do you think?'

Seány shakes his head. 'My teacher says biting will get you in lots and lots of trouble.'

I laugh and Lainey stirs and groans. There's a moment where I think all three of us are holding our breath, before we hear contented snoring again.

'Can we go beach now?' Seány asks.

Fionn nods.

'Okay byeeee,' Seány says, clearly done with this conversation.

'Wait. Wait! You're not really going to take him to the beach in the dark, are you?'

Fionn smirks. It's mischievous and cocky and it melts me.

'Where you from? Dublin?'

'Yeah.' I nod, wondering if my accent has given me away. 'Clondalkin.'

'Right, so you spend your time in shopping centres, cinemas, arcades? That sort of thing.'

He sums up my weekends effortlessly.

'As you can see, we have water. So we go swimming.'

'At night though?'

'Stars aren't out during the day.'

I inhale and enjoy the distinctive smell of the ocean. I would trade every weekend at the cinema or the arcade for one night swimming under the stars.

'Wanna come?'

'Seány,' Fionn scolds, but it's too late; the question is out there, and Fionn watches me with curious eyes as he waits for an answer.

We both know I should say no. But somehow, 'yes' slips pasts my lips.

And we're all smiling. But no one more than Seány.

SEVEN

DEE

I stuff my pillow under the duvet. It doesn't look as much like a sleeping somebody as I would like, but in the dark it's better than nothing. I pull on a tracksuit over my pyjamas and I don't bother with a coat. Although, I regret it as soon as I climb through the window and the night air gnaws at my skin.

'We'll take the car,' Fionn whispers, as he pulls the window closed behind me.

'You drive?'

He nods. I thought he was my age but he must be seventeen or older, I realise.

My heart races as I follow Fionn and Seány across the garden. By the time we reach the gate my palms are sweating. It's both exhilarating and terrifying. I know Lainey is going to kill me for not waking her so she could come too. But I didn't want to share. The realisation shocks me. I don't want to share Fionn with anyone except Seány.

A silver car is tucked at the side of the narrow road. I don't know much about cars. I know my dad drives a Nissan because it says so on the back. This car says nothing and I realise there's a small hole where the emblem should be. There's a large hole in the bonnet. I can see parts of the engine and battery and pipes and wires. Two of the wheels are without hubcaps and rust eats the bottoms of the doors. I wait for Fionn to call out the joke and tell me we're walking.

'We need to give it a push,' he says. 'Just to the bottom of the hill. Can't start it up here. It'll wake my mam.'

He hops into the driver's seat and Seány walks round to the back of the car and places his palms, still chubby with baby fat, flat against the boot.

'Come on, Dee-Dee,' he says. 'You gotta push too.'

The sense that I shouldn't be doing this is overwhelming. *God, I wish I woke Lainey.*

Fionn rolls down the window and sticks his head out. 'Three... two... one... push.'

Seány and I grunt and force our weight into the back of the car. Slowly, it starts to move. At first our feet slip and slide on the gritty road and I find myself warning Seány to be careful.

'Don't fall,' I say. 'Don't fall.'

His legs pick up pace. We're running and pushing and the car is gathering speed. Soon we're racing just trying to keep up, but the car gets away from us. I hear the splutter and purr as the engine chugs to life and Seány jumps in the air, cheering. I feel his hand slot into mine like a jigsaw piece finding where it belongs.

'Let's go,' he cheers.

At the bottom of the hill, we jump into the car. Me in the front next to Fionn and Seány in the back. We wind our way down the narrow roads and back to the port. If possible, the island is even more whimsical in the moonlight, and the magic of a place time has left sleeping snatches my breath away.

EIGHT

FIONN

I take it handy driving to the port. Dee is gripping the edges of the seat so tight her knuckles are white.

'Are you driving long?' she asks me.

'About four years.'

'What? How old are you?'

I can see her staring at me from the corner of my eye.

'Sixteen. Nearly seventeen. I started driving when I was twelve.'

'Twelve!'

'Everyone drives young up here.'

Her grip on the seat grows even tighter.

'My brother showed me how. My older brother. He lives in London now.'

I don't talk about Oisín much. But if she asks me questions, I'll answer them. She doesn't.

Dee glances over her shoulder and says, 'He's asleep.'

The winding and bumpy journey to the port always rocks Seány to sleep. I've never actually taken him into the water at night. Mam would hit the roof if I so much as let him dip a toe. But I look forward to the day he's old enough to swim beside

me. The way I used to with Oisín. And in the meantime, I'll
enjoy the drive. Never more so than I enjoy the drive tonight.
Dee spends most of the journey looking out the window. At
what, I can't tell. There's nothing to see. I find myself embarrassed by the nothingness of it all. The empty fields that roll on
for miles. The empty roads that twist and turn. The empty
ruins of old cottages dotted here and there like broken
Monopoly houses. At least the sky is full, I think, taking my eyes
off the road for a second to glance at the countless stars shim-
mering overhead.

I don't know where all that bullshit about swimming under
the stars came from. I must have seen it on TV at some stage
and regurgitated it like some wannabe surfer. Mam would kill
me if she found out. Panic momentarily rises but I try not to
think about it. Because even if we make it no further, even if
just sitting in the car next to her is as far as tonight goes, then it
will all have been worth it. Because already, this is the best
night of my life.

All too soon we're at the beach and I have to figure out my
next move. I wish I'd thought this far ahead. I park, turn off the
engine and the lights and we sit in silence for a moment. I can
hear Seány's deep breath and the waves lapping the shore.

'What are we going to do now?' Dee asks, looking at Seány
again. 'He was so excited. But I really don't think we should
wake him.'

'No. No. Definitely not.'

'Should we go back?'

'We're here now. Might as well dip our toes, at least.'

The bridge of Dee's nose wrinkles while she mulls it over.
I'm certain she's going to ask me to take her back to the house
and I've no doubt the disappointment is written all over my
face.

'It's cold,' she says. 'Shouldn't we cover him with a blanket
or something?'

I can't pull my jumper off fast enough. I lean into the back and tuck it around him.

Then I get out of the car and wait for her. She doesn't follow. I run my hands up and down my arms trying to keep warm.

'I must be mad,' I tell the moon and the stars, and they blink back, disagreeing.

I make the snap decision to pull off my clothes, right down to my boxers, and wade into the water as if I'm auditioning for *Baywatch*. It bites as if the sea has teeth and I regret the decision. But, when I turn look back, she's out of the car.

'Come on,' I call to her, waving my arms above my head.

Balancing on one leg, she peels off a runner and a sock. She wobbles as she repeats on the other side. I give her time to adjust to the damp sand between her toes. I can't tell if she likes it. Slowly, she tiptoes closer. Her feet barely graze the sand, like a delicate pixie.

I hold my breath as she lets a wave roll over her feet. Then another. And another.

'It's freezing,' she announces.

'It's not so bad once you're out a bit. Roll your pants up.'

She shakes her head. 'No way.'

'You don't know what you're missing.'

'I do actually. Hypothermia.'

I can't fully feel my legs any more as I wade back to her. Her teeth chatter.

'C'mere,' I say, not thinking about it as I envelop her in my arms.

The tip of her head sits just under my nose. Her hair smells like Mrs Clancy's orchard in summer. The water dances around our toes for a long time. I should suggest going back to the car. Going home. But I could stay here all night if she let me. Finally, when I'm not cold any more and I hope she isn't either, she pulls away from me.

'You've never done this before, have you?'

'Done what?'

'Taken your little brother for a swim in the middle of the night.'

I think about lying. I lock my eyes on hers ready to tell her she's wrong but my mouth doesn't open. She sees right through me as if I am made of glass. For her I am. Lying to her would shatter me.

'How did you know?'

She smirks. 'Seány told me he can't swim. He said he's starting lessons in September.'

'The little shit. I'm gonna kill him...'

Dee folds her arms and sighs and I think she might be mad until I notice she has a dimple in her left cheek. How did I not see that before? It suits her. The more she tries to keep a straight face, the more her dimple tells me she wants to smile.

My heart soars.

'And what else did he tell you?' I ask, glancing over my shoulder to check on the car.

'He said you buy him lollipops when you want him to keep a secret. Usually from your mam.'

'I... eh...' I search my brain for words to defend myself but all that comes out is a deep throaty groan.

Dee giggles. 'S'okay. I won't tell anyone. But you might have to buy me a lollipop too.'

'Deal.'

The corner of her lips twist into a half smile, half smirk, and she tilts her head as she says, 'And he said you'd buy him an ice pop if you got a kiss—'

'What? No I didn't. Dee, I swear. I never said that.'

Dee's smile widens and her laughter that follows makes the fine hairs on the back of my neck stand to attention.

'He didn't say that, did he?' I say, catching on.

She shrugs. 'He mentioned the lollipop. The ice pop was my idea.'

'Do you want me to kiss you?'

I cringe. I can't believe how naïve my question sounds.

She nods.

My heart races and I'm suddenly roasting. Sweating maybe. Thankfully, she takes the lead. I feel her body against mine once more. Her chest, her hips, her arms round my waist. I can't catch my breath and I pray she doesn't notice. Then I feel them. Her lips against mine. Warm and soft. Home. I don't know if she leaned closer or if I did. It all happened so fast. And now time has stopped. The waves don't roll, the stars don't twinkle, the world doesn't spin. There is nothing but Dee and me, standing with our bare feet in the sand kissing. It is everything.

NINE

DEE

I grip each side of the open window as if I'm about to stretch the gap wider to fit through. I bring my knee onto the sill and I pause and turn back. Fionn is watching.

'Did you really say I'm the prettiest girl you've ever seen?'

'I. Am. Going. To. Kill. That. Kid.'

My cheeks are warm and in daylight I think they'd be pink.

'Goodnight, Fionn.'

'Night, Dee.'

I climb through the window and close it behind me. I peel off my tracksuit and dump it on the floor before I climb into bed and pull the duvet right up to my chin. My feet are still numb and I shiver.

'Dee, what the hell did you do?' Lainey's voice slices through the air.

'You're awake.'

'Are you mad? Are you trying to get yourself sent home?'

I loosen the duvet around my neck, suddenly feeling choked. I don't want to go home. Not any more.

'Your parents will kill you, you know. And, they won't get a refund.'

'Shh, shh,' I tell her.

'I hope it was worth it,' she says, sounding exactly like her mam did that time we got caught drinking in the park round the corner from her house.

It absolutely was not worth it. I puked for two days and I was grounded for a week. This time is so different.

The bed creaks and moves and even in the dark I know Lainey is sitting up.

'Tell me everything,' she says. 'Is he a good kisser?'

Lainey and I whisper until we can't keep our eyes open. When the alarm goes off the next morning my body feels physically under attack and I stuff my head under the pillow. It's a while before I follow the scent of pancakes, too exhausted to eat.

By the time I reach the kitchen, everyone is almost finished eating. Heads look up and Lainey shoots me a worried glare. I pour a glass of orange juice, and sit in the empty seat next to her.

Two of the girls from Tipperary arrive in the kitchen after me. Erin and Lizzie. I can't remember which is which. They're still in their pyjamas too.

'I can't believe we have to get up at eight a.m. in summer, Liz,' Erin complains.

'So stupid,' Lizzie agrees.

'Eh, there's no pancakes left, girls,' someone at the table says.

I smile at Lainey and she smiles back. We've quickly been sorted into morning and non-morning people and it's all very unremarkable. Thankfully.

Chatting and laughter follows until Lorna pops her head round the door and tells us we need to hurry. The walk to the school will take a half an hour and there's rain forecast.

Lainey and I dress in the outfits we picked out yesterday. Blue hipster jeans and long-sleeve crop tops sitting just above our belly buttons. Lainey's is purple. Mine is mint. We'll swap tomorrow.

We wait for the girls on wash-up duty and all ten of us leave the house together. We bump into a group of twelve boys on the way. They're all from a house further up the hill. One of them counts us as if we're cattle in a pen.

'There's only ten of you. Where's the other two?'

'There's ten in our house altogether,' Lainey says.

'What?' The look of disappointment on his face is priceless. 'But there's twelve of us.'

'Right... and...'

'Well, it doesn't add up,' he says.

'Eh, you don't get one of us each, you know,' Lainey tells him as she twirls a strand of her long blonde hair round her fingers, very clearly hinting that he can have her if he likes.

'You're the prettiest one in your house,' he tells her.

And before they exchange any more conversation, they're at the side of the road with their chests pressed against each other. His arms round her waist and hers are clasped behind his neck and they start kissing.

I walk on with the rest of the girls, knowing Lainey will catch up. She finds me in the schoolyard. I'm huddled with the girls from our house, chatting in broken Irish. Lainey complains that I abandoned her and that he was a dishwasher. She hopes the next one is better. My stomach turns a little.

Above the school door is a commemorative plaque. *St Brigit's 1898* The building looks as if it hasn't changed in its 102-year existence. Inside, there are three very small classrooms. All the windows overlook the ocean.

Class isn't so bad. It's nothing like real school. The lady in the brightly coloured tracksuit that we first met at the port is our teacher. She's wearing a less bright tracksuit today. We sit in a circle on uncomfortable plastic chairs and talk about ourselves.

It reminds me of the AA meetings advertised on telly. I whisper my observation to Lainey and she agrees.

The morning passes quickly. I enjoy the relaxed atmosphere in the classroom, even if my Irish isn't quite up to the near-fluent level of the other kids. When it's time to go home for lunch, Lainey disappears round the back of the school with a boy from the class below us. The boys from our neighbouring house join us again, much to the girls' delight. Most of them break into pairs as they walk. I'm happy to keep to myself and I suspect this is how most of our walks to and from school will play out.

The walk home is mostly uphill, but it's not until we turn the first corner that my breath catches. Fionn, Seány and the other teenagers from the port are sitting on the low roadside wall.

'Are they waiting for us?' Lizzie says.

'I think so,' Erin agrees.

Lizzie's face lights up, much to the other boy's disappointment.

'Hi Dee-Dee.' Seány waves.

Fionn grabs his hand and shoves it back down by his side. Seány's bottom lip drops and my heart aches when I think he might cry. Lizzie and Erin stare at me, questioningly. I shrug.

The boy beside Fionn hops off the wall. His legs are long and skinny and his jeans come to a stop above his white socks.

'Are you staying in Lorna's house?' he asks.

Lizzie nods as if she's lost her voice.

'That's his mam.' The tall boy points to Fionn, who is shaking his head.

'Leave me out of this, John Paul. You're asking for trouble.'

'You're not supposed to be talking to us, are you?' Erin asks.

'No, they're bleedin' not,' a deep voice behind us says.

I turn round to find the owner of the voice holding Lainey's hand. His chest is puffed out as if it's full of too much air and he's glaring at Fionn and John Paul.

'C'mon,' Fionn says, standing up and lifting Seány off the wall. 'We should get back.'

'That's it,' the loud-mouthed boy shouts as they walk away. 'Get back under that rock where you belong.'

John Paul spins round and there's a collective intake of breath.

'Fight! Fight! Fight!' the boys chant.

One of the island girls rolls onto her tiptoes and places her hand on John Paul's shoulder. 'Leave it,' she says. 'He's just a scumbag. They always are.'

'Here, what'd you call us?' Erin says, slamming her hands onto her hips.

'Fight! Fight! Fight!' the boys chant again, but their attention has shifted onto Erin and the girl.

They charge at one and another and there's slapping, and hair-pulling and screeching. Everyone watches, horrified and thrilled. Seány starts to cry and Fionn scoops him into his arms and walks away. And I want nothing more than to walk away with them.

TEN

DEE

All ten of us sit at the kitchen table with our heads bowed. Lorna's words are angry as she daps a wet cotton ball above Erin's eye.

'How dare you? Disgraceful behaviour. Hooligans.'

But behind the hiss in her tone and all her head-shaking is so much sadness. Lorna is a tiny woman, and it feels as if she is that way because the weight of the world has crushed her. I hope later, when we're all gone to bed, Seány or Fionn come inside and hug her for a long time.

'Never, not ever, in all my years as a Bean an Tí, have I seen such shocking carry-on.'

The fight escalated quickly. Everyone threw a punch or received one. My eye hurts when I blink. But Lainey says if I wear purple eyeshadow it won't look so bad. Lorna threatens to have us all sent home. But she makes us soup and brown bread and tells us we can't go to the first céilí tonight. None of us argue and we retreat to our rooms for the remainder of a long day.

I'm in a deep sleep when the knocking on the window

starts. Lainey is on her feet first and I don't rouse fully until I hear whispering.

'Fionn,' I say, scrambling to the end of my bed.

'Hi Dee-Dee.' Seány stands beside him, waving.

'Hi.' I smile.

'You didn't say hello today,' Seány tells me.

I'm searching my brain for a way to explain when Fionn reaches his hand through the window and says, 'You coming?'

Without a second thought I nod.

'Oh, you have got to be kidding me?' Lainey says.

'You won't tell anyone, will you?'

'As if. What do you think I am? A snitch?' Lainey rolls her eyes. 'Anyway, I'm coming too.'

'What?'

'I had a similar problem,' Fionn says.

He gestures towards the road, where John Paul is waiting. Lainey pushes past me and climbs through the window first. She runs towards the road, much to John Paul's delight. I follow and reach for Fionn's hand but I feel small, chubby fingers and look down to find Seány's hand slotted into mine.

'You're my best friend,' Seány tells me.

'You're mine too.'

'Hey.' Lainey turns her head over her shoulder and makes a funny face.

Seány laughs and Fionn warns him to be quiet.

'C'mon, little man. It's piggy-back time,' John Paul says.

He crouches on his hunkers. Seány's fingers escape mine and he charges forward and climbs on board.

'Are you sure about this?' I say, as we cross the garden. 'After today...'

Fionn holds my hand. 'After today, I can't really get in any more trouble than I already am.'

'What? You weren't even there.'

'Try telling that to my mam. John Paul's mam was on the phone to her all afternoon and...'

'And, I know exactly what you mean.'

I think about Lainey's mam and my mam's long, long phone calls. Lainey and I don't stand a chance.

John Paul, Seány and Lainey lead the way and I don't ask where we're going. It doesn't matter anyway. I am happy to follow.

'Apparently Mam is very disappointed in me for dragging Seány into it.' Fionn sighs.

'That's not fair. You protected him. You took him away.'

'That's not the version Mrs Leary told my mam.'

'Oh God. Do you want me to explain? I can tell Lorna what really happened.'

'No. Jesus. No. Then she'll know we've been talking. Would make it all worse.'

'Yeah. S'pose.'

I feel Fionn's fingers tighten round mine.

'Have you been grounded?' I ask. 'My mam always goes with grounding.'

'I wish. I have to go out on the boat with my dad for the rest of the summer.'

'Don't you like fishing?'

'I can't think of anything worse. My parents just sort of assume I'll take over the boat in a few years. But I hate fishing. The smell.' Fionn retches. 'The smell is definitely the worst part. Takes days to wash stinking fish out of your hair and by that time you're back on the bloody boat.'

'You should tell your parents. Maybe they'll understand.'

I wince as I feel hypocrisy sting. I've played camogie since Junior Infants. Twelve years of Sunday mornings on the pitch. Summer's not so bad. But in winter I can't feel my fingers or toes. A belt of the hurl against cold fingers is the worst pain I know. Mam played for her county in the sixties and relives her glory years through me.

'My brother was supposed to take over the family business but since he's gone...'

'Will he come back?'

'No.'

'You must miss him.'

'Yeah. A lot. I'm going to visit though. Maybe even bring Seány with me.'

'Cool. London is cool. I've been a few times.'

'Seány's never been to the mainland. London would blow his mind.'

'No way, really? He's spent his whole life on the island?'

Fionn stops walking and looks at me. I think I've offended him.

'It's not that unusual. We only need to go to the mainland for a big food shop and my mam does that.'

I want to ask Fionn if he's ever been to the mainland. But the question feels rude or loaded or something. Besides, I think I already know the answer.

'We're very different people,' Fionn tells me.

I shake my head. 'No. We're not. We just live in very different places.'

ELEVEN

DEE

After the big fight on our way home from school, the remainder
of my three weeks on Cloch Bheag plays out rather unremark-
ably. The routine is monotonous and yet somehow we don't
grow tired of it. Every morning starts with school, including
Saturday. Then lunch and wash-up duty. Lainey and I volunteer for more than our fair share but we enjoy the time with
Lorna in the kitchen. She shares stories of island life and I make
a conscious effort to play down how invested I am in her anec-
dotes about Fionn and his brothers. Afternoons are filled with
organised games. Basketball, badminton, table tennis, swimming. I never go swimming. If I couldn't get in the water for
Fionn I wouldn't do it for anyone else. Lainey has accused me of
being a dry shite so often now, I'm sure it will stick even when
we go back home. There are céilís every evening. And climbing
through the window every night after. I've seen more of Cloch
Bheag in three weeks than I have seen of Clondalkin in sixteen
years. The beach, the sand dunes, the lighthouse, the hills, the
cliffs. Each place more beautiful and wonderful than the next.

Fionn was right. It is hard to wash the smell of fish out of
hair. It bothers him a lot. I don't mind it. I joke that, when I go

home, I might have to stand beside the fish counter in Dunnes so I'm reminded of him. He doesn't laugh. But John Paul does.

'I wish you didn't got to go,' Seány tells me when Fionn breaks the news to him that I'm going home on the ten o'clock ferry tomorrow.

Fionn, Seány and I sit on the edge of the beach where the sand meets the grassy bank. Seány sits between me and Fionn with his head dropped on my shoulder. We dig our bare toes into the sand and wait for Seány to fall asleep, the way he usually does. Lainey and John Paul's laughter pierces the night air. They splash in the sea and try to duck each other under. They don't seem to feel the cold. I've never seen Lainey so happy. Or known her to kiss a boy more than once before. I honestly believe she will miss John Paul as much as I will miss Fionn.

'When will you come back?' Seány asks.

The question hangs in the air as Fionn looks at me. He's afraid of my answer.

'Soon,' I say.

'You shouldn't lie to him,' Fionn tells me. 'It's not fair. He'll be waiting for you. And if you're never coming back—'

'Why wouldn't I come back?'

'Why would you?'

I inhale sharply. 'Cloch Bheag doesn't belong to you. I can come back whenever I want.'

'That wasn't what I meant. You're doing your leaving cert next summer, so obviously you won't be coming to the Gaeltacht again.'

'And if I'm not a student there will be no one to tell us we can't see each other.'

Fionn makes a face. He doesn't believe I'll come back. It hurts.

'My friends are going on a girls' holiday to Ibiza when we finish school. Maybe I'll come here instead.'

Fionn laughs. 'Sure.'

'I *am* coming back!'

'Yay.' Seány claps his hands.

Fionn shakes his head.

I take Seány's hand and I wrap my baby finger round his. 'I pinkie promise I will come back, okay?'

Seány smiles and soon he's asleep. Fionn lays him flat on the sand and covers him with the blanket we've taken to keeping in the car. He sits on the opposite side of me and we kiss and talk and kiss.

'You pinkie promised,' he whispers. 'Do you know how serious that is to a six-year-old?'

My heart hurts. I'm not ready to go.

I wrap my little finger round Fionn's and he pulls his hand away and digs his heals into the sand. He's angry. Awkward. Scared. I know. Because I feel the same. I take his hand and try again. This time he doesn't pull away.

'I pinkie promise,' I say. 'I pinkie promise Seány I will be back. But mostly I promise you. I promise, Fionn. I promise.'

TWELVE

FIONN

October 2000

I don't hate my time on the boat as much as I thought I would. After mastering the ropes during the summer, I go out with Dad almost every Saturday now. He won't say, but I can tell his old back injury is bothering him. He's walking with a limp, and worry is written all over Mam's face as winter approaches.

I bring my school bag with me, usually. I study a lot, getting As in geography and maths. Mam says if I keep up the hard work, I could have the points to go to Trinity or UCD. Dad says he doesn't know anything about college but if Mam says it's a good idea then it must be. John Paul says I'm a dickhead with notions. He says I have Cloch Bheag in my blood and any man who thinks they can change their blood gets what they deserve.

'We're not built for book learning. We're fishermen.'

I hear his father in him when he talks crap like that. I would study every hour of every day if it brought me closer to Dublin and closer to Dee. I miss her just as much as I thought I would and I know Seány does too.

Seány has started going to the mainland now. He tags along with Mam on Fridays when she's doing her big food shop. She complains that she has to wait until he's finished school to catch the ferry and her whole day is gone, but I can tell how much they love the stolen hours together. They go for hot chocolate and collect our week's post from the mainland post office. I like to think Seány intercepts our letters from Dee before Mam has a chance to set eyes on them. Mam must know Dee has been keeping in touch but she has never said a word. And neither have I.

On Friday evenings I help Seány read his letter and write his reply. I try to save my letter to read on the boat. I'm almost never able to. I write my reply at sea though, always.

Libasheen
Cloch Bheag
Co. Donegal
24/10/00

15 Hilbert Grove
Clondalkin
Dublin 22

Dear Dee,

I miss you too. Is your ankle okay? I can't believe you played on even though it was sprained. How many camogie matches will you miss now? Hopefully lots. At least there's a bright side to an injury.
I haven't told John Paul that Lainey has a new boyfriend yet.

He's still going on and on about her, and I don't want to break his heart.

I think I might be coming to Dublin in February for our school tour. I know it's not as cool as your tour to France but everyone is really excited. It's an overnight thing too, so maybe we could meet up? I'd probably have to sneak out a hotel window or something, but you did it enough times for me. I'm sure we can make it work. Will keep you posted.

Lots of love,

Fionn x

THIRTEEN

DEE

February 2001

'Dee, phone?' Mam calls out.

I'm in the middle of changing from my uniform into my gear for camogie training. I hurry into the hall in my jersey paired with my school skirt and my tights.

Mam looks me up and down and shakes her head.

'Don't be long. I'm waiting for your Aunty Kitty to call. Her gallstones are at her and I want to hear how she got on at the doctor.'

I take the phone and wait for Mam to walk back into the kitchen and close the door behind her before I speak.

'Hello.'

'Hey. Hi,' Fionn says.

'What's wrong?'

'What? How do you know there's something wrong?'

'Just do. You sound funny.'

I hear him swallow.

'I can't come to Dublin after all.'

'Oh.' I shrink. The disappointment is almost overwhelming. It's Tuesday. Fionn was supposed to get here on Thursday afternoon. There was a load of touristy crap he had to do with his class and then, at 11 p.m., I was going to meet him outside Jury's Hotel at Christchurch. We've been talking about it for months. Making a foolproof plan. I know it meant as much to him as it did to me. Something must be very wrong for him to back out now.

'Is everything okay?'

'My mam read our letters.'

'What?' I grip the phone tighter, furious with Lorna. 'Why would she do that?'

'I don't know. She's never read them before and I'm pretty sure she's known for ages that we're keeping in touch.'

'Do you think she suspected something?'

'Yeah. Definitely. She has some sort of bloody sixth sense. Anyway, she won't let me go on the tour anymore. Says she can't trust me.'

'Oh Fionn. I'm so sorry. I feel like this is all my fault. If I hadn't written that whole big thing about going to the park in the dark and showing you the Ha'penny Bridge and stuff. I'm so sorry.'

'It's not your fault, Dee. I should have been more careful. Hidden the letters. Or burned them after I read them or something.'

'Can you talk to her? Promise that you'll behave and stuff.'

'No. Her mind is made up. She said I'm just like my brother and if she doesn't step in now I'll ruin my life.'

Fionn has never told me why Oisín moved to London. But it doesn't take a rocket scientist to work out that he was running away from something. Or someone.

'I really wanted to see you.' My voice is a barely audible whisper. Fionn's is equally soft when he says, 'Yeah. Me too.'

The kitchen door creaks open and Mam's head appears in the gap. 'Right, love. You need to get ready for training. Lainey's mam will be here in fifteen minutes.'

'Okay. In a minute,' I say.

The kitchen door opens fully and Mam steps forward. She glares at me.

'Not in a minute, Deirdre. Now.'

I nod. 'I've gotta go,' I whisper into the receiver.

'Okay. I'll call you tomorrow.'

'Okay. Bye.'

'Bye.'

Mam's face returns to normal as I hang up and she's smiling when she says, 'I've a toasted sandwich made for you.'

'My ankle is sore,' I tell her. 'I think I should skip training.'

'Really?' Mam folds her arms.

'Yeah. I think my old sprain is acting up.'

'I know what's acting up and it's not your ankle. Get dressed and eat your sandwich. You can't keep Mrs Burke waiting.'

I nod and shuffle back to my room to finish changing. I'm dreading training tonight. Not because my ankle hurts. It doesn't. But I can't bear the thoughts of listening to Lainey drone on for an hour about how she was right.

FOURTEEN

DEE

'You're never going to see him again, you know,' Lainey says as we clatter the sliotar back and forth to one another, warming up. 'The summer was great craic but it was forever ago. You need to move on. Like me. I'm so over John Paul.'

Lainey reverted to her old ways as soon as we set foot on the ferry home. She'd kissed a boy at the back of the bus by the time we reached Letterkenny and a different one in the loos at the halfway stop. And so many more since then that I've lost track.

'You need a new guy,' she tells me as we move on to laps of the pitch. 'Next disco you're shifting someone and that's final.'

'Fionn will be here for college in September,' I remind her, as I do often.

I'm more out of breath than usual and the coach barks at me to stop talking and keep running.

'If Fionn gets the points,' Lainey says.

'Why wouldn't he?'

'Just sayin'...'

'Well don't just say,' I tell her, picking up my pace.

'Jesus. Are we in a race?' Lainey puffs.

'And he'll probably be here a good bit over the summer,' I

continue, my breath noticeably laboured. 'He'll be eighteen then so his parents won't be able to stop him.'

Lainey begins to lag behind.

'What are you two doing?' the coach shouts. 'Stop messing and run properly or I'll have you lapping the pitch ten times more.'

'He'll be stuck on that boat all summer, Dee. You know it. I know it. And if he's honest, Fionn knows it.'

'What's wrong with helping his dad out? I think it's admirable.'

'It is. But it also means he won't be up here for trips to the zoo, or the beach or the cinema or all that other stuff you two talk about. He's a fisherman, Dee. Fishermen have to fish.'

'Not all summer.'

'Girls!' the coach shouts, again. 'I swear...' His face is puce. It makes Lainey and me laugh. 'Right, that's it. Off. Off the pitch. You're both on a one-match ban.'

I smile, delighted. We step off the grassy pitch and onto the gravel. Our boots crunch with each step, calling our teammates' attention.

'For fuck's sake.' Lainey grunts. 'I'll never make captain now. Thank you very bloody much, Fionn.'

FIFTEEN

FIONN

May 2001

Seány hasn't spoken to me in almost two whole days. I bought him a lollipop in Dickies' shop yesterday and he said he didn't want it – although he did sneak it out of my jacket pocket later. I broke it to him yesterday that I might be moving to Dublin soon and it didn't go down well. The worst part is, I know exactly how he feels. My heart broke when Oisín moved to London. I've never told anyone that. I probably never will. I recognise the same pain in Seány's eyes. But I'm not Oisín. I *will* come back.

'I'll be home for Halloween,' I try to reassure him as he sits on the edge of my bed, swinging his feet with just socks, no shoes, back and forth. 'I'll take you trick-or-treating. I'll even dress up,' I say.

Seány is unimpressed.

'And Christmas. There's no way I'd miss Christmas. And I'll be back for mid-terms.'

'And weekends?' he asks, bringing his legs to a stop.

'Erm... some...'

'Fridays?'

'Maybe not that many Fridays,' I say.

'But we gots to write our letters to Dee-Dee on Fridays.'

I think about my future Fridays. With Dee. Lazy afternoons in the pub, maybe. Or the park if the weather's nice. There'll be so much to do in Dublin, there won't be enough Fridays in a lifetime. I can barely contain my excitement as I count down the months.

'You're a big boy now. You can read the letters yourself.'

'No I can't,' he says, and the disappointment on his face makes me look away.

Seány is a good reader. Mam says he reads more like a ten-year-old than someone who's only seven.

'I'll tell you what? How about some Fridays, when you're bigger, you come to Dublin to visit me. We can go to the zoo. You'd like that, wouldn't you?'

Seány's face lights up and my guilt abates.

'I love elephants.'

I nod. I know.

'And can Dee-Dee come too?'

'Yes. Absolutely!'

I am equally as excited as my little brother about a potential trip to the zoo. I've seen it on TV but I've never been, of course. Maybe that's where Dee and I could go first. Although I'm sure she's already been. Lots of times.

Seány jumps off my bed and scurries across the floor, almost slipping in his stocking feet.

'Hey, hey, hey. Where are you off to in such a hurry?'

'I gots to write to Dee-Dee. I gots to tell her we're going to the zoo. You're the best, Fionn. The best.'

Seány crashes into Mam in the doorway and a basket of laundry nearly tumbles out of her arms.

'Slow down, young man,' she says, 'You'll split your head open if you fall.'

Mam has spent our whole childhoods worrying for the safety of our skulls. 'Don't climb those rocks, you'll split your head open. Don't jump on the bed, you'll split your head open. Don't run around in the dark, you'll split your head open.'

I turn eighteen in four weeks, coincidently the day the leaving cert starts, and my head is perfectly fine. I'm sure Seány's will be too.

'He's just excited,' I tell her. 'We were talking about the zoo in Dublin.'

'You two are friends again, then?' She smiles as she sets a basket down at the end of my bed.

'Yeah.'

'Good. Good.'

She begins to fold clothes from the basket and put them away in my drawers.

'Much more to do?' she asks, glancing at the geography book open on my desk.

'Nah,' I lie. 'Does Dad need some help?'

Mam smiles and dots a kiss on the top of my head.

'Thanks, love,' she says. 'You know it won't be just your little brother who misses you when you go to college, don't you?'

'I know.'

I try not to think about how much I'll miss them all too.

SIXTEEN

DEE

Wednesday, 7 June 2001

Why is the day the leaving cert starts always the hottest bloody day of the year? It rained all last week. But today? God is trying to melt rocks!

After school I drop my bag on the hall floor and hurry upstairs to fetch my phone. There are two text messages waiting for me. Both are from a new number. I don't need to read them to know who they're from. I flick my eyes over the first message. It was sent this morning but hadn't come through before I left for school.

> :) Gt a fone 4 bday!
>
> Gud Luck 2dy
>
> Fionn x

And the second was sent just seconds ago...

I can barely punch out my reply fast enough.

English paper two was exhausting, to be honest. All the poets Mrs Livingston predicted came up and I almost ran out of time brain-spilling every last thing I knew about Kavanagh and Heaney. Lainey said she thought it went well too.

'Yeah, yeah. It was grand,' she said, as we walked the long way home so we could stop into the shop and get some Kool Pops. 'My Nanna Linda lit a candle for me, so I'm not worried.'

It was hard to keep a straight face.

'What?' Lainey said, opening her Kool Pop with her teeth.

'You didn't study a single poet. Your granny could light every candle in the church; I don't think it's going to help.'

Lainey shrugged and sucked on her brown-black, cola-flavoured ice pop.

'Well, we've Irish paper one tomorrow,' she said. 'Let's see who's laughing then.'

Lainey is right. Despite last summer in the Gaeltacht, Irish is still by far my worst subject. I'm not worried I'll fail, but I am worried a crappy result will bring my overall points crashing down.

I try not to think about it as I change into my favourite Adidas tracksuit and hang my uniform up so it's ready for tomorrow. My tummy rumbles and I head downstairs towards the smell of a roast. I'm surprised Mam hasn't followed me upstairs with a million questions about my day.

In the kitchen, I find Dad's home from work already. He's sitting at the table in his high-visibility county council jacket. His hands are cradled round a cup of tea and he doesn't look up to acknowledge I've walked in. The small TV next to the microwave is on. Mam and Dad are glued to it.

'English went well,' I say.

Mam waves her hand as if she's swatting an irritating fly. 'Shh. Shh.'

I bend and look into the oven. A chicken is browning. 'All the ones I studied came up,' I continue.

'Dee.' Dad sounds strange, as if he's in the distance. He points towards the TV. 'Dee. Look. Isn't that where you were last summer? That island out past Donegal.'

I stare at the screen. It takes a moment before my jaw drops and my chest constricts.

I stare past the reporter on the screen and focus on the familiar scene behind him. The sea. The beach. The port. *Cloch Bheag.*

'It's not known at this time what caused the crash between two fishing vessels this afternoon. There are a number of fatalities, with a child suspected to be among the dead.'

The camera zooms over the reporter's shoulder. The sea shimmers and sparkles under sun-kisses. The water with the audacity to behave as if today is ordinary. Acting as if it hasn't just gobbled a nightmare.

My first thought is of Fionn. The fear that he was at sea steals my breath. What if he was there? Hurt. It takes longer than is reasonable to realise that he couldn't be in two places at once. Fionn was sitting safely in an exam hall today. The relief that follows almost brings tears. I choke them back as Mam, Dad and I continue watching the news.

'Do we have an idea of how many people were aboard?' the lady in the studio asks.

The reporter presses his finger to his ear and shakes his head. 'Not at this time, Rebecca, no. The vessels would have names too, of course. But as yet none of the information is available.'

'Who in their right senses would bring a child out on one of those boats,' Mam says. 'Reckless. Completely reckless.'

I wish I knew more about Mr O'Connell's boat. Did Fionn tell me what colour it was? Blue, or maybe green. Did it have a name? I don't think so. Mostly, I search my exhausted brain for what he said about the boat's safety. Something about it being no place for a child. Mr O'Connell said Seány wasn't allowed on the boat. *Thank God.*

'Are you all right, love? You're awfully pale,' Dad says, finally pulling his eyes away from the TV and raising his cup of tea.

'It's so sad,' I say. 'They're just people doing their job and now they're gone.'

'Whole families destroyed,' Mam says. 'Fishing is usually a family business.'

'Yeah. Yes it is,' I say, knowingly.

I try to remember if John Paul's dad is a fisherman too. I think so. I hope it wasn't his family involved. I wonder if Lainey is watching. Cloch Bheag disappears off screen and the lady in the studio shifts the focus to something about fuel prices due to increase next week.

Mam rolls her eyes. 'Brilliant. As if we're not paying enough already. I'm never voting for that shower of feckers in government again.'

'Sure it's the same no matter who's in power, Bernie,' Dad says.

I leave the room and Mam calls after me. 'Deirdre. Come back here, young lady. How did the exams go?'

'Grand,' I shout back, and continue to make my way up the stairs.

I grab my phone and hope I've credit.

> Did u c d news?

Lainey's reply is instant.

What news?

> On TV.
>
> Cloch Bheag.
>
> d boat crash.

What? No.

Is it on now?

> No. Over.
>
> So sad. Ppl dead.

Did u txt Fionn?

> No. Dnt no wht 2 say.
>
> fraid he mite no sum1

Txt him

> OK

I try several approaches to the message.

~~Hi. I saw d news.~~
~~Hope ur ok~~
~~Hi. Jst checkin ur ok~~

~~Hi. If u need 2 tlk~~
~~Im here~~

In the end I decide not to talk directly about it.

> Hey. Hope u had nice bday.
>
> Gud lck 2moro.
>
> Not dat u need it 4 Irish.
>
> Wish I cud say d same.
>
> D xx

I stare at my phone for a long time. Mam calls me for dinner and I find it hard to eat. We talk about how my exams went today and how I'm feeling about the rest. We don't talk about what we saw on the news earlier. After dinner I return to my room and I hear Mam and Dad talking about me.

'Do you think the exams went badly today?' Mam says.

'She said they were good,' Dad replies.

'But she seems very off. She was very pale earlier. I hope she's not coming down with something. Not in the middle of her exams. That would be terrible.'

'I think she's more upset about that boat crash than she's letting on,' Dad says.

'Ah, not at all. Sure she couldn't stand it up there. Do you remember the fuss she kicked up about having to go?'

I close my door so I don't have to hear any more. I text Lainey again.

> He didnt txt bk

> JP no txt 2

> I hav bad feelin

> Me 2

Want 2 go 4 wlk

Yeh. C u at d shop in 5min

OK

SEVENTEEN

DEE

I check my phone again before bed. Fionn still hasn't replied to my last message. Worry sits inside me like a physical thing. A rock. A stone. Something big and hard, taking up too much space and crushing everything else. I want to cut it out and throw it away. Today my biggest worry was doing badly in Irish. I wish that was all I had to care about now.

Sleep comes until my phone rings. The sound cuts through the night air where it doesn't belong. Groggily, I hold it to my ear.

'Hello.'

'They're gone. Dee. They're gone.'

I sit up, wide awake.

'Who?'

'He's gone.'

Fionn's words are slurred. He's drunk, I think. I try again.

'Who?'

There's no reply. Fionn is still on the line. I can hear heavy breathing. I can hear his heart breaking.

'Is it JP?' I ask, barely able to push the words out past tears that want to fall.

John Paul is younger than Fionn. By a couple of months. He's still seventeen. Technically a child. A child like on the news.

Fionn swallows hard.

'Seány's gone.'

I almost drop the phone. I can't breathe. I don't think I can breathe.

'But... but... but... no. He can't be. Your dad doesn't let him on the boat.'

'Dad's dead. Dad and Seány are dead. They drowned, Dee. They fucking drowned.'

I stand up and pace in a circle. I say something about this not being right and something else about this can't be happening. And then I cry. And Fionn cries and he feels so incredibly far away. No one has ever felt further away than Fionn does from me right now.

'I have to go,' Fionn says. 'Mam's in bits. I can't leave her on her own for long.'

'Yeah. Yeah, of course. Is there anything I can do?'

'No. There's nothing anyone can do now.'

The line goes dead without a goodbye and I sit on my bed and cry myself back to sleep.

EIGHTEEN

DEE

I sit at the kitchen table in my uniform. I'm twirling my spoon around a bowl of Coco Pops and watching as the milk turns brown. The sun is blasting through the kitchen window and warming my back. It's seven thirty and already another glorious day. I think about Seány running around warm sand in his bare feet.

Lainey has heard the news. She texted me to say John Paul told her. She said John Paul's family weren't involved. I didn't reply. There is nothing to say. Lainey didn't text again. I don't think she has words either.

'Ah love, you need to eat something,' Mam says, as she fills the kettle and flicks it on. She's wearing her fluffy pink dressing gown and matching slippers as usual. 'I know Irish isn't your best subject. But worrying about it isn't going to do much good.'

'I'm not worried about it.'

'Good. Good. Glad to hear it. Eat up, then. I thought you loved Coco Pops.'

I've never loved Coco Pops. They always go soggy before you get to the bottom of the bowl. But how little that seems to matter today. The kettle begins to boil and I concentrate on the background sound as I stand up and scrape my cereal into the bin. Mam is furious about the waste and goes on and on about it until the doorbell rings, cutting her off as she walks away to answer it.

'Lainey's here,' Mam shouts back.

Lainey never calls to the door. I meet her at the end of my road, always. But I suppose today is nothing like always. I grab my bag and pass Mam in the hall.

'Good luck, love.'

She kisses my cheek and goes back to making tea for my dad.

Lainey wraps her arms round me, knocking my bag off my shoulder.

'Fuck, Dee. I can't believe it. Fionn must be in bits. Have you heard from him?'

'Yeah. Just for a minute. He couldn't talk for long. Couldn't leave his mam on her own.'

'Oh God. Poor Lorna. Can you imagine?'

I can't. I don't want to.

'Should we go to the funeral?'

I break away. I hadn't thought about the funeral. How had that not come into my head?

Lainey bends down and picks up my bag. 'Could your dad give us a lift?' she asks.

I shrug.

'John Paul says the funeral is this Saturday so...'

'Girls.' Mam's voice reappears behind us. 'What are you doing? You're going to be late.'

'Did you see the news, Mrs McKenna?' Lainey asks.

Mam looks confused for a moment before she nods and says, 'I did. I did. Terribly sad, isn't it?'

'I was just telling Dee we should go to the funeral. Show our respects, you know.'

'The funeral. For the fishermen?'

My eyes narrow, willing Lainey to shut up, but she's looking past me and at Mam.

'Lorna was our Bean an Tí and it's her family who died, so—'

Mam clutches her chest. 'The child who drowned?'

'Yeah. Seány. He was seven.'

'Oh Christ. Dee, why didn't you tell me?'

I exhale. I don't know why.

'God, that's just so, so awful. We'll have to send flowers or something. That poor woman.'

'Yeah, it's really sad,' Lainey says. 'Do you think Mr McKenna might be able to give us a lift?'

I want to cover Lainey's mouth with my hand.

'We'll send flowers,' Mam reiterates.

'My dad's working this weekend but I could ask him to switch his days around. He probably won't mind,' Lainey says.

'It's the middle of Dee's exams,' Mam says, as if Lainey and I haven't been in the same class in school since we were five. 'No road trips, I'm afraid. But as I said, we'll certainly send flowers and a card so they know we're thinking of them.'

'But—'

'Now off you girls go,' Mam says. 'If you're late they won't let you in.'

'But—' Lainey is painfully stubborn and I wonder how after all these years she still doesn't know when my mam is putting her foot down.

'Dee,' Mam says, and I know that's my cue to link Lainey's arm and walk away before Mam's temper explodes.

NINETEEN

DEE

Later That Day

'So who's this Matilda girl?' Mam asks as we sit at the table after dinner.

'I told you about her before,' I say. 'Her mam's French. You met her at the parent–teacher meeting last year.'

Mam scrunches her face, trying to remember a fictional woman.

'I think it's great, love,' Dad says. 'I wish I had a real French lady to help me before my exams.'

I can't make eye contact with Dad. It's harder to lie to him.

'Yeah. So, eh, we're going to study all weekend at Matilda's house with her mam. It's like getting a free grind.'

'And her mother really doesn't mind?' Mam says.

'No. She's so cool.'

'Right.'

'And Lainey's coming,' I say.

'Um-hmm.' Mam spoons rice pudding into her mouth and

makes a face that tells Dad and me it's still too hot to touch ours. 'I'll give her mam a call. A weekend is a long time. And with Lainey there too. She'll have a full house.'

I pass Mam a page with a phone number on it. Poor Lainey has been waiting for over an hour in the phone box next the butcher's in the village for Mam to call.

'You should call her now,' I say. 'They go to bed early.'

'Right. Okay.' Mam nods, standing up. 'Probably a Mediterranean thing.'

Mam walks into the hall and I hear her clearing her throat ready to pick up the phone. Dad and I eat our dessert in silence. I'm certain he knows I'm lying and I can't bear it.

Mam is surprisingly quick.

'Right,' she says, sitting down. 'That's all sorted. She seems lovely. A little hard to understand, but that's just the accent, isn't it?'

'Yeah, probably.'

'So, you'll go up to Matilda's house straight after your maths exam tomorrow. Her mam is making frogs' legs. Now, you're not to turn your nose up, Dee. I'm sure she's going to a lot of trouble.'

Frogs' legs? I can't believe Lainey said that. Another time I might laugh. I nod. I'm afraid to open my mouth in case the lie starts to unravel.

'You're a good kid, Dee,' Mam says, unexpectedly. 'And you're a good influence on Lainey. We all know she wouldn't spend a weekend studying if it wasn't for you.'

TWENTY

DEE

Maths paper one is a stinker. Actually, worse than Irish yesterday. I spend much of my time staring out the window. I try to remember theorems; stuff that has been drilled into my brain since transition year. But angles and proofs sit behind a thick, dark cloud inside my head. In the end I hand up a paper that I have no memory of completing and I meet Lainey in the bathrooms beside the first-year classrooms. We change into jeans and t-shirts and stuff our uniforms into our bags. Our friends ask us if we have any nice plans for the weekend and we tell them we're going to study French.

'It's best to keep the lie consistent,' Lainey said. 'In case our mams are talking to anyone.'

We get the bus into town and buy a Dublin-to-Donegal ticket at the main bus station. I text Fionn when we're on the bus. He doesn't reply. I wasn't expecting him to. Lainey talks for a while and I nod but I'm not listening. We don't get off at the halfway point to pee and for the remainder of the journey I drift in and out of fitful sleep. Then there's the ferry and checking into a B&B on the island. Lainey pays upfront in cash. She has a job in McDonald's. I promise I'll pay her back for my half when I get summer work.

The lady who owns the B&B shakes our hands and introduces herself as Maureen. Then she separates a tenner from the money and passes it back to Lainey.

'It's a discount,' she says. 'Usually I offer a cooked breakfast but tomorrow you'll have to make do with tea and toast or some Weetabix. I've a funeral to go to.'

'Yeah. Us too,' Lainey says.

Maureen nods. I suspect she already guessed that's why we're here.

'Weetabix sounds good. Thank you,' I say.

Maureen's bungalow is almost identical to Lorna's in shape and size and layout. The only noticeable difference is the decor. Maureen has opted for floral carpet, curtains and wallpaper, as opposed to Lorna's bold, block colours. Maureen shows us to our room. A small room at the end of the corridor with bunk beds pushed up against the window. The window overlooks grassy hills instead of the sea, but nonetheless it's all so painfully familiar. Silent tears trickle down my cheeks and I wipe them away before Maureen or Lainey notice.

'If you need me for anything I'll be in the sitting room,' Maureen says. 'Sleep well.'

Maureen didn't show us where the sitting room is, but she didn't have to, we know.

Lainey and I climb into bed in our clothes. We take some popcorn and Coke out of our bags but we're too tired to eat. With the last of my energy, I text Fionn.

I'm here

Dee x

TWENTY-ONE

DEE

I've never been to a funeral before. Lainey has been to a few. Both her grandads passed away last year and her uncle died when she was younger. She said funerals are just like a normal mass except you have to wear black and shake hands with the family. I don't think I can shake Fionn's hand. Even if it's what you're supposed to do, I think it'll be too weird. I wake at 7 a.m. and it's all I can think about until Lainey wakes up over an hour later.

We get dressed. In black. Lainey's black jumper has a giant silver eagle on the front that sparkles under light. We don't bother with toast or Weetabix. My stomach rumbles but I don't feel hungry. Lainey complains about the heat as we walk to the church.

'Can't take my bloody jumper off,' she says. 'My t-shirt is yellow.'

My t-shirt is black. But I'm cold.

The church is packed. There is no doubt that every man, woman and child on the island is here today, dressed in all sorts of colours. Lainey takes off her jumper.

Inside smells of newly treated timber, old leather and tears.

I try to seek out Fionn and Lorna but there are too many people stacked between me and the front of the church. Subtle music plays from a speaker somewhere and you have to concentrate to hear it over the hum of weeping and whispering. My eyes settle on the altar. In front is a pine coffin with gold handles. A framed photo of Mr O'Connell sits on top. He's younger then; in a bright red raincoat and a navy woolly hat. I've never seen him without his hat. A smaller, white coffin is next to it. The handles are a bright blue. Seány's favourite colour is blue like the sea.

Seány's photo is harder to look at. He's smiling and missing a tooth in front.

'My tooth is wobbly, see?' he said, on our way to the light-house last summer. He let go of my hand so he could wiggle it. 'The tooth fairy brings you money when your tooth falls out. I'm going to buy lollipops. Strawberry ones.'

I hope the tooth fairy came. I hope the magic of finding money under his pillow filled him up with happiness. I look away.

I'm overly aware of my stomach and the feeling it produces. The nausea. The shaking. That moment when you feel you're coming down with something. I wish I felt this way because it was a flu.

A group of young women gather at the back of the church. They're older than Lainey and me. Mostly in their twenties, I guess. Some in their thirties. Sadness and a sense of not fully belonging is written on their faces. They second-guess themselves about whether or not they should be here. But a summer that meant so much to them means they couldn't stay away. Lainey and I slide into the pew beside them, knowing that's where we belong. We are all past pupils. Past guests of Lorna's hospitality.

The mass is beautiful. There are many stories of the man Sean O'Connell was. Fisherman, friend, father, husband.

There are many hopes for the man little Seány might have become. His school friends bring some of his artwork to the altar. A soft toy from his favourite TV show. The once-plush Pikachu is missing an eye and the fur below his ear is thread-bare from hugs. A lollipop – his favourite treat, I know. A bucket in the shape of a castle and a bright red spade. And a paper boat, made from blue card, with one sail slightly larger than the other. Seány has written his name in green crayon on the side and the letters are all different sizes. Simple tokens that sum up a little boy so full of life and colour and happiness.

I finally set eyes on Fionn when he gets to his shaky feet and stands between Mr O'Connell and Seány's coffins. He places a hand on each. Without them for support, I think, he might tumble to the ground.

He speaks for some time. Choking often on his words. I try so hard to listen. To hear what he is saying; but the words float over me like bubbles, popping only when they've passed me by. His pain is palpable. I feel it like a knife twisting in my gut. I yield to it, bending in the middle, and I can't sit up straight even though I want to.

'Dad will be there to mind Seány and Seány will make sure Dad is never lonely. When I think of them now, they will always be together. Sailing and smiling with the wind always on their backs.'

Fionn's final words sink in and I can't hold my tears back any longer. Seány will be forever seven. A little boy playing above the clouds with his dad.

When all is said, music plays, louder than before, and men in black suits raise the coffins onto their shoulders. It takes six men to carry Mr O'Connell and just two to lift Seány.

Outside, two black hearses wait at the church gates. The little white coffin is surrounded by flowers, so many they rest on top of each other and their petals are pressed against the windows. The white box doesn't belong. It's too small. Too lonely. Too wrong.

The winding roads seem narrower than I remember. Lainey and I stand with the group of young women from the church.

'I spent three summers in Lorna's house when I was a teenager,' one of them says. She's wearing fancy clothes. The type of skirt and tights and shoes that someone working in an office wears. 'It feels like a lifetime ago. Lorna's eldest was just a teenager then.'

'Is he here?' one of the other girls asks.

'Oisín? Yeah, somewhere. I saw him earlier. He was in an awful state.'

'Did you hear he's living in London now?'

'Oh. Really?'

'Apparently he moved over to the UK when Seán junior was just a baby and he hasn't been home much since.'

'Seány,' I correct them.

'Seány,' someone else echoes.

'You'd wonder how well he knew the little boy at all?' fancy office clothes lady says.

'Must be awful to be estranged from your family like that and have to come home for their funeral.'

'So sad.'

'It really is.'

'Have you seen the middle boy?' Someone else joins the conversation.

'Absolute spitting image of Oisín, isn't he?' office lady says. Clearly the self-appointed leader of the conversation.

'I thought he *was* Oisín. I was thinking London must be the fountain of youth.'

There's collective laughing, followed quickly by hushing. I want to scream.

'You okay?' Lainey asks, placing her hand on my lower back the way older people do.

'Yeah. Yeah. Just thinking about Fionn.'

The hearses begin to move. Mr O'Connell leads the way, followed by his son. Lorna and Fionn walk behind them. Fionn's arm is draped over his mother's shoulder and she turns her head into his neck. Her shoulders shake and I'm not sure she'll make it. She struggles to put one foot in front of the other. A man in a black suit walks beside them. He's older than Fionn but with a face so similar. Oisín. He has no one to hug or hold and I think he must be the loneliest person I have ever seen.

I watch silent tears trickle down Lainey's cheeks as the coffins are lowered into the ground. The priest makes some reference about *into the loving arms of the Father* and Lorna crumbles. Oisín tries to catch her but she pushes him away and lets her knees sink into the soil. She leans over the open ground and her pain spills in angry, tearful wails. Fionn bows his head and a community watch, helpless, as a family shatters.

At some point Lorna stands, and people disperse like blackbirds flying home. The group of past pupils talk about going to the pub for the soup and sandwiches. Lainey and I break away from them and find some shade under an old oak tree.

'What should we do now?' Lainey asks.

'Talk to Fionn, maybe?'

'What are you going to say?'

'I have no idea.'

Stragglers continue to shake Lorna, Fionn and Oisín's hands. Lorna catches Lainey and me in the corner of her eye. She walks towards us with two muddy patches on the knees of her tights.

'Girls,' she says, squinting as the sun shines on her face.

Lainey steps forward and I think she's going to hug her but she doesn't.

'It's very good of you to come,' Lorna says, followed by a sharp intake of breath.

She almost falls apart but she catches herself.

She puts her mammy hat on and asks, 'Do your mothers know you're here?'

Usually, lies slip off Lainey's tongue much easier than mine. But Lainey doesn't open her mouth as she looks at me.

I simply say 'no.'

'Oh girls.' Lorna sighs. 'What am I going to do with you?' And then she says, 'Dee. He's over there.' She tilts her head towards Fionn.

Lorna has known about Fionn and me for a long time. Ever since she found our letters. I thought she might want to keep us apart. I thought she might be mad. But how little any of that matters now. She's not angry. She has no room for it.

She takes my hands in hers and squeezes them gently. 'He will be happy to see you. Thank you, Dee. Thank you.'

Then she walks away with her shoulders shaking once more.

TWENTY-TWO

FIONN

People think that because they cover their mouths or lower their voices we don't know they're talking about us. It's Dad and Seány's last day but the name on everyone's lips is Oisín. The rumours about why he left. The surprise of his return. Gossip drives Cloch Bheag and, much as we don't deserve it, today my family are the fuel for the fire.

Everyone is crammed into Reilly's pub. Mr Reilly is pulling pints like there's a drought on the way and Mrs Reilly has made enough egg salad sandwiches to feed half of Donegal. The distinctive smell of onion and booze turns my stomach and I step outside for some fresh air.

The back of Reilly's sits on a cliff edge. Too many steps forward and I'd topple over. I stand back, avoiding the temptation. It must be the warmest day of the year. Maybe even the hottest day in years. It's not long after midday. I know without checking my watch. Dad was teaching me to tell the time from the sun's position. We should be somewhere in the wide Atlantic now. We'd fish and chat and I'd write to Dee. Instead, Dee is here. Right here. I can feel her presence behind me as if I have a sixth sense. She's been standing there for a few seconds.

Probably searching for the right words. I don't turn round. I don't know how I'll react when I see her and that scares me.

'Fionn,' she says, at last.

Her voice is gentle like the summer wind.

'Fionn, it's Dee.'

I feel a hand on my shoulder. My knees buckle.

'I'm sorry,' she says. 'I'm so, so sorry.'

I stare ahead. The ocean sleeps, tucked under a glistening blue blanket. Too lazy to toss and turn today. Too stubborn to show remorse. The sea is a thief. A murderer. A villain. I will never forgive it.

'I was talking to your mam,' Dee says.

I can't move.

'And your brother's here.'

She waits for a reply. Again, none comes.

'It must be nice to see him again. I mean, not nice, that's so not what I mean. Just good that he's here. Because you miss him.'

'Everyone is talking about Oisín,' I say, words finally tumbling out from somewhere deep inside me.

'Yeah.'

'I haven't talked to him,' I say.

'What do you mean?'

I turn round. Dee is dressed in all black. The only hint of colour is her blue eyes. She looks older than I remember. Older than she is. The window of the pub is behind her. Inside I see people chatting and drinking and eating. I'm sure they're saying how terrible it is. *A shocking tragedy*. Everyone says that. Even the people on the news. But in spite of the shock and the tragedy, they are enjoying the food and drink and their day out. I see Oisín sitting at the bar. There's a pint of Guinness in front of him. He picks it up, drinks, lowers it and repeats. He doesn't open his mouth for any other reason, even when people approach to talk to him.

Dee takes a step towards me.

'Do you want to go talk to him now? I could go with you,' she asks.

'No.'

'Why not?'

'I wish he wasn't here.'

'What? But you're family.'

I shrug. 'I wish you weren't here too.'

Dee's eyes are red and puffy. I only notice now that she's been crying.

'I can go,' she says.

I stare past her and at my big brother. His pint is empty. Mr Reilly takes the empty glass and places a fresh pint in front of him.

'Lainey and I aren't getting the ferry until tomorrow,' Dee says. 'We have it booked. But I can go back to the B&B. The lady there said we can come and go any time so...'

'Lainey is here?'

I sound surprised. I'm not. I didn't think Dee travelled alone. I want to thank her for coming. I want to tell her that even though I wish she didn't *have* to be here I am so glad that she is. But nothing comes out when I open my mouth.

Suddenly, boisterous sound carries through the pub window and pulls Dee and me away from each other. People are on their feet and standing in a semicircle to observe the commotion. Oisín isn't at the bar any more.

'C'mon,' I say.

I take Dee by the hand without thinking. I feel her reluctance for a second. But she follows.

It's quieter inside than I was expecting. There is just one voice. Oisín's. He's shouting.

'You promised you'd take care of him.'

His words are slurred. The Guinness is making its presence known. Mam is standing in front of him. She's even smaller than usual and I realise I haven't seen her eat since the accident. Oisín is pointing a finger at Mam and wagging it.

'You told me to go. You sent me away.'

'Please Oisín. Not here.' Mam is wearing an expression I've never seen on her before. She's begging.

Oisín throws his arms in the air. 'Still so fucking worried about what the neighbours think. Fuck the neighbours.'

There's a communal gasp and some whispering.

'You told me leaving was the best thing for Seány. You said he'd have a more normal life without me.'

'I did my best,' Mam says. 'Your father did too.'

'You did what suited you best, you mean.'

Oisín's face is puce. I've never seen someone so young so full of anger before.

'Stop,' I shout.

I let go of Dee and race to place myself between my brother and my mother.

'Fionn,' Oisín says as if he's seeing me for the first time. 'Leave. Run. Get yourself the hell out of this place. It's toxic.'

'What are you talking about?'

'Look what it did to me. What it did to Seány and Dad. You're next. This fucking island eats men alive.'

'You're drunk, Oisín. Drunk and talking shite.'

Mam nods. 'Help me get him home, Fionn.'

Mam links Oisín's arm but he shakes her off.

'Home? That's some joke. I haven't had a home here since the day Marie told us she was pregnant.'

I look at Mam. Her expression worries me. It's another look I've never seen before. She's scared. I don't know who Marie is but Mam clearly does.

'Not here, Oisín. I told you.'

'I am done with you telling me what to do, Mam. Done. I never should have listened to you. I should have taken Seány to London with me like I wanted to.'

A stranger steps forward from the crowd. A woman about Oisín's age. Her clothes are expensive and office-like and they stand out. A skirt, tights and high heels that I've never seen any woman on Cloch Bheag wear.

'Ois, stop. Your mother is right. Now is not the time or the place to talk about this,' she says.

Mam glares at her. She seems disappointed to see her but not surprised. Mam knows her. I don't need an introduction. This woman in fancy clothes is Marie. A name I've never heard before, but I already know all about her. I've heard the rumours. The whole island has. The mainland girl that an island boy got pregnant one summer. *How long ago was it?* Six, maybe seven years. Shortly before Seány arrived. I try to remember when Mam was pregnant with him. I was twelve and in my final year of primary school. I remember plenty from back then. Football on the beach with Oisín. Driving around the island in the back of his car. My car now. Sharing a bedroom. My last day of school. Mam isn't pregnant in a single one of my memories. I try to remember her with a round belly. I search my brain until it hurts but an image won't come. It won't come because it never happened. Mam and Dad weren't Seány's parents. Oisín and Marie were. Oisín is a father. *Was* a father. *Oh my God!*

TWENTY-THREE

FIONN

I left everyone in the pub. Including Dee. I've been walking since. It's still bright but it's late. Past Seány's bedtime. I haven't stopped to sit down, even when my ankles hurt. I don't know where I'm going or if I'm going anywhere but, finally, I find myself at Aisling's front door.

I knock but no one answers. I assume they're all still in the pub. I saw Aisling in the church with her parents. She waved and I waved back and I was glad when she didn't come to talk to me.

I knock again. Nothing. I walk round the back of the house. I pass the kitchen window, and the bathroom and a bedroom, until I come to the end bedroom window. The curtains are drawn but I knock nonetheless. The curtains twitch and when they draw back and I see Dee's face, I begin to cry. It's the first time I've let tears fall and now I don't know how to stop them. The window opens and she climbs through, stands in front of me and gathers me into her arms all in one seamless motion.

'Oh Fionn,' she says. 'Oh God. Oh God.'

'I loved them, Dee. They drove me up the walls sometimes but I really, really loved them.'

'I know. I know.'

'Seány wasn't my little brother.'

Dee doesn't say anything. But she knows. She heard every word in the pub.

'Can you believe it? Mam has been lying to me his whole fucking life. Who does that?'

I wait for Dee to defend Mam. To tell me she was doing the right thing or at least what she believed was the right thing. But she doesn't.

'Do you want to go to the beach?' Dee asks.

I can't bear to walk another step.

'What about Lainey?'

'She's still in the pub. She got talking to John Paul.'

'Oh right.'

John Paul was drunk when I left at lunchtime. I can only imagine the state he's in by now.

'Are you here on your own?' I ask.

'Yeah. I didn't know where else to go.'

'Sorry. I shouldn't have left you like that.'

Dee shrugs. 'That's okay.'

'I just had to get out of there, you know.'

She smiles. 'Let's go to the beach.'

It's not a question anymore and I nod.

TWENTY-FOUR

FIONN

The beach is just down the road and round the corner, but by the time we reach the sand my ankles give way and I know I can't take another step. Dee doesn't flinch. She lowers herself onto the sand to sit next to me. Despite the sunshine today the sand is cold and damp. Dee sits on her feet with her legs crossed under her. I take off my suit jacket. It was Dad's and it's too big. Mam said he had shoulders as wide as a football pitch. I'll never be that strong. I'm slighter, like Mam. I've never thought about shoulders much before. But suddenly they're all I can think about. I drape it over her shoulders and try hard not to cry.

'Thanks,' she says.

We stare at the water in silence and wait for the sun to set.

'Do you believe in heaven?' she asks once it begins to get dark.

I shrug. I've never thought about it before.

'I do. I think you go somewhere, you know? Like somewhere that would make you really happy and you just sort of stay there.'

'So Seány is in the zoo for ever?' I say.

'Yeah. I think so. Hanging out with the lion cubs.'

'Elephants,' I say. 'Elephants are—eh, were... his favourite.'

'Elephants are very cool, to be fair.'

Dee talks some more. About Dad and Seány and heaven. I stop listening. It feels as fanciful as the bedtime stories I read to Seány.

After some time she squeezes my hand and says, 'Are you okay?'

I nod. It's easier to lie without words.

'What do you think will happen now?' she says.

'What?'

'Do you think Oisín will stay now that he's back?'

'No,' I say, taken aback by the suggestion. It never came into my head that Oisín would be here for any longer than a couple of days. 'He's lived in London for years. He can't just turn round and move back. What would he even work at?'

'Fishing?'

'Oisín doesn't fish. He never went out on the boat with Dad.'

'Oh. Okay.'

Dee fidgets.

'There's no boat any more anyway,' I say.

'What's your mam going to do, then? For money and stuff.'

I shrug. I hadn't thought about money before right now.

'Would she move?' Dee says. 'Maybe she could come to Dublin with you. She'd get a job there no problem. My mam works in Dunnes Stores and she says they're always looking for staff.'

'Mam would never move to the mainland. She was born here.'

'But she'll be all alone.' Dee's voice cracks.

'No. She won't.'

Dee bows her head and begins to draw circles in the sand with her finger.

'I can't go to college any more. I've missed the Irish and maths exams,' I say.

'Not this year. But you can repeat. Loads of people do.'

I shake my head. 'You know, for the last six years all I thought about was school and study and the fucking leaving cert. I thought if I did well in my exams it was my ticket out of this place.'

'You can still do it. I know right now—'

'No.' I cut across her. 'You don't know. Please don't say you know what any of this is like. You should have seen Seány's face when I told him I was going to leave. His eyes were so full of sadness. So instead, he left me.'

Dee straightens and shakes her hand to flick the damp sand off her finger.

'He was such a lovely boy,' she says, sniffling back tears. 'He would want you to be happy.'

I was happy. But I took it for granted.

I shuffle closer to Dee until my thigh is pressed against hers.

'I want to come to Dublin,' I say. 'Like we talked about. But that can't happen now.'

'But—'

'Dee.' I say her name softly.

She nods. 'Your mam. I know. You can't leave her.'

'I can't.'

'What will you do?'

'I don't know.'

Dee leans in to kiss me. I nearly pull away. But her lips are warm and soft and I am weak when they touch mine. I kiss her back and for a blissful moment all the pain and sadness and fear spill out of my brain.

TWENTY-FIVE

DEE

Fionn's lips are salty. His tears or mine, I'm not sure. We kiss for a long time as my mind races. I've kissed Fionn countless times on this beach. Each time more wonderful than the last. I used to think it was so wonderful because our days were numbered. A summer fling that would forever leave us with beautiful memories. All winter I daydreamed of seeing him again. Of the first words I would say. How it would feel to lock eyes. I couldn't possibly have imagined it would be like this. Feel like this.

I'm no longer kissing some boy I fancy with a belly full of butterflies. I'm kissing a boy I love, with my heart breaking. I don't just want to kiss Fionn. I need to. I need to feel him close. I need him to know that I'm here for him. I wish so hard that I could take his pain away.

Fionn pulls away first. I miss his lips. His eyes are on mine, searching for comfort. I hold my breath and hope he finds some in me.

'Thank you,' he whispers.

'For what?'

'For being here. I never should have said I wish you weren't.'

'I wish I wasn't. I wish I was here next month. After our exams, like we talked about. I shouldn't be here now. Not like this.'

'Yeah. Not like this.'

'But I'm glad I'm here. I want to be here for you.'

'I'm glad too.'

Fionn's fingers slip between mine and we kiss again. I've never felt anything like this before. Every inch of my body tingles. He needs me and I need him, and all I can't think about is being one. I've never thought about sex before. Lainey goes on and on and on about. She says she's done it. With a few different guys. I don't believe her. But none of that matters right now because I'm not thinking about sex the way she does. It's more. So much more. An ache, a hunger, a need. Like air.

I stop kissing Fionn and open a button of his shirt. He doesn't flinch. I slide my hand against his skin. He gasps and his breath rushes from his mouth into mine. I open another button. And another until I expose his whole chest. His skin is dimpled with goosebumps.

'Cold?' I whisper.

Fionn shakes his head. I untuck my feet from under me and lean closer to him. My hands are shaking.

'Cold?' he whispers.

I shake my head too.

He stands up and reaches his hand out to me. I take it and he pulls me to my feet.

'Not here,' he says, glancing over his shoulder. 'People can see us here.'

I cringe. Thinking about what comes next makes me feel awkward. I think of the parts of me he might see and feel. I can feel my ears get hot.

Fionn starts walking with my hand in his. His open shirt flaps by his sides and he doesn't bother to close it. We continue to the edge of the cove, where you can tell by the colour of the water that it's deep. I've been in this spot before. The sand is scarce; sandwiched between long grass and breaking waves. We make our way into the grass. Lifting our knees high as if we're on a jungle expedition.

Fionn stops walking and lets go of my hand. We stand face-to-face. He has grown since last summer, I realise. The top of my head used to rest just under his nose. Now, it barely reaches his chin.

Without a word his hands find their way under my top. I feel his fingertips against my belly first. Slowly they move behind me and reach for the clasp of my bra. He pauses and looks at me. My cheeks are hot and my heart races. I nod and feel the clasp unhook.

Fionn guides me back, until I'm lying on the grass. Despite his jacket, spreading out like a blanket beneath me, it's cold and damp. Thick blades tickle the sides of my face but I don't want to stop.

'Are you okay?' he whispers, lowering himself to lie beside me.

I kiss him.

'Are you sure you want to do this?'

'Yeah. Do you?'

He looks at me, silent and thoughtful, and for a desperate moment I think he's going to say no. I think he doesn't want me as much as I want him.

'I think so,' he says.

'Are you scared?' I ask.

'No. Are you?'

'Yeah. A little.'

'Do you think it will hurt? I don't want to hurt you.'

'Lainey says the first time is a bit sore.'

Fionn pushes himself away as if just being too near right now could hurt me.

'It's okay,' I say. 'I'll be okay.'

He's so unsure. So shy. So vulnerable.

I shuffle closer, closing the gap between us almost completely. My fingers tremble as I unbuckle his belt. His inhale is sharp and the sound of it makes the fine hairs on the back of my neck stand up. I try to unbutton his pants but there's a clasp and a button and a zip. My fingers don't know what to do. Fionn helps and then he pulls his pants down until they're round his knees.

I stare at a boy's body. A body so different to mine. I never even dared imagine these parts of him. I don't know how long I watch. Long enough until he grows comfortable with my gaze. My heart races when I follow his lead. I lift my bum and shuffle my pants down. I'm glad they've an elastic waist. I close my eyes. It's less embarrassing this way as I feel him looking.

I open my eyes again when he climbs above me. His hands are at either side of my shoulders.

'Tell me when you're ready?' he whispers, already breathless as if he's just finished playing a match.

'I'm ready.'

I feel skin against me. Warm. And I *am* ready. I want this. But my breath catches and it hurts in a way I wasn't prepared for. I stiffen. I don't ask Fionn to stop. But he does. He pulls away.

'I'm sorry.'

I kiss him. The awkwardness melts away and I'm left with desire and longing.

'Keep trying,' I whisper.

He shakes his head.

'Please.'

We try again. And again. We stop and start. It takes longer than I ever imagined to make progress. But slowly I feel him edge deeper. Each gentle nudge takes my breath away and we kiss and kiss and I promise I'm okay.

With one hard, deep push I yelp. Fionn becomes still and

his eyes lock on mine. We are one. As close as two people can possibly be. I feel him share my body. Not just physically.

He's an imprint now. A permanent mark on my soul. The boy I've lost my virginity to. A once-in-a-lifetime moment and I'm so glad it's with him.

'Are you okay?' he whispers.

'Yeah.'

I feel all things. Pressure, stretching, stinging. But pleasure too. Warmth and comfort. His shaking chest against mine.

'Are you okay?' I ask.

He doesn't answer. He doesn't have to. I feel him like a broken thing inside me. A person who used to be whole but the pieces of him are scattered now like fine china after it hits the ground.

Fionn pulls out of me.

'I'm sorry,' he says. 'I shouldn't have done that.'

'What? No. I wanted you to.'

He stands up and pulls up his pants. I pull mine up too and get to my feet.

'What's wrong?' I ask, picking up his jacket and passing it to him.

There are tears in his eyes. 'I should get back. My mam and Oisín will be home from the pub. They'll be wondering where I am.'

'Em. Eh. Okay.'

'I'll walk you back to Aisling's.'

'Aisling's?'

'My friend,' he says. 'Her mam owns the B&B.'

I stuff my hands into my pockets. I'm cold.

'It's okay,' I say. 'I can walk back by myself.'

Fionn insists on walking with me. We walk the whole way back in silence. I think about reaching for his hand but I don't and he doesn't reach for mine. Lights are on at the house.

'Everyone must be home from the pub,' I say.

'Yeah.'

'How long will it take you to walk home?' I ask.

'An hour.'

'Can you call JP, maybe he could give you a lift.'

'JP is drunk. Anyway, I need the walk.'

The bedroom window opens and Lainey's head pokes out. 'Where the hell were you? I've been on my own here for ages.'

Fionn looks at Lainey and squints. He looks back at me. 'Are you on the eleven o'clock ferry tomorrow?' he asks.

I nod.

'Can I come see you off?'

I pick at my nails, breaking one by accident. 'Have I done something wrong?' I say. 'Back there. Did I...'

'It's me.' Fionn taps his chest with his finger. 'It's all me, Dee. I'm just so fucked up right now. I'm so sorry if I ruined your first time. I just, I just—,'

'You didn't.'

Fionn tilts his head.

'I swear.'

He sighs.

'Do you have to go?' I ask. 'You could stay here? No one would know.'

'What are you two whispering about?' Lainey shouts.

I turn round and press my finger against my lip. Lainey rolls her eyes and disappears out of view.

'No. I can't,' Fionn says. 'I have to go home. I need to check on my mam.'

There is so much sadness in his eyes I can't bear to look at him. I can feel his guilt that he lost himself for a moment with me. Maybe I should be hurt or offended that he pulled away from me so suddenly in the most intimate and important moment of my life, but my mind is so far from there. All I can think about is his pain. It's intense and it's choking both of us.

'I'll see you in the morning,' I say. 'To say goodbye.'

'Yeah. In the morning.'

Fionn turns and walks away and I know he will most likely cry the whole way home.

TWENTY-SIX

FIONN

I don't go home. I intended to, but, somehow, I find myself sitting on the beach again. I scoop up sand with my hand and part my fingers to let it slip through. I do it again, and again and again. I don't watch the sand fall but I feel it slipping away.

I'm torn between glancing out to sea and turning my head over my shoulder to stare at the spot where Dee and I were. I wonder if this is what my life will be like from now on. Slipping away like grains of sand. Always torn. Not sure where to look. Not sure how to feel. Not sure what to say or do or how to act. I am empty. I've been tipped over and spilled out.

I close my eyes and when I open them again it's bright. The sun sits just above the horizon, rising slowly to supervise the day. I've flopped onto my side at some point during the night and sand is stuck to my face. I brush it away and pull myself to my feet and begin to run. I slip on the sand at first, but as soon as I reach the road I gather pace. My leather shoes dig into my heels. They used to belong to Dad and they're a size too small. I feel the bite of a blister forming but I keep running. I stop only to catch my breath.

The island is sleeping as I race by neighbours and the school and up the hill towards home. I'm panting when I open the front door and I bend in the middle because it hurts. I tiptoe towards my bedroom and I hear voices in the kitchen. Two women. I recognise Mam's voice. The door is open and I can't creep past without her laying eyes on me. I decide it's best to face the music instead.

'Mam,' I say.

Mam doesn't look up. She's sitting at the table with her back to the window. It's Seány's spot. Another beautiful day is coming to life behind her as the sun shines and the sea sparkles. The woman from the pub is making tea. She's still wearing fancy clothes but she's in her bare feet now. Her shoes are lying on their sides next to the door. I search my brain for her name but it won't come.

She doesn't say hello to me. And I don't know what to say. She takes two cups of tea with steam swirling out the top over to the table. She places one in front of Mam and keeps the other for herself. Then she sits down.

I wait for their conversation to begin but the only sound is the woman blowing on her tea.

'Mam,' I say again.

I've a stitch in my side and it's hard to stand up straight.

'Mam, are you okay?'

Mam stares into her cup as if she'll find Dad and Seány at the bottom.

'Mam?'

Finally, when the silence becomes unbearable, the woman turns towards me.

'I'm Marie, by the way. I don't think we've been properly introduced. You're Fionn, right?'

'Yeah. Fionn.'

'I'm a friend of Oisín's. Or I was. A long time ago.'

'You're Seány's mother?' I say.

Mam's cup flies across the table. It hits the wall with a loud smack and shatters. A brown stain trickles down the wall and pools on the ground. I grab a cloth from the cupboard under the sink and begin to clean up.

'Where's Oisín?' I ask.

'Gone,' Marie says.

'Where?'

'We don't know. Home, I guess.'

'London, you mean?' I say.

'I guess so.'

'He can't. There's no ferry until later.' I prick my finger on a shard of porcelain and I instinctively suck it.

'You all right?' Marie asks.

I don't reply. 'What happened?' I ask instead, pulling my finger out to examine it.

It's not too deep but it stings. Marie's eyes narrow. Mam's too. But their expressions are so different. Marie wants to talk. Mam distinctively does not. Mam wants everyone to shut up.

'What happened in the pub?' I continue. 'After I left.'

'Nothing.' Marie sighs and I can tell she's exhausted.

She's travelled to be here. From Dublin or London maybe. Maybe even further. New York, I think. She looks like someone who could live in New York. I want to ask but I won't.

'Nothing,' I echo.

'Yeah, nothing. He just walked away,' Marie says. 'There wasn't anything more to say. Not really.'

'Oh, he said his piece, all right.' Mam finally speaks. 'He blames me.'

'No. Lorna.' Marie reaches across the table and places her hand on top of Mam's. 'It's just the shock. He's shocked. We all are.'

'He blames me,' Mam says again, louder this time. 'And he's right. You should too, if you have any sense.'

Marie shakes her head. 'Well, I don't. Not for any of it. Oisín and I were sixteen. We didn't know the first thing about having a baby. We didn't even know the first thing about each other. We spent three weeks together. It shouldn't have changed our lives for ever but it did. It did because of Seány.'

'Did you love him?' I ask. 'Were you and Oisín in love?'

Marie snorts. 'No. No we weren't. Maybe we thought we were, at the time. But it wasn't real.'

'Why?' I say.

Silent tears trickle down Marie's cheeks. She wipes them away before she says, 'Because we were just a couple of kids.'

'It can be real. People can be in love when they're young,' I say.

Marie pulls her shoulders up to her ears for a moment and holds them there. 'We had a lot of growing up to do.' She exhales and drops her shoulders. 'Being parents when we were just kids ourselves would have made that impossible. You did the right thing, Lorna. You gave Seány the best possible life. You were a great mother. And I am grateful. So, so grateful.'

'Seány is dead and Oisín is gone,' Mam says, standing up. 'Don't thank me. Please don't sit there and thank me.'

Mam opens the back door and I'm about to go after her when I feel a hand grab my arm. Marie's grip is tight. I try to shake her off but she's having none of it.

'Leave her,' she says. 'She'll be okay. She just needs time.'

'Where are your parents?' I ask. 'Why didn't they come? If Seány was their grandchild...'

Marie lets go of my arm.

'We don't speak,' she says, standing up and picking up her shoes.

'You don't forgive them?'

'It's complicated.' She sighs. 'I should get to bed. I've to catch the early ferry tomorrow. And then a flight back to Melbourne.'

'Melbourne. Wow.'

'It's nice there. I like it.' Marie's eyes glass over.

'Erm... when you're talking to Oisín, will you tell him I'm sorry. I wish it was all different. Could you tell him that for me, please?'

I nod. I think Oisín would like to know.

'Well, goodnight. It was really nice to meet you again after all these years.'

I watch Marie walk towards the spare room. Dee's room. And her words play over in my mind. *After all these years.*

When Oisín and I were kids we used to drop a Polo mint into a glass of 7up. We'd watch the bubbles fizz, sometimes spilling over the edge of the glass. Suddenly, inside my head is fizzing like that 7up as memories spill over. Marie and Oisín kissing on the beach. Holding hands. Sneaking through windows. And Oisín begging me to keep his secret. I kept it so well, I didn't even tell myself.

TWENTY-SEVEN

FIONN

I lie in bed and stare at the ceiling. Dad painted it last summer but there's already a crack showing in the corner. I hear Mam come back inside the house after half an hour or so. She closes her bedroom door but I can still hear her crying. I can hear Marie crying too. Softer, gentler sobs. Guilty sobs. My teeth clench. I press them so hard against each other they crunch and grind. My jaw protests. It aches and begs me to realise but I press even harder. It's the only way I can hold my own tears back.

I don't think anyone sleeps. We get up and pretend like we did. I offer Marie a lift to the port and Mam says I'm a good kid.

The silence in the car is awkward but it's worse when Marie breaks it.

'You drive Oisín's car now,' she says.

'Yeah.'

'You know he was about your age when we met.'

'Younger,' I say. 'I just turned eighteen.'

'Eighteen. Wow. Now I feel old.'

Silence returns and I think about driving faster, but something is rattling every time I go round a bend. I hope it's nothing expensive.

'Is he happy?' Marie asks.

'What?' I grip the wheel tighter. I know what she's asking but I need time to process an answer.

'In London. Is Oisín happy in London? You know, it's funny how we both ended up in big cities. Just at the far side of the world.'

I take my eyes off the road for a moment to look at Marie. She's wearing black jeans and a cream blouse that's too big for her. She almost looks like she belongs here.

'He's happy,' I say.

I lie to myself and to her because I think we both want to believe it.

I park outside Dickie's shop and take Marie's small case out of the boot.

'Well,' she says.

I know I should say something. There is so much to say. And yet it doesn't feel right to say anything at all. I settle on a head-nod as I look around the port for Dee. I spot Lainey first. Her luminous pink *I Love Westlife* school bag slung over one shoulder is hard to miss. She sees me too and waves. Then she elbows Dee in the ribs. Dee turns and smiles. A lump forms in my throat and I think I might choke on it. There's a moment when we lock eyes and I think Dee might walk towards me and when I think I should walk towards her. But neither of us move and the moment passes.

'Thanks for the lift,' Marie says, pulling my focus back to her.

'No problem.'

She leans in and kisses my cheek. 'Take care. And mind your mam, won't you?'

'Yeah. Yeah I will.'

Marie nods and I can tell she's about to cry as she pulls the handle of her case up and drags it down the ramp and onto the ferry.

When I look up again Dee and Lainey are gone. I take my phone out of my pocket and text Dee.

> Tank u 4 bn ere x

Dee texts back instantly.

> xxx

I push my phone back into my pocket and walk towards my car. I'm opening the door, about to sit in, when I see Oisín hurrying towards the port from the far side.

'Hey,' I shout.

He doesn't look up.

'Oisín,' I try again, louder. 'Ois. Oisín!'

The ferry rumbles to life, spitting out waves from under its belly.

Oisín picks up pace. He races down the ramp, waving his arms. He makes it. He's wearing my red New York Yankees baseball cap. It's my favourite and he's taken it without asking. I'm glad. I'm glad he has a reminder of me with him. He stands at the back of the boat with his arms folded and his head down. Marie appears beside him. She knocks her shoulder against his and she points towards me. Oisín doesn't budge. He doesn't look ahead towards the mainland. Or back towards home. He doesn't see me waving. Not even when the ferry leaves Cloch Bheag and me behind.

Dad and Seány left without saying goodbye. And now Oisín has done the same. The sea takes everyone away. One way or another.

PART TWO

TWENTY-EIGHT

DEE

December 2001

Lainey says Christmas is a load of shite. But she's just pissed off because she broke up with the guy she's been seeing since freshers' week and now she has to go to the UCD student ball on her own.

'I'm not sure I'll even bother going, to be honest,' she says, as we wander around town trying to find evening dresses within our budget.

We started out on Grafton Street and definitely couldn't afford anything there. Now we're down some side street that we don't know the name of, and my stomach is rumbling.

'What? No. You have to go. It'll be no fun without you,' I say.

'You have Trevor, though. I'll be a big feckin' gooseberry.'

'You won't be. He's not like that. Anyway, do you want to get McDonald's or something? I'm starving.'

'Yeah. Grand. What time do you have to be back at UCD?'

'I've a lecture at four but I think I'll skip it. I want to be home by six.'

'Does Trevor know you're spending Friday night at home by the phone, waiting for a call from your ex?'

'You're making it sound weird. And anyway, Fionn was never my boyfriend.'

'So, Trev is cool with you guys being in touch?'

'Yes, Lainey,' I snap. 'He's fine with it. Like a normal person.'

Lainey and I have this conversation a lot. I'm never in the mood for it, but Lainey never seems to pick up on that. It bothers her that Fionn and I are still in touch. I don't know why. Especially since it's not like it used to be. We don't write to each other anymore. I wrote a couple of letters after Seány died but Fionn didn't write back. Maybe the tradition he shared with his little brother was too hard to keep alone. I miss those days. The excitement of coming home from school and finding two white envelopes in the pile of post on the kitchen table. One from Fionn and one from Seány.

We text instead now. Once a week or so. I tell him all about college. He says media studies sounds crazy but he's glad I love it. I haven't told him about Trevor yet. I keep meaning to, but it's hard to find a way to say it in 160 characters. Fionn shares less news. He tells me how his mam is doing. She has good days and not-so-good days, he says. He never mentions his own feelings, even when I directly ask. He regularly promises to make the trip to Dublin and I've long stopped hoping it will actually happen. However, Fionn has texted more than usual this week and I've wholly enjoyed each snippet of news he's shared.

She arrives on Friday

Have 2 go 2 d mainland 2 get her

Will sail her straight home

> She's called The Two Seans

> She's smaller than Dad's boat

> Perfect for a 2 man crew

I can sense the excitement in Fionn's texts. After months of red tape crap, the insurance money came through and Fionn and Lorna can finally afford a new boat. I didn't ask how they've made ends meet these previous few months, but it was on my mind often. Fionn said he'd call this evening when *The Two Seans* is home at Cloch Bheag port. Much as I won't admit it, Lainey is right... I will be waiting by the phone for that call.

Besides, it will be nice to take a Friday night off. I'm usually on self-appointed chaperone duty, making sure Lainey's drunk arse gets home safely. I take my phone out of my pocket and text one of our college friends.

> Hey.

> I wont b out 2nite.

> Can u share taxi home with Lainey?

> No way. Sorry.

> She puked last time.

> Pls?

> Fine.

> But u owe me!

> Shots on me nxt time.

> Deal :) xx

'Who you texting?' Lainey asks.

I slide my phone back into my pocket and link her arm.

'Zara, she was wondering if you could share a taxi with her later.'

'Ugh. So needy,' Lainey says, but I can hear her relief that she has a safe plan for getting home later. 'Yeah, fine, if she needs to.'

'Cool.'

By the time we reach McDonald's we're both tired and hungry, and we eat without talking. I'm thinking about Trevor. I told him I had to study tonight. He offered to come over with a takeaway and a few cans. I said my parents wouldn't approve. But Mam and Dad love Trevor. Mam denies it's because he's from a sea-front, detached house in Blackrock and his father drives a brand-new Mercedes. Dad hasn't said a word.

'I'm going to get more chicken nuggets,' Lainey says, standing up. 'Want anything?'

I look at my watch. 'No. Thanks. I should probably get the bus.'

Lainey rolls her eyes but she's smiling. 'Right. I'll see you tomorrow so.'

'Have a good night,' I say. 'And remember to find Zara. For the taxi, you know.'

'I might not be going home after all.' Lainey winks, turning her phone round to show me a chain of texts with someone. 'Loads of the med students are heading out tonight. I fancy me a student doctor. I bet they're animals in bed.'

'You're gross.'

'I know.' Lainey shrugs. 'Right. Go on. Say hi to Fionn for me.'

'Yeah. I will. See ya.'

TWENTY-NINE

DEE

The house is empty when I get home. There's a note on the fridge.

Gone to dinner.
Pizza in the freezer.
Empty the dishwasher.
Mam + Dad x

I can't remember the last time I came home and Mam and Dad were here. They're gone to a restaurant, or the cinema, or playing golf all the time. Mam says she never realised how much time camogie took up when I was in school and Dad says it's nice to have his wife back. Lainey joined the UCD camogie team, and despite Mam's newly developed hectic social life I think deep down she's disappointed that I didn't.

I like having the house to myself. I'm especially glad this evening. I pop a frozen pizza in the oven and grab a shower. I've a missed call from Trevor when I get out. I call him back.

'Hey,' he answers.

'Sorry. Was washing my hair. Everything okay?'

'All good. Just missing you.'

'Is Lainey there?' I ask.

'She was.'

Trevor is tipsy. I can hear it in his exaggerated vowel sounds.

'But she left to get chips or something.'

'Sounds like Lainey,' I say, and I make a mental note to text Zara to check Lainey's not wandering around the city drunk and alone.

'Anyway, we're going to be here for a few hours,' Trevor says. 'If you finish your study and want to come in. You could stay over in my house tonight.'

I'm glad he can't see me as I grimace. Trevor's parents make him sleep on the couch when I stay over and I feel weird in his room by myself.

'Yeah. Maybe. I'll text you.'

'Okay.'

'Okay,' I echo. 'Gotta go, I've a pizza in the oven.'

Trevor blows kisses into the phone and I hold it away from my ear.

The landline rings.

'Mwah. Bye,' I say, and then I hang up and toss my mobile onto the bed.

I race downstairs with a towel wrapped around me and my wet hair dripping onto my shoulder and pick up the phone.

'Hello.'

'Hi. It's Fionn.'

'Hi. How are you? It's great to hear from you.'

I feel awkward. I hope Fionn can't hear it in my voice. Maybe it's the towel thing. I know he can't see me, but I'm still uncomfortable.

'Are you okay to talk? Like is it an okay time to call? You're not busy with college stuff or anything.'

'Actually, could you hang on for two seconds?'

'I can call back—'

'No. No don't go. Just give me a sec.'

I race into the kitchen and turn off the oven on my half-cooked pizza. My stomach is knotting and I'm not hungry anymore. I hurry back into the hall and pick the phone up again.

'Okay. All good,' I say.

Fionn doesn't say anything. For a moment I think he has hung up, but I can hear him breathing on the other end.

'How are you?' I ask.

'I'm good. How are you?'

'I'm okay.'

My face scrunches. This is like the cumbersome conversations I have to endure with my Aunty Kitty every time she calls and Mam takes painfully long to come to the phone.

'So did you get your new boat?'

'I did.'

'Oh wow. That's exciting.'

'Yeah.'

I stare at the carpet. Mam had a new one fitted at Halloween. It's dark green with no pattern. I like it, yet right now I find myself drawing out the pattern from the old carpet with the tip of my toe.

'So, will you be fishing every weekend now?'

'That's the plan.'

Fionn sounds deflated. I wasn't expecting this. I thought he'd be delighted to finally have a family boat again.

'Is JP still going to be your right-hand man?'

'My skipper,' Fionn says. 'He is. I couldn't do it alone.'

'He's a good friend.'

'Yeah.'

The conversation dries up. I think about saying something about Lainey. That usually gives us some mileage. Fionn talks about his best friend. I talk about mine. Instead I say, 'How's your mam? What does she think of *The Two Seans*?'

'She won't step foot on board.'

'Oh.'

'Yeah. A bit too much for her, you know.'

I don't know what to say. I wish I'd talked about Lainey instead.

'She's glad you have it though, yeah?'

'She is. A good haul is one of the few things that makes her smile these days. I managed to fill all the cages this week. The trick is to kill the engine so the lobsters don't know you're there.'

'Wow, that's fantastic. You're such a good fisherman.'

I can hear Fionn smiling.

'Well, I'm a fisherman now whether I like it or not.'

'Don't you like it?' I say, and I immediately want to take my words back.

'So, how's college?' he asks, and I know better than to fight the change of subject.

'Yeah. Good. Getting a bit hammered with assignments and I've exams coming up soon so lots of studying.'

'Sounds tough.'

I'm beginning to shiver. My wet hair is cold on top of my head and my legs need pants.

'Nah. It's grand really,' I say. 'We go out a few nights a week. Tuesdays and Fridays, mostly. Actually, we've a black-tie ball coming up soon.'

'Wow. Living some life, Dee.'

'Ah it sounds posher than it is. It's just a Christmas thing they do for the first-years every year. Everyone will be pissed by eight o'clock and not so classy then.'

'Still. It's something. Something fun,' he says.

'You could come, you know?'

'What?'

'I mean it. You don't have to be a UCD student to go. Loads

of the girls are bringing their boyfriends and they're in college in Cork or Galway or wherever.'

'Do you have to be in college somewhere?'

'No. Not at all. My friend Zara's boyfriend is doing an apprenticeship. He's training to be an electrician.'

'That would be a cool job,' he says.

'Yeah. He likes it. So will you come?'

I know Fionn will have an excuse. I don't even know why I'm asking.

'Could JP come?'

The question catches me off guard and I choke as if there's something in my mouth. I don't know how Lainey would feel about seeing John Paul again.

'Yeah. I'm sure, if he could get a ticket.'

'Okay,' Fionn says, determined. 'I'll come.'

'Really?'

My heart is racing.

'Yeah. If you want me to, I'll come.'

My thoughts scramble. I try to catch them and rearrange them in some sort of order but they're spinning out of control. Finally, I grab hold of one. *Trevor*. I have to tell Fionn about him.

'Of course I want you to come,' I say, my voice higher-pitched than it was before. 'You could meet my boyfriend. I've been telling him all about you.'

'Okay,' Fionn says.

Fionn's coolness shocks me. I don't know if I'm upset or relieved that he has no reaction to the news that I'm no longer single.

'Can you get me a ticket. And one for JP too please, and I'll give you the money back?' he says.

'Yeah. Sure. No problem. They're forty pounds. Is that okay?'

I hear Fionn's intake of breath.

'They're expensive, I know,' I say, 'but there's a meal and so—'

'Forty is fine.'

He's lying. I can hear it. I want to get off the phone.

'Okay. Well, I'll get them on Monday when I'm back in college and I'll text you.'

'Thanks.'

'Fionn...'

'Yeah.'

'It will be really good to see you.'

'It will be great to see you too.'

'Okay, well, I better go. I have a pizza in the oven.'

I cringe. I hate that I've shooed Fionn off the phone with the same lame excuse I gave to Trevor.

'No problem,' he says.

'Bye, Fionn.'

'Bye, Dee-Dee.'

I hang up and sit on the ground. I hug my knees into my chest and I start to cry.

'Dee-Dee,' I say aloud, just so I can hear how it sounds.

No one has called me that since last summer. I miss it.

THIRTY

FIONN

Two Weeks Later

'Fucking forty pounds. My mam will throttle me if she knows I spent that,' John Paul says.

He's moaned the whole bus journey from Letterkenny to Dublin. I chose the back seats, hoping to get some sleep. We've spent the last three days at sea and my eyes are burning with exhaustion.

John Paul spent the whole time bombarding me with questions.

'Will Lainey be there? Is she seeing anyone? Does she know I'm coming?'

I did my best to answer, but I know very little about Lainey these days. Truth be told, I don't know much about Dee either anymore, and deep down I'm as nervous as John Paul about seeing them.

'Do you think we stink?' John Paul asks.

My head is pressed against the window and I'm drifting in and out of sleep.

'Who knows,' I mumble.

'I don't want to smell like fish,' John Paul says.

'No one does.'

'I don't usually worry about it. Everyone at home is used to it. But I don't want Lainey to get a whiff and run the other way.'

'You smell very nice,' the elderly lady in front of us says.

She turns and peeks her head above her seat. 'Maybe a little too much aftershave. But that's just what boys your age do, isn't it? They drown themselves in the stuff. My grandson does the same and I'm always telling him...'

I drift towards sleep, relieved that I don't smell. I'm excited and nervous about the ball. Mam took in Dad's old suit and I took a trip to the mainland last week to buy a new white shirt and shoes that fit. Mam took my photo when I tried it all on together. She said I looked just like Oisín and then she went to her room for a while. She spends a lot of time alone in her room. I never know if I should check on her or not. The only time I hear her laughing anymore is when John Paul's mam comes over on a Friday night and they open a bottle of wine and watch *The Late Late Show*.

I wake to someone shaking my shoulder. I open my eyes expecting to see John Paul but instead I find the bus driver. The bus is empty and he's walked all the way down the back to call us.

'Come on, you two. Rise and shine.'

'Are we in Dublin?'

'Is there somewhere else you were expecting to be?' He laughs.

'JP, get up,' I say, looking at John Paul stretched out across the row of seats beside me.

He's snoring.

'Right lads, c'mon. It's time to go. The cleaner will be getting on in a minute.'

I give John Paul a shove. His feet flop off the seat and the rest of him almost follows but he wakes and jolts upright.

'I'm up. I'm up.'

'Could you give us directions to O'Connell Street, please?' I say.

The driver inhales sharply, losing patience.

'Are you serious?' he says.

'We've never been in Dublin before,' John Paul says, rubbing his eyes.

The driver tilts his head.

'Where are your parents?'

'We're nineteen,' John Paul says.

The driver doesn't look like he believes us.

'Have you somewhere to stay?'

'Yes,' I say. 'We've a hotel booked. And we're meeting friends.'

'Right.' He nods. 'Just walk down by the quays so. You'll find your way.'

'The quays?'

'Oh lads.' He shakes his head. 'The Liffey. The big main river running through the city.'

'We know the Liffey,' John Paul says, sounding offended. 'We learned about it in school.'

'Right, well, stick beside that. There's a footpath the whole way. And mind yourselves. Keep an eye on your wallet and that sort of thing. Kids like you stick out like a sore thumb.'

'Thanks,' I say, standing up.

I throw my rucksack over my shoulder, shuffle down the aisle and get off.

John Paul follows me.

'What do you think he means by kids like us?' he says, as we start walking.

'I don't know.'

But I do know. He means teenager fishermen, with thick Donegal accents and too much aftershave. The nearest we get to fancy nights out are a couple of drinks in Reilly's pub on a Friday night. Where old men sit on high stools at the bar, staring into pints of Guinness, only lifting their head to tell me that my dad was a good man and that he'd be proud.

I lead the way, keeping the Liffey at my side like the bus driver said. My hand is in my pocket, curled round my wallet, and I keep my head down, careful not to make eye contact with anyone. I am not someone to be proud of.

THIRTY-ONE

FIONN

O'Connell Bridge is exactly as it is on the telly. I stop walking and stand for a moment to take it all in. My mouth is open, I think. I don't care. It's louder than I was expecting. Car horns, engines, construction work in the distance, dogs barking, babies crying, people talking. So, so many people. They walk past in large groups. Couples holding hands. People by themselves. Pushing a buggy. Walking a dog on a lead. Holding a child's hand. No one notices me and John Paul, standing watching. I feel invisible and invigorated all at the same time.

'Are we lost?' John Paul asks.

'Isn't this place great?' I say.

'Are we lost?' John Paul repeats, and there's a slight wobble in his tone now.

I point across the bridge at a red-brick building with large windows.

'Lynches on the Quays,' I say, reading the name across the front.

'Oh right. Good,' John Paul says. 'Looks very fancy.'

'It does. Let's go check in.'

John Paul and I begin to walk again and we're quickly swallowed into the flow of pedestrians. The bridge crosses the Liffey and roads cross each other on the far side. It's busy and loud and I still haven't closed my mouth. The traffic and the people all seem to understand one another. Buses, cars, trucks and walkers all take their cue from traffic lights dotted sporadically around the city. John Paul twitches and, if he was younger, I think he'd reach for my hand.

The hotel is less impressive from the inside. There's some green and red tinsel tacked round a teak reception desk and the area smells of stale beer. We wait our turn to check in, behind some American and Japanese tourists.

'Room 209,' the girl on reception tells us.

Her uniform is grey, and so is her face. She's wearing a Santa hat and she makes no effort to hide how much she doesn't want to be here.

'Breakfast is from seven to ten. It's not included in your room and it's ten fifty each.'

'Another tenner. Jesus.' John Paul rolls his eyes.

'I need to swipe your credit or debit card,' the girl says. 'No money will be taken from your account now, but...'

'Cards?' John Paul says, his eyes darting from the girl to me.

'Is cash okay?' I say.

The girls eyes narrow. More tourists have filled in behind us and I cringe.

'That's fine,' she says. 'But I need to take the payment upfront.'

I take my wallet out of my pocket and pass the girl three twenty-pound notes. I nearly fell off the phone last week when I rang around hotels and discovered the price for a single night in Dublin. Sixty pounds was the cheapest I could find.

'And what about breakfast?' she says, counting the notes.

There's one more twenty-pound note in my wallet. I'm one pound short.

'At that price, are you joking?' John Paul says.

The girl smiles for the first time and passes me the key. 'Enjoy your stay.'

THIRTY-TWO

FIONN

John Paul's suit is much nicer than mine. It fits him like a glove, and there's no manky light grey pinstripe. I recognise it. It's the suit he wore to Dad and Seány's funeral. His mother must have bought it on the mainland after the accident.

Mam did her best with Dad's old suit, but one shoulder is tighter than the other and it chaffs slightly under the arms. The pants are too wide but they stay up with the help of a belt. Unfortunately, there is nothing I can do about the length, and my socks are firmly on display.

'Jaysus, would ya look at us. We're like a couple of film stars,' John Paul says, eyeing himself up in the full-length mirror that's stuck to the front of the wardrobe.

'Do you hear yourself?' I laugh.

'What?' John Paul's cheeks turn pink.

'It suits you, JP,' I say, and I'm telling the truth.

John Paul throws his bag on the bed and pulls out a plastic Lucozade bottle filled with dirty brown liquid.

'It's whiskey,' he says, noticing me pulling a face.

'Where'd you get it?'

'It's my dad's. He'd go apeshit if he knew I had it.'

John Paul unscrews the lid and takes a sip. 'Oh Jesus.' He gags and chokes and then takes another swig.

He shoves the bottle towards me and I do the same. It burns my throat the whole way down. I take another mouthful and another. We swap the bottle back and forth until it's all gone.

'Ready?' John Paul says, his eyes beginning to glass over.

I finally look at myself in the mirror. I see Oisín staring back at me in Dad's suit. I wish there was another sup in John Paul's Lucozade bottle.

'Ready,' I say.

It's dark outside. A group of middle-aged women stand on the corner near our hotel singing Christmas carols. There's a bucket on the ground in front of them and people passing by drop coins into it. John Paul and I cross the road before we reach them.

We asked the girl on reception for directions to the venue and she told us we'd need to get a taxi. John Paul made a face and she quickly explained that we could get two buses instead and she wrote down the numbers and told us where to wait. I begin to regret the whiskey as we try to find the stop for the 46a.

However, when we turn the next corner there's a swarm of guys in suits and girls in fancy dresses. We follow them and get on the bus. My phone rings just as we sit down and Dee's name appears on screen.

'Hello,' I say.

'Heeeeeyyyy.'

'Hi.'

'Where are you?' Dee says.

'On the bus.'

'Oh brilliant. We'll just wait outside for you so.'

'We?'

'Yeah. Lainey and me. And Trevor's here too.'

'Trevor.' I sigh. 'Okay. Great.'

'Yeah. He can't wait to meet you.'

'Yeah. I'm sure.'

The background becomes noisy. I can hear chatting. Dee is distracted for a moment. I guess it's friends asking her to join them.

'You should go on inside,' I say. 'It's freezing.'

I think of Dee in a pretty dress. Long and swishy like the other girls. I think of her standing at the side of the road, shivering as she waits for my bus. I wonder if Trevor has given her his jacket. I hope so. And yet the idea makes my skin crawl.

'Can't go in,' Dee says. 'I have your ticket. They won't let you in without it.'

'Oh. Right. Sorry.'

'It's grand. I'll see you soon, okay?'

I hear more background chatting and Dee hangs up.

The bus stops and there's some argy-bargy when everyone tries to shuffle off at the same time, as if suddenly they can't wait a moment longer to get here.

'Fionn. Oh my God, Fionn.'

I hear Dee before I see her. I turn round and freeze when I spot her. I can't believe how beautiful she looks. Her hair is pulled off her face and pinned to the back. Small plastic butterfly clips seem to hold it all in place. Her shoulders are bare and her dark purple dress sits across her chest with no straps and falls to the ground. The other girls on the bus tried similar looks, but none of them are as stunning as Dee. There is no suit jacket keeping her warm.

The crowd disperses quickly and we make our way towards Dee and Lainey and the tall, thin guy beside them. Lainey seems surprised and I suspect Dee didn't tell her John Paul was joining me. But her surprise soon twists into a smile as she lunges forward and wraps her arms round his neck.

'Oh my God. Oh my actual God. I can't believe you're here,' she says.

John Paul hugs her back and I never realised before how good they look together.

I want to hug Dee but the guy beside her drapes his arm over her shoulder as he stares at me.

'I'm Trevor,' he says, extending his hand the way old people do.

I look at Dee and she nods. I shake.

'It's nice to meet you, man. Dee has told me lots about you,' Trevor says.

'Oh,' I say, not sure what the hell else to say.

Dee passes me a rectangular piece of card. It's bright blue and at a glance it has words like, *party the night away, DJ until 2 a.m. and shots.*

'It's your ticket,' she says.

I reach into my pocket for my wallet but Dee shakes her head and winks.

'On me,' she says.

'She's too generous, this one,' Trevor says, kissing her forehead, before he's distracted by a group of guys calling to him.

'Go on,' Dee encourages him, and she slips out from under his arm. 'Catch up with the lads and I'll see you inside.'

Trevor seems unsure. He looks at his friends and then back at Dee and then at me before making a decision.

'Okay,' he says. 'I'll give you guys a chance to catch up.'

'See you inside,' Dee says.

Trevor nods and calls out to his friends. 'Hey, guys. Wait up.'

'He seems nice,' I say.

Dee smiles. 'It's so good to see you. I can't believe you're really here. Finally here.'

'Me neither.'

Dee's bottom lip trembles and without thinking I take off

my jacket and drape it over her shoulders. She crosses her arms and grabs each side to stop it slipping.

'I remember this jacket,' she says. 'It fits you better now.'

I blush as I remember the last time Dee wore my jacket, just like this. The night on the beach. The night we made love. I can't believe I ever pulled away from her. If I could go back, I'd hold her in my arms and never let her go.

'My mam took it in.'

'Good woman, Lorna,' Dee says.

We're distracted by the sound of laughing and we turn to find Lainey bent in the middle because she's laughing so hard.

'What's so funny,' Dee says.

'Oh nothing,' Lainey says, straightening up.

Lainey is wearing John Paul's jacket. She has her arms in the sleeves, although her fingers don't poke out at the ends.

'C'mon,' Lainey says, 'it's bloody Baltic out here. Let's go inside. I'm dying for a drink.'

THIRTY-THREE

FIONN

Lainey leads the way through the vast university grounds and towards a large building made mostly of glass. John Paul reaches for Lainey's hand and I'm surprised when she takes it. He turns his head over his shoulder and gummy-smiles. Dee giggles.

We join the long queue at the door and make stilted conversation until we show our tickets and someone stamps the date on my hand in red ink. Dee notices me examining it.

'It's just so you can get back in without your ticket,' she says.

Inside is pretty. There's a floor-to-ceiling Christmas tree dominating the decorations. Tall, round tables are draped in purple silk and impersonate some of the girl's dresses. There's a vase with flowers on every table and soft lighting bathes everything in a pinkish-purple hue. I snap my mouth shut when I realise it's gaping and I hope it hasn't been wide open for long. My eyes struggle to take it all in. This place is huge. And elegant. And busy. And sophisticated. Everyone wears fancy suits that look as if they have been crafted seamlessly to fit their bodies. My stomach knots and it makes me want to double over. I hate their suits. I hate their carefree laughter and their college brains spilling over with knowledge. But much more than that, I hate myself for feeling this way. Dad and Seány are gone. A big college brain is no use to Mam. She needs broad shoulders like Dad's to heave and ho with lobster nets.

We gather round a table.

'Drinks?' Lainey says.

John Paul nods. 'Sure.'

'Dee, whatcha having?' Lainey asks.

'Erm, eh, Smirnoff Ice, please?'

'Grand.'

'Fionn?'

'I'm okay, thanks,' I say.

Lainey makes a face. 'You're going to need a drink. Dinner isn't for an hour.'

I glance at the guys in well-tailored suits and girls in elegant dresses surrounding us. Suits that fit them and dresses that no doubt cost a fortune. Most of them have a drink in their hand.

'Water, then,' I say.

'Water.' Lainey snorts, turning towards John Paul. 'Is he serious?'

'Is the water free?' John Paul asks.

'How would I know?' Lainey says.

'Maybe try a Smirnoff Ice,' Dee says. 'They're nice.'

I think about the forty pounds in my wallet. I was planning to drop it into Dee's purse later to pay her back for my ticket.

Dee cranes her neck and sieves through the crowd with her eyes. I've no doubt she's searching for Trevor.

'Yeah, okay,' I say. 'A Smirnoff Ice sounds good. I'll try one of those.'

Dee smiles, then she takes off my jacket and passes it back to me. I tuck it under my arm and it feels bulky.

Lainey takes John Paul's hand again and says, 'C'mon. Come to the bar with me.'

Despite the countless people dotted around us I am hyper-aware that Dee and I are very much alone at the table. Silence falls over us and I search my brain for something to say.

'I've never had a Smirnoff Ice before.'

I cringe, hating myself that *that's* the best I could come up with.

Dee tucks a strand of flyaway hair behind her ear. 'They're nice.'

'Yeah. Yeah. You said.'

The silence returns. Dee searches harder through the crowd with her eyes. I find myself doing the same. I try to see where John Paul has gone and I will him to hurry up.

'Oh. My. God.' A voice behind me shrieks and, before I have time to turn round, I feel arms round my neck.

I look at Dee for a clue but she's as startled as I am. I pull away from the bear hug and turn round.

'Aisling,' I say, recognising the girl in a silver evening dress straight away.

'What are you doing here?' she says before she hugs me again.

I hug back, still a little shaken.

'Just getting a drink,' I say.

'Right. Yeah. Sure.' Aisling smiles but she seems confused and a little drunk. 'But I meant, what are you doing in Dublin? I didn't know you were coming. My mam never said.'

Maureen Purcell is the biggest gossip in Cloch Bheag. She considers it a public service to spread everyone's business like wildfire. She managed to tell half of the island about Dad and Seány's death before Mam had a chance to break it to me.

'My Aisling is off to UCD,' she told Mam one day when we bumped into her in Dickie's. 'It's in Dublin. The biggest university in the country. Very prestigious. Costing an arm and a leg, mind you. But that's the joys of teenagers, isn't it? Aisling is studying science. The best choice for her. What with being so maths-minded.'

I've been in Aisling's class since we were four. Maths is not her thing. Mam asked Mrs Purcell to wish Aisling all the best and then she put down her basket and left Dickie's empty-handed despite having an equally empty fridge at home.

'Do you go here, now?' Aisling asks.

I tug at the top button of my shirt that feels too tight. 'UCD? No. Just visiting.'

'Of course. The Gaeltacht girl.' Aisling turns her attention towards Dee and waves as if they aren't standing side-by-side. 'Hi.'

Dee forces a smile. 'Hello.'

'I think you're in my statistics lecture?' Aisling says.

'No,' Dee says. 'I'm doing media studies.'

'Oh. Right. I could have sworn it was you.' Aisling shrugs and turns back towards me. 'Anyway, it was so great to see you, Fionn. Maybe we could catch up later?'

'Sure. Later.'

Aisling walks away to join a large group of girls at a nearby table. She fits in effortlessly among them. And Mrs Purcell was right. Dublin really is the best place for her.

Lainey and John Paul return from the bar and place the drinks on the table. There's two glass bottles of Smirnoff Ice with plastic straws poking out the tops.

'Try it,' Dee says.

The whiskey from earlier sits in my otherwise empty stomach and I dread adding more liquid on top, but I curl my lips round the straw and suck.

'Whatcha think?' Dee asks.

'It's good.'

We drink and talk. Lainey talks the most and John Paul joins in sometimes. Dee and I are both much quieter.

'Another drink?' Lainey says.

Dee passes Lainey some money and I realise we've entered an unspoken agreement to take turns paying for a round of drinks. I can't afford four drinks, but even if I switch to water now it's too late. I still have to buy Lainey, Dee and John Paul something.

Trevor finds us at last. He approaches our table with a glass bottle in each hand. He places one of the drinks in front of Dee and kisses her. It's a slow, passionate kiss and I don't know where to look. I catch Aisling looking over in the corner of my eye. She waves and I wave back. Dee and Trevor finally separate and Trevor places the other bottle in front of me.

'Here, mate. The queue is mad, so I got this for you.'

I panic, afraid this means I have to buy Trevor a drink now too. We're less than an hour into this thing and already it's spiralling, financially, out of control.

'Thanks, but I'm okay. My friend has gone to get me a drink.'

'Ah man. Let me buy you a beer.'

'No, really. It's okay. But thank you.'

'Seriously? You're not going to take a free beer?' Trevor says.

'Thanks again. But no.'

'Look, I don't want to embarrass you, but Dee has told me...' Trevor places his hands on his hips. He's quite a bit taller than me and, whether he means to be or not, it's intimidating. 'Well, she's told me about... well, you know...'

'I know?' I question.

'Eh yeah, about how hard things are for you,' Trevor says, and he makes a face that I think is supposed to be sympathy. 'About the boat and your family. I just want to buy you a drink, if it helps?'

Dee's face is on the floor. At least she has the courtesy to feel ashamed that she's told a perfect stranger the most intimate details of my life. Aisling should introduce Dee to her mother, they'd get on great, I decide. I glare at Dee but she won't look at me.

'I'm sorry,' Trevor says, 'I'm just nervous. I know you and

Dee go back a long way and I want us to be friends. I didn't mean to offend you.'

I stare at Dee without blinking. My eyes burn.

'Can you stop looking at her like that?' Trevor says. 'I said I'm sorry. I was out of line. Look, skip the drink. It's not important.'

I pick up the bottle of beer. I don't recognise the label but I chug it nonetheless. I don't stop guzzling until the bottle is empty. I slam it down on the table with such force I expect it to break. Everyone seems relieved when it doesn't.

'I shouldn't have come,' I say.

The liquid tries to work its way back up and I beg my stomach not to be sick.

'Fionn, I'm sorry,' Dee says. 'But it's not like you think. I was just telling Trevor all about you, and stuff like that just sort of explains you.'

'Stuff like that explains me?' I say.

Acidy vomit swells up my throat and I swallow it back down.

'I mean like how you describe someone; you know. Like if someone was to describe me they'd probably say, has long brown hair, goes to UCD and used to play camogie.'

'Yeah. Maybe,' I say.

'So, you see what I mean? I was just describing you.'

'Poor fisherman with a dead father and brother,' I say. 'That's me.'

'No. No. That's not what I said.'

I raise my hands in mock surrender. 'Why not? It's an accurate description.'

'No it's not,' Dee says, pulling away from Trevor to get closer to me. 'Was the best big brother in the world and now takes care of his mam working on the family fishing boat. That's you.'

'Same thing,' I say.

'It's really not,' Dee says.

'Look. I've clearly created a shitshow here,' Trevor says, edging closer. 'It definitely wasn't my intention. As I said, I *do* want to be friends. And I'm genuinely sorry if I upset you. I've probably had too much to drink already. Can't hold my beer for shit. I think I should probably piss off for a bit and leave you two to talk.'

'Yeah. Maybe that's a good idea,' Dee says.

Trevor kisses her again. Quickly this time. And then he backs away mouthing, *I'm sorry*.

Dee folds her arm and cups her elbows in her hands. She watches as Trevor joins a group in the corner and soon he's chatting and laughing effortlessly.

'He's not a dickhead. Please don't think he's a dickhead,' Dee says.

'I don't think Trevor is a dickhead.'

'It's me, isn't it? You're pissed with me for telling him all that stuff about you?'

'Yeah.'

Dee inhales. I can't hear it above the background noise but her chest puffs out and when she lets go she seems smaller and more fragile than usual.

'It's just... I feel a bit like it happened to me too. And I know, I know how selfish that sounds. Seány wasn't my little brother. But I really, really cared about him, Fionn. And sometimes it's just so hard to believe he's gone.'

I don't know what to say. It comes as no surprise that Dee cared about Seány. I knew how much she enjoyed her time with him. But, still, hearing her say it here and now pulls the ground out from under me.

'Sometimes I pretend he's still here. I let myself believe he's still in Cloch Bheag with you and maybe I can go visit someday.'

I have no words. The whiskey and vodka and beer are swirling in my stomach and the ground is spinning beneath me.

'Do you want to go somewhere?' I say.
'Yeah.'

THIRTY-FOUR

FIONN

I take Dee by the hand and lead the way. If you saw me, you'd almost believe I knew what I was doing. I try to spot John Paul as we sift our way through the crowd and back towards the door we came in. I can feel Dee searching for Lainey. Her feet drag and she tugs on my arm every so often to pause and look around.

'Where are they?' Dee says, and I struggle to hear her above the background music and noisy chatter. 'They're not at the bar.'

'Maybe they left,' I say.

'Together?'

'What?' I say.

Dee leans forward and cups my ear. 'Look over there, by the Christmas tree.'

I turn and find John Paul and Lainey deep in conversation. His hands are on her hips and she's smiling and throwing her head back with laughter.

'I think they'll be okay on their own,' I say, and then I take Dee's hand again.

This time she holds me a little tighter and we walk. Leaving UCD and our friends behind. Outside is dark and cold.

'Shit,' I say, looking at the tiny goosebumps that appear on Dee's arms. 'I left my jacket inside. I must have put it down somewhere.'

'Oh, okay. Let's go back in.'

I stiffen. I don't want to go back inside and risk bumping into Lainey or John Paul or, worse still, Trevor, and not being able to slip away again.

'It's fine,' I say. 'It didn't fit anyway.'

Mam will kill me when she finds out I've lost Dad's jacket. I try not to think about it.

'How long do you think we'll be waiting for a bus?' I ask.

'Not sure, at this time of night. Maybe we should just walk?'

I grimace.

'It's not that far, really,' Dee says. 'An hour, maybe a little more. Shorter than one side of Cloch Bheag to the other for sure. And we'll be warm if we keep moving.'

I smile. I think about all the times Dee and I strolled around the island late at night. We weren't going anywhere in particular. We just enjoyed walking and talking. The sense of nostalgia takes my breath away.

We talk a lot on the walk in the city. Dee tells me about her course. She likes her society lecturer but her creative writing lecturer is a bitch apparently. She sees Lainey most days and they have a small but close group of friends. She avoids mentioning Trevor. Sometimes I can tell he has a role in one of her stories but she edits him out.

'Did you know your friend from Cloch Bheag goes to UCD?' Dee asks abruptly at the end of a story about drunk Lainey getting lost in the ladies' bathroom in some pub.

'Aisling? Yeah. I knew. Her mother couldn't wait to tell my mother when the offers came out.'

'That was a bit insensitive,' Dee says.

I inhale. 'Not really. Aisling did well in the leaving cert and got the points to go to the college she wanted.'

'But after what happened... just seems a bit—'

I cut across her. 'People can't watch everything they say in case they upset us.'

'Yeah. You're right. Sorry.'

'See, like that. You don't have to apologise all the time,' I say.

'Gotcha. Sorry. Oops, sorry, I did it again.' Dee slaps her hand over her mouth. 'Jesus.'

I laugh and slowly so does she.

All too soon we're in the city centre and I don't know where to lead us from here. Pubs are bustling. People gather and queue outside and music spills onto the street.

'Do you think we're overdressed?' Dee asks, tilting her head towards a stony, grey pub overlooking the Liffey.

Two lads about our age stumble onto the road outside, throwing punches at each other. They spend more time zigzag-ging and staggering than making contact with one another.

'Where's your hotel?' Dee asks.

I point to the far side of the river.

She squints and reads: 'Lynches on the Quays.' Then she makes a face as if its reputation precedes it.

'It was the cheapest I could get,' I say.

'Want to go up to your room?'

I balk.

'Just to talk,' Dee says. 'I'm freezing.'

She rubs her hands up and down her arms. The thought of being alone in a hotel room with Dee makes me nervous. If I'm being honest, being alone with Dee at all makes me nervous. I want to hold her and kiss her and feel her skin against mine. But I'm afraid to get too close because I'm not sure I could ever let go.

THIRTY-FIVE

DEE

Lynches is a shithole. Everyone knows it. The bar downstairs runs a student night every Tuesday and drinks are only one pound each. Some of the girls from our year go but Lainey and I never do. It's a rough crowd and there's almost always a fight outside. Trevor got the shit kicked out of him one night there because some guy thought he was hitting on his girlfriend. Trevor said he wasn't talking to her and she wasn't even that good-looking.

I keep my head down and I follow Fionn past reception. I'm overly aware that we stand out like moving Christmas ornaments in our fancy clothes.

'Swit swoo,' some eejit whistles, and slaps my arse, as we wait for the lift.

'Did he touch you?' Fionn asks, his eyes narrowing as he glares at the man, who has already walked away.

'He was drunk,' I say.

'That's not an excuse.'

The lift dings and the doors open.

'People are assholes,' I say. 'Especially in this city.'

Fionn and I step into the lift; a rattly old thing with just about enough room for us both. He presses '3', and there's a clunk-and-grind sound above our heads and we begin to move. When the doors open again there's a smell of damp, and the carpet on the corridor looks as if it's been there since the seventies. I'm almost certain we walk past a drug deal on the way to Fionn's room. Fionn doesn't seem to notice and I don't say anything.

He fiddles with the key in the lock for long enough to make us both uncomfortable. Finally, the door opens and we step inside. The smell of aftershave nearly knocks me over, but it's still a pleasant change from the nasty stench of the hall. The room is bigger than I expected, with two single beds, a large floor-to-ceiling window overlooking the Liffey and an en suite bathroom.

'That's JP's bed,' Fionn says, pointing at the bed nearest the window. 'This one's mine.'

'Okay,' I say. 'Mind if I sit down? These shoes are killing me.'

'Sure. Yeah. Grand.'

I sit on the edge of Fionn's bed and slip off my silver sandals. My feet sting a bit as the blood rushes back to my toes.

'How do you walk in these?' Fionn says, picking up one and examining the five-inch stiletto.

'You get used to it.'

He puts my sandal back down and shoves his hands into his pants pockets. I wait for him to come sit beside me but he stays standing and stares out the window.

'Do you and JP have any drink up here?' I ask. I can feel myself sobering up.

He points to an empty plastic bottle on John Paul's bed. 'We had JP's dad's whiskey.'

I scrunch my face and poke my tongue out. Just thinking about the taste of old people's whiskey turns my stomach.

'We could order something. Room service,' I say.

Fionn looks horrified at the suggestion and I feel awful. Money is obviously even tighter than I thought.

'Or we could watch some TV?' I glance around and realise there isn't one in the room. 'Or go for another walk.'

'It's freezing outside,' Fionn says, and he stares out the window again.

'Are you okay?' I ask. When he doesn't reply I answer for him. 'It's just you don't seem to be.'

'I'm okay.'

'Do you not like Dublin?'

'I like it.'

'Really?'

'Really. I think it must be kind of cool to live here. Even if the people are assholes, as you say.'

'Not everyone.'

'No. Not everyone.'

Fionn finally sits down beside me and I can't hold my relief in. I puff out as if I'm exerted from running uphill.

'Thank you for coming tonight,' I say.

'I ruined your night,' he says. 'I didn't mean to make things awkward with Trevor.'

'You didn't.'

'I understand that you're going to talk to your boyfriend about stuff. I just wasn't expecting him to say it all back to me. Not like that.'

'It was all a bit weird,' I say, and I fidget with a loose thread at the edge of my dress. 'He was just nervous. I talk about you a lot.'

Fionn runs his hand through his hair and tosses it a bit. And all I can think about is kissing him.

'A lot,' he says, and he's blushing.

I tut. 'Not like a lot, a lot. Just sometimes. Like when you got *The Two Seans*. I told Lainey and Trevor all about it 'cause I was so happy for you.'

'Thanks Dee. That really means a lot.'

'I really am happy for you, Fionn. It must be amazing having your own boat.'

Fionn snorts.

'You're only nineteen and you're totally independent, sailing around with JP. And I'm here sitting in an auditorium every day learning crap I'll probably never use in real life.'

'You'll use it, Dee. Someday I'll turn on the telly and I'll see you staring right back at me.'

I slap his shoulder playfully. 'C'mon. As if.'

'You will, Dee. And I can't wait to watch.'

I can't remember what I was about to say next because as soon as Fionn's lips press against mine, all my thoughts tumble out of my head. I have waited six months to feel him like this again and it has been worth every second.

THIRTY-SIX

FIONN

It's nothing like last time. I don't dart my eyes away, afraid to look, in case I embarrass her. I unzip Dee's dress and watch it fall off her shoulders and into a pile on the ground. She takes off her bra and knickers and lies naked on my bed. I stare and take in every inch of her skin. The freckle above her right knee. Her hourglass shape. Her small breasts. Her long hair. Her dark eyes. I don't want to blink and miss a fraction of a second of her beauty.

'Your turn,' she says, and then she giggles and I know that under that new, sexy surface is the same shy girl I made love to on the beach.

Dee helps me undress. She unbuttons my shirt and kisses my chest. My belt is stubborn and her nail scratches me as she tries to unbuckle it.

'Shit. Sorry.'

'It's okay,' I say.

I take over the unbuckling but my hands are shaking. Dee notices. She takes her hands off me and her eyes peer into mine. Searching me as if I'm a book she's desperate to read.

'Are you okay?' she whispers.

'Yeah. You?'

'Yeah.'

'Got it,' I say, as my buckle releases and my pants fall down straight away.

Dee's girlish giggling turns to real laughter. I kick my pants away and pull off my boxers. I can feel the heat creep across my nose and cheeks as her gaze sweeps over me. She photographs me with her eyes.

She pulls me close to her with such confidence it takes my breath away. Her skin is silky smooth and she smells like pineapples and summer. I take deep breaths and concentrate not to lose myself already. Dee guides me inside her. She doesn't flinch or squirm. I'm confident there's no pain. Not anymore.

It's nothing like before. The last time I felt Deirdre McKenna beneath me she was a girl and I was a boy. We were both young and curious and unsure. Dee is very much a woman now. Confident, clever, graceful. She's more experienced than me in every way. I think I'm more in love with her than ever.

THIRTY-SEVEN

FIONN

Dee and I lie wrapped around each other for a long time. It's hard not to fall asleep, but we don't have that luxury. We don't say it, but we're both concerned that John Paul could arrive at any moment. With or without Lainey.

Dee gets up first.

'I'm going to grab a shower, if that's okay,' she says.

'Sure.'

'Come with me?'

I swallow hard. 'Yeah. You go ahead. I'll be in in a minute.'

I watch Dee's naked body disappear into the bathroom. The toilet flushes and the shower comes to life. I give Dee some privacy and I listen to the water fall for quite a while. I replay what just happened. Her touch, her smile, her gasps. *Her!* My mind is blown.

My legs are shaky when I stand up and make my way into the bathroom. Dee is standing in the bath with the shower curtain pulled. It feels strange to pull it back and step in behind her. But I take a deep breath and do it. She turns round, smiles and wraps her arms round me.

Her make-up is washed away and I think she's even prettier now. We kiss and cuddle. The words *I love you* are on the tip of my tongue. They have been since the moment I stepped off the bus and laid eyes on her. They almost slipped out when I pushed inside her. And now, as the night comes to an end, it's hardest of all not to say them. So I say something else, instead.

'How long are you and Trevor together?'

I can see the question takes her by surprise.

'Nearly three months. We met at the start of college.'

'That's not that long.'

Dee shrugs. 'Suppose not. Still though. It'll be hard to tell him about this. I don't want to hurt him.'

'He's a good guy?' It comes out like a question but I wasn't asking. I genuinely believe Trevor is a nice person. I see the way he looks at Dee. Like he can't believe his luck. I know how he feels.

'He is a nice person, Fionn,' Dee says, as if she needs to defend him to me. 'I know he put his foot in it earlier—'

I close my eyes and shake my head, cutting her off. I don't want to talk about that again.

'Don't tell him,' I say, opening my eyes again to see her confusion. 'Don't tell him about tonight. About us.'

'What? I have to. I have to explain.'

'No. No you don't.'

Dee takes a step back. The taps on the wall must dig into her back but she doesn't acknowledge them. Her face scrunches and her lips quiver.

'Don't say it. Please don't say it,' she says.

'Say what?'

'Don't say we shouldn't have done this. I can't bear to hear that again.'

'I won't. I wasn't going to. This was amazing. You are amazing.'

'Then why don't you want me to tell Trevor? He'll understand. I think he's always known.'

'I'm going home tomorrow,' I say.

Dee sighs. 'I know.'

'And that's it, really.'

'What's it?'

'We'll be apart again.'

'People make long-distance work,' Dee says, enthusiastically. 'We can split weekends or something. You can come up here. I can go there.'

I open my mouth but no words come out.

'I know it's not ideal, but it's Cloch Bheag, not the moon,' she says.

'It might as well be,' I say. 'Dublin is expensive, Dee. I couldn't afford a round of drinks tonight; I definitely can't afford trips across the country regularly.'

'Okay, I'll come to you, then. I love Cloch Bheag.'

'You don't have time.'

'I'll make time,' she says.

'Dee...'

'No seriously, I will. I only have two lectures on a Friday morning. I can skip them. I could get an early bus and be up to Cloch Bheag by dinnertime and then we'd have all day Saturday together.'

'And what about work? You work Saturdays.'

'I'll figure it out. I'll work evenings after college instead, or something.'

Dee is so convincing. It almost sounds doable. I want so desperately to agree, or to at least try. My chest is tight and my heart aches when I know I can't. I can't let her shape her life around me. I'm shackled to Cloch Bheag but Dee deserves to be free.

'Do you know the first thing I thought about tonight when I saw Aisling?' I ask.

Dee rolls her eyes. It's obvious she likes talking about

Aisling as little as I like talking about Trevor.

'What did you think?' she says.

'I thought she looked exactly like the other girls. She fitted in with them.'

'Is that not a good thing?'

'It is. I'm happy for her.'

The water begins to grow cold and I reach behind Dee and turn off the tap. I get out first and fetch the towels. I pass Dee one and wrap another round my waist. I take her hand and make sure she doesn't slip as she steps out.

'What are you trying to say, Fionn?'

'I don't belong here. I want to. I think Dublin is so cool. But I stand out like a sore thumb. Jesus, the bus driver took one look at me and he knew that.'

'I'm not asking you to belong here,' Dee says, shivering.

'You don't belong on Cloch Bheag either.'

Dee looks at me with heartbreak-heavy eyes. I can't look. Instead, I focus on her hair and how the water drips from the ends and onto the floor tiles.

'You have such a great life, Dee. I mean, I always knew it sounded great when we talked about it on the phone. But seeing it for real tonight. Wow. Look at you. You're stunning. Your life is fancy balls, college guys and beer I don't recognise.'

'None of that matters to me,' she says.

'You say that now. Maybe you even believe it. But not so long ago I dreamed of this life too, and if I had the chance there's no way I'd give it up.'

'Fuck's sake, Fionn. How can you do this? Again. Use me for sex and then basically tell me to piss off when you're done. You're right. You don't belong here. Because even the biggest bastards in Dublin don't behave like that.'

I reach for her, but she pushes me back and we both almost slip on the wet floor.

'I love you,' she shouts. 'I love you so much. But if that's not enough for you...'

Dee opens the bathroom door and it slams against the wall with a loud bang. I follow her into the bedroom. She doesn't look at me as she gathers up her underwear and her dress and shakes them out. I pull yesterday's tracksuit out of my rucksack and bundle my suit in. We dress without speaking, but our puffy exhales say so much.

Finally, when we're both fully clothed, I catch Dee's hand and pull her close to me. I kiss her and she doesn't pull away, but she doesn't kiss me back.

'You're my favourite person in the whole world, Deirdre McKenna,' I say.

'Then why won't you try...'

'Because you're my favourite person. It won't work. People want stuff like this to work and it never, ever does. They grow apart and end up hating each other. I couldn't bear it if you ever grew to hate me.'

I feel Dee's stiff pose soften and a silent tear trickles down her cheek. 'I could never hate you, Fionn.'

'Promise?'

'I promise,' she says, her voice breaking. 'You're my favourite person too.'

My heart hurts. I know this feeling. I felt this way when Mam sat me at the kitchen table and told me Dad and Seány weren't coming home. I'm not losing Dee, I'm giving her away. But I think, if possible, it's even harder to bear.

'Don't tell Trevor,' I suggest, again.

'I have to.'

'He's mad about you.'

'Yeah. He's nice to me. That's why I have to tell him about tonight. I can't lie. I can't pretend.'

'Don't break his heart, Dee. It's not worth it. Let him be nice to you. Let him love you. And let yourself love him back.'

'I will miss you,' Dee says, tears gathering in the corners of her eyes.

'I know. I'll miss you too.'

I lead Dee to the bed again. We lie side-by-side, fully clothed, and we let ourselves sleep at last.

THIRTY-EIGHT

DEE

Sneaking out past reception is worse than sneaking in. Last night's dress feels wrong on my body this morning, and despite a long shower I still feel grubby. My hair is frizzy, without conditioner and a brush, and my make-up-free face is pale and tired.

Fionn leaves the room key in reception and exchanges generic chit-chat about his stay with the girl on the desk. I wait for him outside.

'Where are they?' Fionn asks, joining me.

I like his all-black tracksuit and I try not to think about how good dark colours look on him and how much I fancy him.

'McDonald's on O'Connell Street,' I say, and I point in the general direction so he knows it's not far away.

'Who's with them?'

'It's just Lainey and JP.'

'Trevor?' Fionn asks.

I inhale sharply. I don't want to talk about Trevor with Fionn.

'Just Lainey and JP,' I say.

Fionn waits for me to lead the way. We walk side-by-side.

My hand dangles by my side and sometimes I think he'll reach for it and I'm disappointed when he doesn't. We don't talk and I'm glad McDonald's is just round the corner.

Lainey squeals and jumps up from her seat as soon as she sees me. Thankfully the place is nearly empty, and heads don't turn.

'Oh my God, was that the best night ever or what?' Lainey says, throwing her arms round me. Her breath smells like beer and Egg McMuffin.

'Yeah. It was great.'

'Here. I got you brekkie,' Lainey says, and she points to a large Coke and an apple pie. 'You too, Fionn.'

'Thanks,' he says.

Fionn and I sit in the seats next to Lainey and JP and we tuck into our apple pies as if we haven't eaten in days.

'Can you believe they don't serve chicken nuggets until after ten thirty? Like what a load of bollocks. I wanted a Happy Meal,' Lainey says.

Lainey and John Paul fill us in on everything we missed at the ball. The food was shite, apparently. Lumpy mash and soggy vegetables. John Paul ate most of Lainey's. The shots were only two pounds so they had a lot of them. There was a band and a DJ after. Some girl slipped on the stairs and they think she might have broken her ankle, and someone else threw up under the Christmas tree. One of Trevor's friends was stocious and got in a fight with the bouncers, and the whole group got kicked out before the meal even started.

'Poor Trevor,' Lainey says between sips of Coke. 'He was all like, *oh tell Dee I'm so sorry. I'll make it up to her, I swear.*'

I slip my phone out of my purse and realise I have fifteen texts and five missed calls. Probably all from Trevor.

'I see flowers and chocolates in your future.' Lainey laughs.

'So, what did you two get up to?' John Paul asks, when Lainey finally lets him get a word in.

'A walk,' I say, quickly.

'A walk?' Lainey looks wholly unimpressed. 'So you just wandered around the city for hours, in the middle of the night.'

'Yeah. Pretty much,' Fionn says. 'Never been here before so a lot to see.'

'Fair enough,' Lainey says, and then she looks at John Paul.

He shrugs.

'Right, I need to pee,' Lainey announces loudly, and the guy at the next table looks over. 'Dee, come with me, yeah?'

I don't need to pee but I know that's not why we're using the bathroom.

'Sure,' I say, standing up, and John Paul looks as excited as Lainey to get his best friend all to himself for a moment.

'Oh my God.' Lainey links my arm. 'I have sooooo much to tell you.'

I look back over my shoulder. John Paul has launched into a story with lots of hand movements. Fionn is listening and nodding.

The cleaner is in the bathroom so we have to wait outside for a while and Lainey hops from one leg to the other.

'Seriously. I'm bursting.'

'Me too,' I say, although I'm not.

'What the hell happened you last night?' Lainey says. 'We came back from the bar and then you were gone.'

'You didn't say anything to Trevor, did you?' I ask.

'Like what?' Lainey says. 'The truth? That you pissed off with your ex without telling anyone?'

I wince.

'No. Of course I bloody didn't say anything to him.'

I think about reiterating that Fionn was never my boyfriend, but Lainey calls him my ex regularly and now doesn't feel like the time to argue about that.

'So where did you *really* go?' Lainey says.

The cleaner pushes a metal cart loaded with cleaning products out the door and says, 'The flush on the loo nearest the wall isn't working.'

'Okay. Thanks,' Lainey says, darting inside and using the other stall.

I wash my hands while I wait for her, as if the water can erase the way I treated Trevor last night. The toilet flushes. Lainey reappears, washes her hands and looks at me very seriously.

'You okay?' I say, suddenly concerned. I've never seen Lainey like this before.

'John Paul and I did it last night.'

'Oh.' I puff out, realising I'd been holding my breath.

'"Oh!" That's all you're going to say?'

'Erm, eh...'

I stare at Lainey. One of the spaghetti straps on her dress is broken. Her hair is even messier than mine and her make-up is still there, but just about. I can only imagine Lainey and John Paul didn't have the luxury of a hotel room last night and I try not to think about them in the park or a public loo somewhere.

'Dee,' Lainey says, her eyes wide and glaring at me. 'Say something. This is a big deal.'

'I didn't know you liked him that much,' I say.

'Neither did I. Not until last night. It was amazing, Dee. Like so good. I mean, it hurt a bit, but that's to be expected, right?'

'Yeah.'

I don't remind her of all the other guys, all the other times. We both knew Lainey's stories of hot dates and amazing sex when we were in school were tall tales. Beside, none of that matters now. We've grown up since then and she's found a guy she really likes. But he's leaving. Just like Fionn.

'Oh Lainey.'

I hug my best friend and my heart aches for her as much as it does for me.

'I'm really glad last night was so special for you,' I say. 'And I'm sorry it's so shit now. If it helps, I know exactly how you feel.'

Lainey breaks away from me and looks me up and down. 'Are you still drunk?' She laughs. 'I said I like him. Like I proper like him. It was the best night of my life. It was like butterflies and fireworks. I get it now. I mean, it's like Ross and Rachel. We were on a break but we're meant to be. You know?' She takes my hands in hers and raises them above our heads as if we're catching the ends of rainbows. 'This must be how you feel when you're with Trevor.'

My heart sinks and I pull my arms back as the rainbow instantly disappears. This is never how I feel when I'm with Trevor. But I understand. I do. Because this is *always* how I feel when I'm with Fionn. And Trevor doesn't deserve that. He deserves butterflies and fireworks. He deserves to be the Ross to my Rachel. Guilt sits in my stomach like a rock, too heavy to hold, and I regret that apple pie. I am going to make it up to him. I am going to be the best girlfriend ever.

'Dee, are you even listening?' Lainey waves her arms in front of me, demanding my attention. 'Did Fionn say anything? Has JP been talking about me?'

'Sometimes, yeah, I think so.'

'Oh God, Dee. I'm so excited. This morning, before you guys came in and we were just sitting having breakfast and talking and stuff, I would just look at him and start thinking about last night all over again. I just want to do it again, you know.'

I nod.

'Imagine how fun this summer will be? JP said people camp out on the beach on Cloch Bheag when the weather is good. Wouldn't that be so cool.'

I swallow.

'We'd have to go before the Gaeltacht kids arrive. Those

little fuckers take over the whole island. So, June. The bank holiday weekend would be perfect. June third or fourth or something.'

'That's a week before Seány's anniversary,' I say.

'Shit. Sorry. I forgot.'

'S'okay,' I say. 'I'd like to be there for Fionn. But I don't think he'd be up for much partying.'

'Dee...' Lainey says my name as if it's a mouthful. 'Did something happen with the two of you last night? I mean, you were gone for pretty much the whole night, and I know the boy likes to walk but that's pushing it a bit.'

I think I'm going to start crying.

'I need to pee,' I say, hurrying into the stall.

'Flush doesn't work in that one,' Lainey shouts after me.

I lean against the stall wall and ignore her. I take some deep breaths and dab some tissue around my eyes. When I open the door Lainey is waiting, and she gathers me into her arms.

'What the hell happened last night?' she says.

'We're just friends.' I sniffle. 'We're going to be just friends.'

'Fuck him, Dee. He's not worth it. You have Trevor. What does Fionn have? Nothing. Just a stupid boat and a stupid island.'

Finally, I let myself cry. Because Lainey is right. All Fionn has is *The Two Seans* and Cloch Bheag. This isn't how it was supposed to be.

THIRTY-NINE

FIONN

We finish breakfast. The city came to life all of a sudden as we ate, and when we step outside the street is scattered with cars and people. Dee and Lainey walk to the bus station with us. Heads turn as they pass. People smirk or point at the girls' dresses, evidence of a party last night. Dee takes off her sandals and carries them in her hand. She keeps her head down and I can sense how self-aware she feels.

Lainey and John Paul hold hands and I've never seen my best friend happier. Lainey looks at him every so often as if he's a lollipop she wants to lick. Then she turns towards me and glares at me as if I'm someone who just killed her cat.

At the bus Lainey and John Paul kiss the way people in films do and they reassure each other that it's all going to be okay. Dee and I stand back and give them some space.

'JP says he's going to come to Dublin at the weekends,' Dee says.

I nod.

'But Lainey says she's going to go to Cloch Bheag sometimes too.'

I nod again.

'So, I might go with her and then maybe we could all meet up.'

'C'mon, Dee,' I say. 'You know as well as I do Lainey is going to forget JP the moment he steps foot onto the bus.'

Her face scrunches.

'You don't think she's serious about him?'

'Of course not. Lainey is never serious about anyone. It's just the way she is.'

'You're wrong,' she snaps. 'Just because you didn't want to make long-distance work doesn't mean they won't.'

'That's not what I'm saying.'

Dee raises her hand. 'Just leave it, Fionn. Okay. We've said everything we need to say. You're going home and I'm staying here. And, look, if it's going to be a problem for you then I won't come to Cloch Bheag. You already made it clear I don't belong there, so...'

Dee folds her arms. Her sandals dangle from her hands. I think about her sitting on the edge of my bed in her bare feet, waiting for me to touch her. I hope I never forget what she looked like in that moment. What she felt like.

'If Lainey comes to Cloch Bheag then it would be really great if you came too,' I say.

'There's no if, Fionn. Lainey will go. I've never seen her this determined.'

'Okay.'

One of Dee's shoes falls and we both bend to pick it up. There's a moment when we're crouched on the ground, face-to-face, and I think if I don't kiss her I'm going to burst. I stand up and leave her sandal for her to pick up.

John Paul comes to stand beside us and he drapes his arm over my shoulder.

'You've our tickets, right?' he says.

I tap my pocket. 'Yeah.'

'Don't worry, Dee. I'll take good care of him for ya,' John

Paul says.

Dee smiles and I'm almost certain I can see a lump work its way down her throat.

'Keep an eye on my girlfriend,' he says.

Lainey appears beside Dee, giggling at the mention of girlfriend.

I want to scream.

'Right,' I say. 'We better get on.'

'It's the same driver as before,' John Paul says.

'Text me when you're on the ferry. And when you get home,' Lainey says, like a worried mother.

Dee rolls her eyes. 'As if he's not going to be texting you the whole way home too,' she says.

Lainey giggles again. I didn't know she could make that sound. It's so girlish and innocent, and it doesn't align with the person I thought she was.

John Paul kisses Lainey again. And I think I'm going to have to physically drag him onto the bus.

'Bye,' Dee says. Her eyes water and glisten.

'Bye,' I say.

'You'll text me too. When you're home?' she says.

'Yeah. Of course, I will.'

John Paul and Lainey finally part, and John Paul slaps my back and says, 'Right. Let's go.'

A shrill Nokia ringtone cuts through the air and Dee rummages in her purse for her phone.

'Hello,' she says, and then she smiles and her shoulders round. 'It's okay. Don't worry. I'm just in town now but I'll come straight over. Um-hmm. Um-hmm. See you in half an hour or so. Um-hmm. Love you too.'

I turn away and walk up the bus steps. I don't wait for John Paul and I don't look out the window. I take a seat at the back of the bus, keep my head down, and I promise myself that I am never coming to Dublin ever again.

PART THREE

FORTY

FIONN

Three Years Later – May 2004

Four days at sea always feels longer than it actually is. My arms and back ache from pulling and tugging the lobster cages. Canned food keeps the hunger at bay, but I daydream about a juicy steak and Mam's mashed potatoes. The sun shines overhead, but nonetheless the Atlantic breeze could slice strips off you. My navy woolly hat itches and Mam says it's seen better days. She bought me a new, dark-green one for Christmas last year, but this flimsy navy one belonged to Dad and I can't bear to part with it.

This trip feels especially tiresome. John Paul has spent the whole time talking about Lainey's graduation from UCD.

'There's a ceremony. Probably in that fancy building we went to before. You remember, the one with all the glass.'

I remember.

'Can you believe that's the night Lainey and I got together. God, imagine if I hadn't gone with you.'

'Destiny,' I say, jokingly.

John Paul muses over my words. 'It was,' he says. 'I think it really was.'

John Paul talks for hours more about the graduation. All the while I think about Dee. Lainey graduating means Dee is too. I try to imagine her all dressed up. All grown up. My heart hurts when an image won't come. All I see is the disappointment in her face the night I told her to go back to Trevor. I'll never forgive myself for causing her to look at me that way.

'Mam gave me a right bollocking over me suit,' John Paul says, cutting into my thoughts. 'She's fuming that the one I have doesn't fit me anymore. As if growing out of it is my fault. Dad is six two, what does she expect?'

John Paul is a giant. He's at least two inches taller than his father and a head and shoulders taller than me. We were always the same height growing up, but when I stopped growing he continued to shoot up.

'Mam won't come shopping with me,' he says.

I strain to hear him over the squeak of the pulley as I heave-ho and drag nets laden with plaice from under the water. In six months I reckon I'll have enough money to invest in an electrical pulley. I never thought the idea would excite me, but it does.

'Do you think I'm made of money?' John Paul mimics his mother with a hand on his hip and a finger wagging. 'If your girlfriend wants you all dressed up, then she can go shopping with you. It's far from suits you were raised.'

'I'll go shopping with you, if you like?' I say.

'Really?' John Paul sounds strange, as if the idea of me stepping foot on the mainland for an afternoon surprises him.

'Sure. How about tomorrow?'

John Paul smiles and nods, and I look forward to my first day out in months, maybe even a year.

The following morning, I take a long shower, shampooing

my hair twice to make sure I get the smell of the ocean out, and I meet John Paul at the pier. We catch the mid-morning ferry followed by the bus to Letterkenny.

We spent hours trying to find the perfect suit. John Paul's long legs make it difficult and every pair of trousers he tries on stops too shy of his shoes. I buy a pair of jeans for myself and some chocolate for Mam. She's so thin lately that the bones in her cheeks look as if they could pierce through her skin.

'My mam's just in a pisser because she's sick of me going to Dublin,' John Paul vents from behind the curtain in an umpteenth changing room.

'You are there a lot.'

'Lainey is there,' he tells me, as if I didn't know or don't understand his reasons.

'You're the eldest, JP. You have responsibilities.'

'Says who?'

He pulls back the curtain and stands in a navy suit with a white shirt and pink tie.

'It fits,' I say, relieved.

He closes the curtain again and I hear him change back into his tracksuit. He pays for the suit and we go for lunch in the fish and chip shop next door.

'Fish isn't great here,' John Paul says. 'Def not as fresh as ours.'

'You're right,' I say. 'Hang on.'

I stand up and walk towards the counter. I ask the young girl frying chips if I can speak to the manager and I return to my seat ten minutes later.

'Fish is shite because it's frozen,' I say. 'I said I could get them fresh for the same price. So, we're officially their supplier now.'

'Oh fuck, Fionn,' John Paul says, clearing his plate. 'I wish you'd told me you were going to do that.'

'What difference does it make? The deal's done now. We've

another client. If we keep up like this, we'll have to hire some help.'

'You'll have to hire help,' John Paul says.

'We're partners, JP. If we're taking on someone else, we'll do it together.'

John Paul stands up and walks outside as if he's suddenly desperate for fresh air. He forgets his suit bag. I pick it up and follow him outside.

'What's wrong?' I say.

'I'm moving, Fionn.'

I swallow hard. I know what comes next.

'I'm moving to Dublin to be with Lainey. Her dad is fixing me up with a job laying timber floors.'

'Timber floors.'

'It's a good job. And it's her dad's own company so...'

'When do you go?'

'As soon as we find somewhere to live. Flats in Dublin are crazy expensive. We can't afford the city but we can probably manage something on the outskirts.'

'Is that why your mam is like a demon. She doesn't want you to go?'

'She does want me to go. She wants me to make something of myself.'

I look at the ground.

'Shit. That's not what I meant. Staying in Cloch Bheag is different for you. You've taken over where your dad left off. *The Two Seans* is your boat. Your business. I was always only helping out.'

'Yeah,' I say.

I remember a time the thought of leaving Cloch Bheag horrified John Paul and now he's buying fancy suits and he can't wait to get away. He's living the life I always wanted. I'm happy for him, and at the same time I'm so jealous I want to punch something.

'Sounds like the dream, JP,' I say.

'You'll have to come visit,' he says.

I'm about to say something redundant about city prices but I know John Paul was offering me a spot on his couch. But if I couldn't make trips to Dublin work three years ago, I doubt I could start now.

'We okay?' John Paul asks. 'I know I've let you down. But I won't leave until you find someone to give you a hand.'

I wonder where I'm possibly going to find help. Anyone with experience has their own boat or works on a family boat. I guess it's just me now.

'We're okay, JP,' I say. 'C'mon. If we head back now we'll have time for a few pints in Reilly's.'

'You're a good friend, Fionn,' JP says, slapping my back. 'A good friend.'

FORTY-ONE
DEE

I can smell sausages and rashers as soon as I wake up, and I hear Mam in the kitchen. The radio is on and the sound of voices on a talk show hums beneath my bedroom and the lawnmower is working away outside my window. A cupboard bangs and a utensil clangs every so often as Mam cooks up a fry. It's the smells and sounds of a busy morning and I lie in bed for a few moments and take it in.

I check my phone. There's a text from Lainey.

Holy Shit.

We did it.

C u soon xx

I've similar texts from most of my college friends and I reply with equally profound texts about graduating.

Whoop! OMG! YEEEESSSSS!!

I get up and pee and then spend a ridiculously long time staring at my cap and gown hanging on the back of my door. I spent stupid money on a purple dress for underneath and Mam says she's not sure about it. Apparently, it makes me look much older than twenty-one.

Mam has been buzzing with a nervous energy all week. It's as if she has something to tell me. But anytime I broach the subject she shuts me down, loading me with compliments.

'We're so proud of you, Deirdre,' she says a lot. And, 'A first-class honours degree. You deserved it. All that work you put in. Your Aunty Kitty couldn't believe it. That'll really put the pressure on her lot.'

My cousins are still in primary school. I don't think Aunty Kitty has to worry about their degrees or pressure just yet.

'Ah, love, you're up,' Mam says, when I walk into the kitchen.

'Smells great,' I say.

Mam is plating up a mountain of food. Rashers, egg, sausage, black and white pudding and a shrivelled, fried tomato.

'I made us a fry,' she says, passing me the plate. 'God knows when we'll get grub at this thing.'

'We're going for dinner after the ceremony,' I remind her.

Mam rolls her eyes. 'That's not until this evening. You know your father. He'll be like a bag of cats if he's hungry. And what if it drags on? I've heard UCD graduations can really go on.'

I don't argue. My mouth is watering as I set my plate down at the kitchen table.

Mam opens the back door and sticks her head out. 'Dessie,' she shouts. 'Food.'

I can feel the heat of a summer's day creep in the door.

'I don't know why he needs to cut the grass this morning of all mornings,' Mam says, and then she takes off her apron and joins me at the table.

Mam, Dad and I sit and eat. Mam pours tea and Dad thanks her. Dad doesn't read the paper the way he usually does, and

Mam doesn't bombard me with questions about today. It's all very quiet and civilised and nothing like us.

'This is lovely,' I say, polishing off my tomato.

Mam smiles.

''Tis, Bernie. 'Tis very good.' Dad says.

Then the damn silence returns. I can't take it any longer.

'So, Lainey's dress is red and floral,' I say.

'My God,' Mam says, setting down her knife and fork. 'I never thought I'd see Elaine Burke in a floral dress. I remember when she was wild as a goat. Poor Mags didn't know what to do with her. And now look. She's all grown up. You both are.'

Mam's voice cracks and Dad says, 'Ah Bernie, not now.'

'Sorry. Sorry, love,' Mam says. 'You're right.'

'Right, that's it,' I say, slamming my hand on the table with a force that makes the rasher on my plate jump. 'What is going on? You two are acting so weird lately.'

Mam looks at Dad and he shakes his head.

'Seriously,' I say, 'you're freaking me out. Is one of you sick? Please just tell me.'

'Jesus, no,' Dad says. 'What the hell gave you that idea?'

'You. This.' I draw an invisible circle round us and the table. 'Thanking Mam for pouring you tea, like you're all posh. Mam nearly crying because Lainey's dress is flowery. Something is wrong. Please just tell me.'

Mam looks at Dad again and this time he nods. I wait.

Mam puffs out and says, 'Well, for one thing, we're in perfect health, thank God.'

My chest is tight. 'Then what?'

'We wanted to wait until after your big day,' Dad says.

'Just tell me.' My voice is raised and I'm surprised Dad doesn't pull me up on it.

'We're moving,' Mam says as if the words hurt her to push out.

'That's it? That's all? Jesus, Mam. I actually thought you were dying,' I say.

'We're moving to France, Deirdre,' Mam says. 'The house is going on the market and we've found a lovely little one-bed apartment in Cannes.'

'France?' I say.

'I know it's a bit of a shock. But you're graduating, love. You don't need us any more. And I'm pottering around here on my own most days.'

'France?'

'Dad is going to take early retirement; he only has a couple of years to go anyway and we're going to make the most of getting older.'

'He's fifty-nine,' I say. My voice is growing louder.

'Sixty this year,' Dad says.

'Where am I supposed to go?' I ask.

Mam and Dad look at each other again. I wish they'd stop doing that. It's obvious they've been talking about this for a while. I can't believe they never discussed it with me.

'We thought you'd be moving in with Trevor soon enough anyway,' Mam says.

I swallow. Living with Trevor has never come into my head. Lainey and John Paul talk about moving in together all the time but Trevor and I have never touched the subject.

'I can't believe this,' I say. 'I can't believe you're leaving me behind.'

'We're not leaving you behind,' Mam says. 'You're a grown woman now. We're cutting the apron strings so you can make your own way in the world.'

'And we couldn't be prouder,' Dad says.

FORTY-TWO

DEE

I excuse myself from the table without finishing my fry and I flop onto my bed. My cap and gown stare at me. Suddenly, graduating feels like the last thing I want to do. I take out my phone to text Lainey.

~~Ur not going 2 believe dis~~

I text Trevor instead.

~~Can we talk?~~

I don't send either message. Lainey and Trevor will care, of course, but they won't understand. They'll try to say all the right things but they'll just be words.

Finally, I look for Fionn's number. I have to scroll miles back through my messages to find the last time we spoke. It's been almost a year. Our conversation has diluted to wishing each other Happy Birthday, Merry Christmas, and I text every June for Seány's anniversary.

I rarely say Fionn's name out loud anymore and I'm sure

everyone thinks I've long forgotten about him. Even Lainey.
But, it's strange, the only person I want to talk to right now is
him. Because, I know, he's the only person who will truly
understand.

~~Hi~~
~~My parents r moving away~~
~~I dnt want them 2 go~~
~~Ppl leave~~
~~Its not fair~~

I shake my head and toss my phone aside without sending
any text. I go to my desk and open the top drawer, smiling when
I find my old pad of scented notepaper. I take it out and inhale.
It still smells of lavender. I search the remaining drawers for a
pen, find one and sit cross-legged on my bed. Words spill onto
the page without having to think. Just as they always did before.

15 Hilbert Grove
Clondalkin
Dublin 22

15 May 2004

Libasheen
Cloch Bheag
Co. Donegal

Dear Fionn,

*You'd think that writing to you again after all this time would be
hard. But it's not. It feels like the easiest thing in the world. It
feels like being a teenager again. Back in school when life was so
much simpler.*

You were right, when you said time would drag us apart. The more time Lainey and John Paul spent together, the less time we could seem to find for each other. The boat, assignments, deadlines, work. You said life would get in the way. How were you so wise?

I still think about you. I don't tell anyone that. I don't even say your name out loud anymore. But you're there. Taking up space in my head and I wouldn't have it any other way.

I see JP a lot. As you know, he travels to Dublin most weekends. He's changed. He's taller and he has a beard now. I try to imagine you with a beard too, but I can't. I suppose you'll always be baby-faced in my memory. That's where you live now. Somewhere in the back of my mind. For a long time I spent every weekend hoping you would tag along with JP. I hoped you'd want to visit Dublin again. And me. Over time I learned to hide and, finally, to no longer feel the disappointment when you never did.

JP says you spend Saturdays on the boat again. Just like you did with your dad. I think about you sailing alone. I like to imagine you on the deck of The Two Seans *with the sun beaming down on your face. I try not to think about you on board in winter. When the sea is rough and the waves are high. Isn't it strange to worry about someone you haven't seen in three years?*

Do you ever think about me? I hope so. I've changed too. I'm not any taller. But I've cut my hair. It's barely above my shoulders now and my mam says I'm as thin as a rake these days. Lainey and I run in the Phoenix Park three times a week. I can't see myself completing a marathon just yet, but I'm enjoying the fresh air.

I think about Seány too. I can't quite believe he'd be ten soon. Can you imagine what he'd be like? I bet he'd love Saturdays sailing with you and I hope he'd still be writing to me. I think about your mam too. I wonder how she's coping. I'm glad she has you. I finally understand why you couldn't come to Dublin.

*Being with me would mean leaving her alone and no one should
have to be alone. I was selfish to ever ask.*

*I graduate today by the way. All the years of study are finally
rewarded in a fancy ceremony. I need to get dressed and leave as
soon as I finish writing this letter. But all I can think about is
how lonely I am. How lonely I am going to be. My parents are
moving to France. To a one-bedroomed apartment. No spare
room, it seems.*

Abruptly, my words dry up and I drop my pen. I have no
right to compare my parents moving to Fionn's loss. I crumple
up the paper and toss it aside. I listen to the familiar sounds of
Mam washing up and I go down stairs to help her. Then I'll
grab a shower, get dressed and spend ages on my make-up.
Because today is going to be a good day. A big day. A day to
make memories. A day Fionn didn't get.

FORTY-THREE

DEE

October 2004

'Three years, Dee. Can you believe we're together three whole years?' Trevor says, as we pack the contents of my bedroom into cardboard boxes.

I can't quite believe it, if I'm honest. Sometimes it feels as if time is flying and other times I could easily believe a whole lifetime has passed since Trevor and I met. We were just kids back then, although I was convinced I was all grown up. I'm still not as old as I feel. Sometimes I think I must be the oldest 21-year-old in Ireland. I caught myself complaining about back pain last week. Lainey laughed at me for a solid ten minutes.

'You just need a night out,' she told me. 'JP and I found this fab club round the corner from our flat. You should come. You could stay over. You and Trevor. Wouldn't that be fun?'

I haven't stayed in Lainey and John Paul's flat yet. I'm not sure I want to. It's in an area that Lainey and I were afraid to walk through when we were in school and it smells like damp.

Lainey must be aware of its failings because she constantly reminds me that prices are crazy and they haven't much of a budget.

I suggested that her dad could start paying John Paul more for his labour but she nearly took the head off me.

'JP is an apprentice. We had to do our time in college and we didn't get paid,' she said.

If anyone deserves to complain about back pain, it's John Paul but he never does.

'Are we going out this weekend?' Trevor says, pulling me back to the here and now. 'For our anniversary. We could try that club Lainey is always going on about.'

I'm so tired, the thought of clubbing makes me want to curl up and take a nap. But I'm not complaining. I love my job and I know how lucky I am to have it. When Lainey and I both applied for the position as morning radio host, it was just a joke. Neither of us ever dreamed we'd land a job like that straight out of college. But it turns out Trevor's sister used to date the guy who did my interview, and I was a shoo-in. Lainey has never said anything, but I'm not sure she forgives me for getting a job she would give her right arm for. I managed to put a good word in for her and she's working in administration for the station. Her salary is slightly more than my paltry sum, and her mornings don't start at 4 a.m. But still, I'm living her dream and it's taking its toll on our friendship. I ask regularly if any presenting jobs are coming up and I hope as much as she does that one crops up soon.

'Dee, are you listening?' Trevor says.

'Sorry,' I say, folding a woolly jumper and placing it into a box with *clothes* written in chunky black marker across the front.

'You okay?' he says, 'You keep zoning out.'

'I'm fine. Just a lot on my mind.'

'I get it,' Trevor says, although he couldn't possibly. 'I'd feel weird if my parents were moving abroad too. But my dad hates the sun so...' He shrugs and lifts a box full of t-shirts and blouses ready to carry it downstairs.

'Have you thought any more about what I was saying?' He hugs the box close to his chest, resting his chin on top as he stares at me. 'About moving in together.'

'I... I...'

I don't know what to say. I've thought about nothing else since Trevor brought it up a month ago. Lainey seems blissfully happy with John Paul in her shabby flat but I want more. I want different, although something stops me from admitting that out loud.

'It's just so expensive,' I say.

The cost of living is my only reasonable argument but Trevor sees straight through it.

'You have to live somewhere, Dee. Your parents are moving in two weeks.'

'I know. I know.' I hate to be reminded of how soon they leave. 'I'll figure something out,' I say.

Trevor sets the box down and walks towards me, taking my hands.

'I'm worried about you,' he says. 'I think you're in denial. I know you don't want your parents to go. But this is happening. Look, my mam said you're welcome to the spare room for as long as you need, but don't you want our own place sooner, rather than later?'

My chest constricts. Living together seems so inevitable to Trevor. I wonder when he got so far ahead of me.

'Your mam is very good, but I couldn't impose like that—'

'Dee. Dee, love. Could you pop down here and give me a hand with some of the china plates,' Mam calls out from the bottom of the stairs.

I've never been so grateful to hear Mam's voice.

'Go on,' Trevor says, letting go of my hands and tilting his head towards the door. 'Go bubble-wrap the crap out of those plates. I'll bring all this stuff downstairs.'

I turn on the spot. A full 360 degrees, taking in as much of my room as I can. It looks so strange now with all my stuff boxed up. I try to detach myself from the space; the space I grew up in with threadbare carpet and a desk with a broken drawer. I try to imagine a new family living here. A little girl redecorating the room to reflect her personality. There probably won't be a hurl and camogie boots in the wardrobe, or Harry Potter books on the shelf or a shoebox of handwritten letters under the bed.

I gasp, realising that, in a sea of boxes, I'd forgotten all about the one under my bed, and for a moment thinking about it takes my breath away. I crouch and flop my belly onto the carpet and shove my arms under the bed, pulling it out. The large rubber band wrapped round it has changed colour over the years from a sunny, sandy yellow to the dirty brown of wet sand. The box is bowed in the middle like a canoe from the pressure of the elastic band. It's stuffed full of envelopes and the lid tries to pop.

'Oops, did you forget one?' Trevor says, when I stand up and blow the dust off the top.

'Nearly,' I say.

Trevor's eyes measure up the box. He reaches his hands out for it. I pull it close to me for a moment, not wanting to pass it over.

'I'll put it with the other boxes,' he says.

I nod, and I know I have to pass it to him. But even when Mam calls me again, her tone warning me that she's losing patience, I wait in the doorway, reluctant to leave my room and my letters behind.

FORTY-FOUR

DEE

Halloween 2004

Mam and Dad's flight was delayed by two hours. Mam texted me from the airport like a demon. She texted me twice more before they took off. Again when they landed and once more when they reached the new apartment. I wonder if this is what life will be like now with parents who live in a different country. I wonder if my days will be filled with texts and calls and talking to my mam and dad so much more than my friends talk to their families who live down the road. I think I'll be okay with that.

'Did your parents arrive safely?' Lainey asks.

Her expression is concerned but it's hard to take her seriously in a Dorothy costume. Her outfit is complete with sparkly red stilettos, a stuffed toy dog and a wicker basket full of bottles of Miller beer.

I reach in and take one.

'Yeah. All good,' I say. 'The party is great. Everyone looks amazing.'

I glance around Lainey's flat, overflowing with eccentric costumes. A werewolf and Cinderella make out on the couch and knowing I have to sleep there later grosses me out. My back is sorer than ever after a week on Lainey's lumpy couch. But I am grateful for somewhere to stay. I'm trawling the ads section of every paper trying to find accommodation, but most of it is either too far out or only suitable for students.

'Hey. Wow, you look exactly like Hermione,' John Paul says, approaching with a bottle opener. He takes my beer, pops the cap and gives it back to me.

'Thanks. You're a very cool fireman.'

John Paul flexes a bicep and I laugh.

'Where's Trevor?' Lainey asks.

I point towards the policeman chatting to Batman.

'Everything okay with you two? I haven't seen you together much tonight.'

'Sort of,' I say, taking a swig of my beer.

'Is he still nagging you about moving in together?' Lainey asks.

'Sort of,' I say again and drink more.

'I have to say, I think he has a point, Dee. Do you really want to share a house with strangers? It has to make more sense to live with your boyfriend.'

'If he's still my boyfriend,' I say.

Lainey throws John Paul a look. He kisses the top of her head and walks away, understanding. Then Lainey cups my elbow and leads me into her tiny kitchen.

Rainbow Brite and Wonder Woman are whispering next to the fridge.

'Can we have a minute?' Lainey says.

They stare at Lainey as if they've forgotten this is her home.

'There's more beer in the sitting room,' Lainey says. 'Next to the TV. Help yourselves.'

The girls huff and stagger out, both very drunk.

Lainey sets her basket down on the countertop and places her stuffed dog on top.

'What's going on, Dee?' she whispers. 'And don't give me any of that "it's complicated" bullshit.'

I finish my beer and take another, and I'm instantly disappointed when I have no way of opening it.

'Trevor read my old letters. The ones from Fionn and Seány.'

'You still have those?'

'Of course I still have them. Seány is gone. It's all I have to remind me.'

'And what about Fionn? Do they remind you of him?'

'Yeah, I suppose.'

Lainey opens the drawer near the sink and takes out a bottle opener and passes it to me.

'Did Trevor ask if he could read them?' she says.

'What do you think?'

'Wow.'

I pop the cap and it flies into the air, flips and lands in the sink with a clink.

'We were packing up all my stuff and I gave him the box of letters to put with all the other boxes. He read them while I was downstairs.'

'Jesus.'

'And now he thinks he has the right to be pissed off,' I say.

'Well, I can kind of see why. I mean, I don't know how I'd feel if I found a stack of letters from JP's ex.'

'JP doesn't have an ex,' I say, guzzling beer now. 'And anyway, I wasn't hiding them. I literally gave him the box. I wasn't expecting him to dive in and help himself to a read.'

'Hey, hey.' Lainey raises her hands above her head, surrendering as if my tone and words are ammunition. 'I get it. Reading your stuff was a total dick move. So, what now? You're both pissed off with each other?'

I drink and drink, until liquid sloshes around in my stomach.

'He wants me to throw them out,' I say. 'He says they make him uncomfortable.'

A prisoner, complete with a ball and chain, rattles into the kitchen.

'Any more beer in here?' he says.

'Beside the TV,' Lainey says, pointing, and he turns round and shuffles back out.

'Sorry.' Lainey apologises as if her guests inconvenience me. 'You were saying?'

'I'm not throwing them out.'

'Oh Dee.'

'Seány is gone and these letters are all I have. All I'll ever have. I don't even have a photo. I. Am. Not. Throwing. Them. Away!'

'You're choosing old letters over your boyfriend,' Lainey says.

'I guess I am.'

'Okay,' she says. 'If you're sure. I just don't want you to end up with a broken heart.'

'I don't think—'

Commotion coming from the sitting room cuts me off. Lainey and I hurry towards raised voices and the sound of something like furniture breaking. We arrive to find broken glass scattered around the floor like confetti. Trevor is sprawled on his back, in the centre of what was the coffee table.

John Paul is standing, towering over him with his fists raised.

'Jesus Christ, JP,' Lainey says, racing over to him. 'That's the landlord's table. It'll have to come out of our deposit. You better hope that wasn't bloody expensive.'

'What the hell happened?' I say, walking cautiously towards Trevor. Glass pebbles crunch under my feet.

'Your boyfriend has a big mouth. He needs to keep my best friend's name out of it,' John Paul says, and angry saliva sprays past his lips.

My breath catches and the sense that this is all my fault is crushing. I reach my arm out to help Trevor up. He slaps my hand away. John Paul notices from the corner of his eye and I see the flash of temper illuminate his face again. Lainey places her hands flat on his chest and shakes her head. He looks at her as if he would crawl through the broken glass for her and he takes some deep breaths and calms down. Trevor on the other hand looks at me with heartbreak-heavy eyes and I stare back with an equal sense of sadness. We both know that our next conversation will be our last. Although I know it's the best thing for us both, Lainey is right – my heart is breaking.

FORTY-FIVE

FIONN

December 2004

I take out my wallet and hand twenty pounds to the man selling Christmas trees from the boot of his car in the car park at Spar. The mainland is particularly beautiful at this time of year, with low-hanging Christmas lights that sparkle like fireflies, and the smells of mince pies and home-made puddings waft in the air.

'Happy Christmas,' the man says, in an accent that isn't from here.

'Yeah. You too.'

My tree comes in a net and I'll have no idea whether it's full-bodied or a couple of sparse branches until I open it. But it looks pretty green as I examine it through the gaps in the net. I hope it's big and bushy and beautiful. Mam deserves the most beautiful tree in the world. It's our first time putting up a Christmas tree since Dad and Seány died. If what the doctors are saying is true, then it will most likely be Mam's last time too.

I sling the tree over my shoulder and begin walking.

'Where are you parked, mate?' the man calls after me.

'Not far,' I shout back as I set out on the kilometre or two walk back to the port.

I need to hurry if I'm going to catch the last ferry home. A small red car passes me with a tree strapped to its roof. It honks and some people turn in the back seat to wave at me. I don't recognise the car but I wave back, feeling festive. I squint and try to make out the faces in the back, but I have no luck in the dusk.

Despite the minus temperature, I've broken a sweat by the time I reach the port. I set the tree down by the stony wall and catch my breath. I'm taken aback to find the red car on-board the ferry, still proudly carrying a tree, much bigger and no doubt bushier than mine. We don't get many tourists at Christmas, I think. And certainly not the type of tourist that comes equipped with their own decorations.

Darkness falls as we set sail. Cloud cover is thick and hides the stars. It becomes hard to tell where the sea ends and the sky begins. I prop my tree against the side of the boat and adjust my bobble hat to better keep my ears warm. Thankfully there aren't many people on the ferry at this time of day. It's my favourite time to sail, when keeping to myself is easy. Unfortunately, the ferry company has threatened, more than once, to cancel this sailing if demand doesn't pick up.

The people from the red car have made their way up the narrow stairs and they hang over the rusty railing singing Christmas songs. They butcher a Mariah Carey classic first before moving on to George Michael. Something about their tone-deafness is endearing. I find myself humming along and soaking up their joy.

The cold has made its way straight through my coat and into my bones by the time we reach Cloch Bheag. I sling the tree over my shoulder once more and I'm surprisingly glad of the walk home, and the chance to march some heat back into my body.

I make record time. I can't wait to see Mam's face when I bring home a tree. I plan to get all the old decorations out of the attic, and I bought a bottle of Mam's favourite red wine to share while we decorate. I come to an abrupt stop when I see the red car parked outside the house. I peer in the windows but there are no people inside.

I open the front door, set the tree down in the hall, and I'm about to walk towards the sound of chatter carrying from the kitchen when I freeze. I recognise the voices. I hear a distinctive Dublin accent that I could never forget. Dee. My mouth opens and my heart races. I hang my coat and hat on the rack and I listen. There's a second girl's voice. Lainey, I think. And finally, I hear John Paul. Happiness fills me. Then surprise. And a strange feeling that I can't put my finger on. Something between hurt and realisation. John Paul is home for the first time in months and he didn't let me know he was on his way. I guess that's just how it's going to be now.

I run my hand through my hair and glance in the mirror. I hate myself for it. I leave the tree in the hall and prepare to perform as I enter the kitchen.

'There he is now,' John Paul says, as soon as he sets eyes on me.

He jumps up from the table and grabs me. Bear-hugging me so hard I can't breathe. My eyes are on Mam. She's sitting in Seány's spot. Her spot now, and she's smiling brighter than she has in a long time as John Paul and I embrace.

'This is a nice surprise,' I say, as John Paul and I separate.

'Isn't it. Isn't it just,' Mam says.

She's positively glowing and I can't remember the last time we had a visitor in the house that isn't John Paul's mam. There's half an apple tart in the centre of the table. Polished-off plates sit in front of Dee and Lainey. Lainey chases crumbs around her plate with the tip of her finger, helping them into her mouth.

'Hi Fionn,' Dee says, finding her voice after what feels like the longest time.

'Hi Dee.'

'JP is home for Christmas,' Mam says, with a single, celebratory clap of her hands. 'Trish has no idea. Isn't it the loveliest surprise?'

'It's definitely a surprise.'

'Listen, we've taken up way too much of your time,' John Paul says, turning back towards Mam and using a phrase that seems so alien to him.

'Thanks so much for the tart,' Dee says, standing.

Lainey's chair squeaks as she gets to her feet too.

'It was delicious,' she says. 'It reminds me of all the yummy desserts we had when we were students here that summer in the nineties.'

'Oh, those were the best,' Dee says.

Her sense of nostalgia is palpable and it almost knocks me off my feet.

'I'll walk you to the door,' I say.

Dee seems surprised, but she hasn't noticed how Mam has tried to stand and it's taking longer than it should and I can see pain on her face.

'We're here until the new year,' John Paul says, as we reach the door. 'Maybe we could catch up in Reilly's for a few drinks.'

'Maybe,' I say.

Dee notices the Christmas tree leaning against the wall.

'Do you put it just inside the sitting room window?' she asks.

'Yes. You can see the lights best that way.'

'I can't wait to see. I bet it's going to look great.'

I realise Dee has every intention of visiting again before she leaves, but I get the sneaky suspicion she's here to see Mam and not me.

FORTY-SIX

DEE

New Year's Eve 2004

John Paul said we needed to be in Reilly's early if we wanted to get a table. I didn't believe him. I couldn't imagine the unassuming pub in the middle of nowhere being packed out. But I was wrong. Everyone on the island, from toddlers to pensioners, seems to be here to ring in the new year.

Luckily we got a table. It's in the corner at the back and it suits me just fine. Lainey complains that she can't see feckin' anything. But we can hear the music and that's all that matters.

'They're not a band,' Lainey leans in and says. 'They're just some locals who come together every New Year's Eve to belt out a few tunes. It's tradition.'

I smile. Lainey speaks about Cloch Bheag traditions fondly and I can sense the island taking up space in her heart.

'They're very good,' I say.

The sounds of a bodhrán, fiddle, accordion and tin whistle

command the room and everyone's head bobs and their hands clap. I tap my foot along to the beat and sip my beer.

'Is Fionn here?' I ask.

'Hmm?'

I cup Lainey's ear and try again. 'Is Fionn here? I see Lorna. But I don't see Fionn,' I say.

Lainey looks up and waves at Lorna, who's sitting at a table in the corner opposite us. Lorna smiles and waves back. I can't help thinking about how thin she is, and how her hunched shoulders make her seem so much older than John Paul's mam, who sits beside her, chatting.

'He's probably not here yet,' Lainey says.

'Okay.'

John Paul returns from the bar with another round of drinks, and Lainey kisses him.

'Have you seen Fionn, JP?' I ask, as he slides a bottle of beer in front of me.

'Yeah. Just now. He's out the back.'

'Oh good. I was hoping to have a quick word with him about his mam,' I say.

'What about her?' Lainey says.

'Erm.' I shift awkwardly and the leather bench seat beneath me squeaks. 'She's looking a little frail, or something. I just want to check she's okay.'

'She seems fine to me,' Lainey says.

She points towards Lorna and Trish, who are laughing the way best friends do.

'I dunno,' John Paul says. 'Mam's down at the O'Connells' house an awful lot lately. I think she's worried about her too.'

'Really?' I say, the sense of dread gripping me. 'Right.'

I sigh and make the decision to go outside and talk to Fionn. I stand up and I'm nearly trampled by a group of kids playing tag.

'Sorry, missus,' one them says, and then he runs away with his friends.

'Missus.' Lainey snorts. 'You're old now.'

I slip out the back door and the icy air catches my breath, but it's the view that takes it away. The light of the near full moon shimmers on the water and countless stars sparkle overhead.

Fionn has his back to me. He's wearing a woolly, navy hat and curly brown-black hair pokes out underneath. It's almost as long as mine, nearly reaching his shoulders. I'm about to call out to him when I realise he's with someone. A woman. And he's kissing her. I feel unreasonably disappointed. I know I have no right and I mentally scold myself as I turn to walk back inside.

'Dee. Deirdre.'

I cringe hearing my name. I have to turn back, no matter how much I don't want to. I take a deep breath, force myself to smile and turn round.

'Hi Aisling,' I say.

'Oh my God, what are you doing here?' she says, stepping away from Fionn to edge closer to me.

For a moment I think she's going to hug me and I freeze. I'm grateful when she doesn't. I can feel Fionn staring at me but I can't bring myself to look at him. I hate that my heart is hurting.

'Just here for Christmas,' I say.

Aisling seems confused.

'I'm staying with JP and his family.'

'Ah, of course, yeah. I heard JP and Lainey are home for a while.'

I swallow. Aisling refers to Cloch Bheag as Lainey's home, but despite her bright smile and warm tone I can tell her hospitality stops there. Aisling is not happy to see me. And I wonder if she suspects the feeling is mutual.

'Lainey didn't tell me you were coming,' Aisling says.

'Oh.' I try to sound blasé but a fire is burning inside me.

Lainey and Aisling have become good friends over the years. I suppose it was inevitable. Lainey and John Paul are inseparable. If Aisling was hanging out with John Paul, she was hanging out with Lainey too. Whether she liked it or not. Turns out, she liked it, and I sometimes think Aisling and Lainey are closer friends now than John Paul and Aisling ever were. For the first time, I think that Lainey and Aisling might be closer friends than Lainey and me these days. For one thing, Lainey didn't tell me Aisling and Fionn are together. I can't believe she kept something like that from me. I try not to think about it now because it makes me want to cry or scream or both.

'Are you home for Christmas?' I ask.

'Em, I'm not sure, really.' Aisling shrugs. 'I came home after graduation to give Mam a hand with the B&B. It was just supposed to be for the summer. But then I bumped into Fionn and...'

Aisling steps closer to Fionn and strokes his arm as if he's her pet. I selfishly want it to irritate him but it doesn't seem to. Instead, he smiles at her.

'And how about you? How are things with you?'

I open my mouth, but Aisling continues speaking, answering for me. 'I hear you're working in radio now. That's great. Really great.'

'Thanks,' I say, 'I'm really enjoying it.'

'It sounds so exciting. Lainey has told me all about it. And here I am running a B&B for my mam. God, I'm so jealous.'

When Aisling puts it like that it does sound fabulous. Two best friends working in radio for one of the biggest stations in Dublin. But as she stands next to Fionn, holding him, stroking him, I am the one filled with jealousy.

'Is Lainey inside?' Aisling goes on. 'I'd love to catch up.'

I nod.

'Cool. I'll pop in and see if I can find her,' she says.

'I'll be in in a sec,' Fionn says.

'It was great seeing you, Dee,' Aisling says. 'I'm sure we'll be chatting again before the end of the night.'

'Absolutely,' I say, with a smile so wide it almost aches.

Aisling disappears inside and suddenly it feels colder. The see breeze pinches my cheeks and I wrap my arms round myself.

'You still don't wear a coat?' Fionn says.

I finally bring my eyes to meet his. My heart flutters.

'I left it inside.'

Fionn unzips his puffy black coat and offers it to me. I take it, gladly, and slip my arms in.

'You let your hair grow.' I point towards the curls' ends hanging from under his hat.

'Keeps my ears warm.'

Silence falls over us. I listen for the sound of waves breaking on the shore, but the hum of music and chatter from the pub drowns out the sea.

Fionn tilts his head towards the pub. 'I better get in.'

'Is your mam okay?' I ask.

Fionn's eyes widen as if I've winded him. I wait while he gathers himself. He seems to struggle.

'You noticed,' he says, at last.

'How bad?'

'Very.'

'Shit, Fionn. I'm sorry.'

He sniffles and drags a shaky hand under his nose.

'Does Oisín know?'

'No.'

I gasp. I don't know why. I'm not overly surprised. But I am sad. Oisín hasn't spoken to his family in such a long time and the next time he does the news will be awful.

'Are you going to call him, or does your mam want to tell him herself?' I ask.

Fionn stares at me with a guarded expression, as if I'm a

stranger asking inappropriate questions. I suppose in many ways that's exactly what I am right now.

'Sorry,' I say, lowering my head. 'This is none of my business.'

Fionn doesn't agree or disagree.

'What does Aisling think?' I say, trying to redirect the conversation in a more acceptable direction.

'She doesn't know. Nobody does. Mam doesn't want to talk about it.'

'Oh God. I shouldn't have said anything,' I say. 'I just—'

'It's okay,' he says, beginning to shiver. 'It's good to talk to someone about it.'

I smile, relieved.

'It's always good to talk to you, Dee.'

Fionn pulls his hat off and ruffles his hair. He's even more attractive than I remember.

'I better get inside,' he says.

He walks away without taking his jacket or looking back. Something tells me not to follow him. Not right now.

FORTY-SEVEN

FIONN

Reilly's is buzzing. Some kids have started Irish dancing to the music. They don't quite have the steps right but they look as if they're having the time of their life. Mam watches them, clapping in time to the music.

'Are you having a good time?' I ask her, but the answer is written all over her smiling face.

'Isn't the music great?' Mrs Leary says.

'Yeah. Lovely,' I say.

The purple hammocks under Mam's eyes hang lower than usual. I'm worried she'll be exhausted by midnight.

'Do you want me to drop you home?' I ask. 'The car is outside.'

Mam slaps the air. 'I do not.'

Mrs Leary takes my hand and squeezes gently. 'She's having a good time, Fionn. Don't worry.'

'Well as I said, the car is parked outside if—'

'I'm fine.' Mam cuts me off. 'Will you go get yourself a drink and relax? Your friends are over there.'

Mam points towards Dee and Lainey and John Paul. Aisling is sitting with them too. She sees me looking over and waves. I wince, knowing I have to join them. Not because I'm worried that it would be rude not to. It would be. But I don't care. I'll join them because Mam is watching and I know it will make her happy.

John Paul is on his feet as soon as I reach the table.

'What are you having?' he asks, placing his shovel-like hand on my shoulder.

There was a time, not so long ago, that he wouldn't have to ask.

'A pint. Cheers.'

The musicians take a break, and I think, secretly, everyone is grateful for the respite and the chance to talk without shouting.

John Paul takes a long time at the bar. Katie serves him and I overhear some of their conversation. John Paul says something about not seeing her in years and compliments her on how well she looks. She says something about it being good to see him because not many people come back.

Katie's words cut deep. *Not many people come back.* Oisín didn't.

Lainey and Aisling chatter. Dee is unusually morose. And I don't think it's unreasonable to ask her what's wrong.

She shrugs. 'Nothing.'

'Doesn't seem like nothing to me.'

'I'm just tired.'

Dee is a terrible liar.

'Do you want to step outside again?'

Aisling overhears me and shoots me a pointed look. Dee notices and I see a flash of irritation.

'Why didn't you tell me Aisling was running the B&B?' Dee asks.

The question wasn't directed at anyone in particular, but Lainey knows she's the one it's meant for.

'I didn't think it was something that would interest you.'

'You didn't tell me she'd moved home, or started going out with Fionn,' Dee says.

'Again, I didn't think you'd really care. You never mention Cloch Bheag or Fionn. Ever.'

My chest hurts, as if Lainey's words have just stabbed me.

'Just because I don't go on about it all the time doesn't mean I wouldn't want to know something like that, Jesus,' Dee says.

'Sorry.' Lainey makes a face. 'I'll know for next time.'

John Paul returns with two pints of Guinness. He places one in front of me and pats my back, then he takes a massive gulp from his. He eyes Lainey with concern over the rim of his glass.

'What's wrong?' he says.

'Dee is pissed off that I didn't tell her Aisling and Fionn are shagging.'

'Lainey!' Aisling says, and then she looks at me with a cheeky grin.

It makes me uncomfortable and I look away.

'See, what did I tell you?' John Paul says, crouching beside Lainey and placing his hand on her knee. 'I knew you were asking for trouble bringing her here.'

'Are you talking about me?' Dee taps her chest with the tips of her fingers.

'Ah, Dee. Let me just explain...' John Paul stumbles over his words and Lainey glares at him and I can tell he's in for a long lecture later.

Dee stands up. My coat is hanging on the back of her chair, but she bypasses it and puts on her own. I know she's not coming back.

I take a few mouthfuls of my pint, reach for my coat and follow her. Aisling calls after me. And John Paul too. But I block them out and hurry outside.

FORTY-EIGHT

DEE

'Wait up!' Fionn shouts

I don't turn round. Instead, I pick up my pace.

'Jesus Dee. Are you in a race?'

I've a stitch, but I don't slow. I suspect I'll hear Aisling's voice calling Fionn. And Lainey calling her. And John Paul calling Lainey. Like the worst game of dominos ever.

'Dee, please? Slow the fuck down.'

The moon is doing a great job of lighting my way. Although, I actually have no idea of what my way is. I know I'll have to turn back at some point. I'm sleeping in Trish Leary's house tonight after all.

I stop walking and turn round. I hope it's obvious that I'm irked that he's following me.

'Go back inside,' I say.

'Dee.'

'Seriously, Fionn. Please. Just go back to your friends.'

'They're your friends too.'

'So I thought.'

'Don't mind JP, he's got a big gob,' Fionn says.

'He's right. I shouldn't have come.'

'Why did you?'

My mouth gapes. I'm not used to people saying what they think. In college everyone learned how to be guarded and prim. We learned that being grown up meant biting your tongue a lot of the time. And at work, people are so busy playing office politics that I've forgotten what it's like to be blindsided by a real question. A question you might have to do a little digging around inside yourself to find the answer to.

I shrug and I think about walking some more.

'Because I had nowhere else to go,' I say, surprising myself at how easily the honest answer slips out.

'Don't you spend Christmas with your parents?' he says.

'Not this year. They retired to France a few months ago. I think they're done being parents.'

I wonder if I sound as lost as I feel. But Fionn doesn't seem as shocked as most people are when I tell them.

'Do they like it there?' he says.

'Yeah. S'pose so.'

'That's good, then.'

I don't know what to say. I want to be happy my parents are enjoying life to the fullest, but I miss them.

'And Trevor?' he says.

I groan and roll my eyes. 'Gone.'

Fionn smiles. It almost makes me laugh.

'How's your mam?' I ask. 'I mean, is she having a good night?'

'Seems to be.'

'That's good.'

The conversation feels pointless and unnatural. My temper has abated and I regret storming out of the pub. I can only imagine how awkward things will be when I return.

'So, you and Aisling are together,' I say. It didn't sound jealous in my head, but when I hear myself say it out loud there's a bitterness to my tone.

Fionn smiles.

'Since the summer,' I add. I hate myself for how I sound.

'Since the summer,' he echoes.

'And you're happy?'

Fionn looks away. I wish I knew what he was thinking. I wish I knew if he *was* happy. I want him to be. More than anyone else in the world, I want him to be happy.

He checks his watch and says, 'It's nearly midnight. We should go back to the pub for the countdown.'

'Do you want to go to the beach?' I blurt.

His eyes narrow.

'For old times' sake.'

'I can't. I have to get back.' He points as if I'll find the pub at the end of his finger.

His rejection stings. My face flushes and I'm grateful that it's dark. 'Aisling is waiting,' I say.

'My mam,' he says. 'I need to drive her home soon. She's not able to walk far any more.'

My shoulders round and my heart aches.

'Oh Fionn, I'm sorry. I wasn't thinking. Of course you have to get back. Absolutely.'

'Are you coming?' he says.

'I'm moving,' I blurt.

Without context Fionn looks confused. But the decision has just come to me. Right this very moment; as I stand, drinking in the face of a man I don't really know, but who was once a boy I loved very much.

'I have a job offer in London,' I say. 'It's for the BBC.'

'Wow.'

'It's kids' TV.'

He nods and nods, thinking. Approving, I think.

'That's great, Dee. Really great. You'll be good with kids. Seány loved you, remember?'

Tears prick the corners of my eyes. I could never forget.

Being here, in this sleepy place that never seems to fully wake, I'm reminded more than ever.

'I haven't told Lainey.'

'Yikes,' he says, and then he laughs.

'I know, right? She's going to hit the roof.'

'Do you want me to tell JP? Maybe he could break it to her gently.'

'Thanks, but I think I need to talk to her myself.'

'You're right. Probably best she hears it from you.'

'I'm scared,' I say.

'Ah, look.' Fionn scrunches his face. 'She'll probably go apeshit, but she'll get over it.'

I laugh. I didn't mean I'm afraid of Lainey. Although, I probably should be.

'I'm scared about moving,' I say.

His expression changes and he finally moves close to me. Close enough to reach out and touch him. And I want to. I want to touch him.

'I don't know anyone there and it's a big city.' My palms grow clammy just thinking about it.

'When do you go?'

'Next week.'

'I'll come,' he says.

I nearly choke on air.

'You asked me earlier if Oisín knows my mam is sick.'

I nod.

'I can't tell him over the phone.'

'You're serious,' I say.

'I am. I need to talk to my brother and you need some company while you get settled. It works.'

'I... I... I...'

'We both need to do this, Dee.'

I shove my coat sleeve up and look at my watch.

'It's past twelve,' I say. 'We missed the countdown.'

'Happy New Year, Dee-Dee.'

I smile. Bigger and brighter than I have since my parents left for the airport.

'Happy New Year, Fionn.'

I have a feeling it's going to be a good one.

FORTY-NINE

DEE

Ten Days Later – January 2005

I'm disappointed but I'm not surprised that Lainey isn't speaking to me. She didn't take the news of my imminent departure well. She shouted. I cried. We hugged. She sulked. I thought when the station offered her my old job that she'd come round, but it seemed to fuel her annoyance even more. I overheard her tell John Paul that she wasn't interested in my hand-me-downs.

'They can stuff their crappy job. And the BBC can go jump too. I knew Chris better than she ever did,' Lainey grumbled one evening when I was in the loo. She'd had far too much wine and the walls in the apartment are paper thin. I thought when I flushed she'd stop, but she had plenty more to say. 'We were friends. I can't believe he'd headhunt her and not me. It's not fair, JP, Dee is always so lucky. When am I going to get some good luck, eh?'

'I think we're pretty lucky. We have each other.'

'Oh shut up, JP.'

My memories of Christopher Jacobs extend no further than nice producer with round-rimmed glasses and a beard who left a few weeks after I started in radio to take up a fancy job at the BBC. I hadn't thought about him since. When he'd called personally and asked me to come work with him in London, it took me some time to jog my memory and conjure an image of his face.

'And she can find someone else's couch to crash on,' Lainey added before slamming her wine glass down on the counter and breaking the stem.

I don't know how their conversation went after that, but Lainey stopped speaking to me before she could ask me to leave. I suspect John Paul pointed out that I had nowhere else to go. John Paul said bottling everything up was her way of coping. But he didn't need to explain. I've known Lainey Burke since we were four years old. I know we'll get past this; I just don't know when.

'Jaysus, the traffic is bonkers,' John Paul says, as he chauffeurs us to the airport in his new van.

Fionn is sitting in the front of the small, red two-seater next to him. Aisling and I are in the back. We sit on our cases, crammed between John Paul's tools and offcuts of timber.

'I've never been to London before,' Aisling says, and her excitement is tangible.

'None of us have,' Fionn says.

'I can't wait to go to Buckingham Palace,' she says. 'I hope we see the Queen.'

'Don't be stupid, Ais.' John Paul snorts. 'The Queen is hardly going to be sitting in the window sipping tea and waving to tourists now, is she?'

I smile. I like to think of the Queen doing exactly that.

'There's one way to find out,' I say, catching Aisling's eye. 'We can go tomorrow, if you like?'

Aisling looks away.

'Sounds good,' Fionn says.

'But I thought we were going to Trafalgar Square tomorrow,' Aisling says.

'Yeah, we still can. The palace is just round the corner,' Fionn says.

'I thought it was just the two of us.' Aisling pulls her shoulders to her ears and holds them there as she turns back towards me. She's making a stupid face and all I can think about is how much I dislike her.

'I mean, I'm sure you're going to want to get settled in and not spend the day bored with us,' she says.

When Fionn asked me if I was okay with Aisling joining us on our trip, my instinct was to rethink our arrangement and I nearly pulled out altogether. But in truth, I wanted Fionn to come more than I wanted Aisling not to. So, I lied and said I thought it would be nice for them to enjoy some time away together. I haven't regretted my decision until right this minute.

'Oh, I don't mind,' I say, offering her a toothy grin. 'Unless I'd be too much of a gooseberry for you.'

'Of course you wouldn't be,' Fionn says, before Aisling has a chance to say a word.

I try to catch Aisling's eye again, but she's staring at her runners and won't look up.

Traffic is heavy and John Paul sweats more than the rest of us about missing our flight.

'Stay in your own lane, ya big gobshite,' he shouts towards a nearby truck. 'Look at this wanker,' he calls on Fionn to agree as he honks the horn.

John Paul pulls up outside departures with forty minutes until take-off. Fionn thanks him for the lift and they shake hands the way men thirty years their seniors do.

'I really appreciate you keeping an eye on my mam this weekend,' Fionn says.

John Paul winks. 'I'm just in it for the apple tart.'

They both laugh and smile and nod. The type of knowing communication that only comes with a lifelong friendship.

'Just don't let her know I've asked you to check in,' Fionn says. 'I don't want her thinking I'm talking about her. You know what she's like.'

'Too proud for her own good,' JP says as he leans to the side and places a hand on Fionn's shoulder. 'Like I said, I'm just there for the tart.'

Lorna will see straight through John Paul as soon as he rings her doorbell. We all know it. But nonetheless, I find myself relived that John Paul and Lainey are on the island this weekend, in case she needs them. I wonder if I'll ever see Lorna again. Doubt sets in, and, not for the first time, I don't want to get on the plane. As silence falls over us, I suspect we're all thinking about Lorna's health and what the future might hold.

'Right,' Fionn says, opening the van door. 'We need to hurry.'

John Paul opens the back door of the van and Aisling and I hop out. We pull the handles of our cases up and Fionn slings his rucksack over his shoulder. I recognise it as the same blue Adidas bag he brought to Dublin with him when he visited me in UCD years ago.

John Paul hugs me as if he might never set eyes on me again and he tells me I've been a great friend.

'Jesus, JP, relax. She's moving to London, not the bloody moon,' Aisling says.

'Are you going to come home often?' John Paul asks.

Oddly, the question winds me. I don't much feel like I have a home any more. My family home is gone and Lainey's couch isn't somewhere I particularly want to return to.

'Erm...' I say.

'You're always welcome on Cloch Bheag,' Fionn says, reading me as clearly as if my thoughts are written on my face.

And just like that, I remember what it's like to be wanted somewhere.

FIFTY

DEE

Heathrow Airport is almost disappointingly similar to Dublin. It's bigger. But it's not the monumental change of worlds I'd expected. The tube is cool, although there's a constant smell of urine and engine oil no matter what line you travel. I think being underground is going to take some getting used to. Aisling is particularly distressed by the whole experience. When Fionn tells her that we're travelling under the Thames, I think she might pass out.

'Do you hear that dripping sound?' he asks as we rattle along the Bakerloo line.

'The rain?' Aisling says.

'It's not rain.'

'Ignore him,' I say, giving him a warning look. 'We're nearly there.'

An hour later, still underground and on a different line, we are completely lost.

'Should we just get a taxi?' Aisling says. 'Above ground. At least we can see where we're going.'

Aisling's face is flushed and, if we don't ascend steps soon, I'm genuinely worried she won't be okay.

'We need to figure the tube out,' Fionn says.

'No *we* don't,' Aisling says. 'I'm sure Dee will figure it all out in her own time.'

Fionn looks at me with concerned eyes, as if he's worried that I may never figure it out. That I may wander around in the bowels of London lost and alone for ever. I'm worried about it too.

'Look, let's get a taxi for now,' I say. 'Find the flat and get some food. We can try the tube again later.'

The compromise seems to satisfy Aisling. On the street, we're hit with the icy wind of a winter's afternoon, and we all pull our coats a little tighter across our chests and flag a taxi. It almost feels as if I belong here. Or I could, at least.

The flat is bigger and posher and definitely whiter than I imagined. The walls, the carpet, the furniture, the cupboards. All white. It's open plan and there's a floor-to-ceiling window that overlooks a busy shopping street below. There are also two bedrooms; I knew that from my chats on the phone with Sammie in HR at the BBC.

'You have the place for one calendar month,' she said. 'But do give us a shout if you're going to need further assistance. London is a bitch to find housing in at the moment. I had to move back with my parents.'

She seemed wholly disgusted by the idea of returning to her childhood home as an adult, and I had to physically fight the urge to tell her how lucky she is to have that safety net.

'So when does your stuff arrive?' Aisling asks, opening the fridge and being shocked when she finds it empty.

I flick my eyes to my small case.

'That's it?' she says.

I shrug.

'Where's all your clothes?'

'I have everything I need in here. I gave the rest to charity shops before I left.'

'Okay, fair enough. But what about stuff like your CD player. Or your computer?'

I gave those away too. Much more reluctantly. I couldn't clog up Lainey's flat with bulky electrical stuff.

'It's cheaper to buy new stuff here than have it shipped over...'

Aisling seems happy with that explanation and I console myself with the belief that it's probably true.

'We should go shopping,' Fionn says. 'Get some food in. I saw a Tesco round the corner.'

'Are we not eating out?' Aisling says.

Fionn looks at me apologetically, as if he takes responsibility for Aisling's words. He seems uncomfortable in his own skin and I want to help. I want to strip him back to the Fionn I knew before and build him back up from there.

'We're here to help Dee get settled, Ais. A food shop should probably be our top priority, eh?'

Aisling folds her arms. 'Sure. Okay.'

'Anyway, we're meeting Oisín at seven so we're tight on time,' Fionn adds, checking his watch.

'You're both going to see Oisín?' I say, and I can't keep how bad an idea I think that is out of my tone.

'You'll come too, won't you?' Fionn asks.

My eyes widen.

'Oisín suggested a pub nearby. The Knight's Arms. I saw it on the way here. It's walking distance,' he adds.

'I thought you and Oisín were going to talk,' I say.

'We are.'

'But I thought Aisling and I could stay here. Have a girly night.' I catch Aisling making a face from the corner of my eye but I ignore her. 'I thought we could grab a pizza and rent a DVD or something.'

'A DVD.' Aisling laughs. 'Come to London to rent a DVD. Oh Dee, you're so funny.'

She swats her hand through the air as if she's slapping away the joke I didn't make. I don't want to spend the evening with her either, but it's a small price to pay if it gives Fionn time alone with his brother.

'Right. I'm going to go get changed,' Aisling says. 'Dee, where's the loo?'

'Erm...'

'Don't worry, I'll find it.'

Aisling disappears behind a door, and I take Fionn by the hand and lead him to the couch. He doesn't sit until I press my hands on his shoulders.

'This place is nice,' he says.

'It is,' I say, quickly dismissing small talk. 'Are you sure you don't want to see Oisín on your own?'

Fionn doesn't answer.

'It's just...' I pause to choose my words carefully. 'It's just, it's been so long since you've seen him—'

'Exactly,' Fionn cuts in. 'It's been years. I don't want some sort of formal rekindling of our lost years. I just want a few drinks in a nice pub and a chat.'

'But.'

'Dee, I haven't seen Oisín in so long I'd struggle to make conversation about the weather, if I'm honest. At least if you and Aisling are there then there's less chance of things getting awkward.'

I sigh. I understand, but I still think Fionn's approach is wrong. Breaking such huge news about his mother in front of us doesn't feel right.

'You will come, won't you?' Fionn says.

I can't say no. I close my eyes and nod.

'Do you want to get that Tesco shop?' Fionn asks. 'Aisling will be a hundred years getting ready. We'll be there and back while we're waiting.'

'Sounds good.'

'Cool. I'll let her know we won't be long.'

Fionn knocks on the bathroom door and chats to Aisling without opening it.

'Ready?' he asks, returning.

'Ready.'

I'm more excited than I should be at the idea of pushing a trolley around some aisles.

FIFTY-ONE

FIONN

The Knight's Arms reminds me of Reilly's and I wonder if that's why Oisín chose it. It's much larger and there are more people, but there are distinct similarities. The mahogany bar has darkened over many years. In front are old men sitting on high stools with leather that's cracked and peeling. Their arms are folded above round bellies, and their backs are arched like question marks. Round tables with mismatched chairs are dotted haphazardly around the floor. Oisín stands up from his table and waves when he sees us walk in.

It takes me a moment to recognise him. He's wearing an all-black suit. A funeral suit. But he doesn't look as if he's on his way to a funeral. He looks intelligent and sophisticated. He has a beard now and it suits him, I think. There's a laptop on his table, and as we get closer he closes it.

'Fionn,' he says, wrapping his arms round me. 'I can't believe you're actually here.'

'Hi Ois,' I say, hugging him back.

'Ah man, it's been years. Bloody years.'

Oisín and I part and take a moment to look each other up and down.

'Look at you,' he says. 'All grown up. My not-so-little little brother.'

His accent startles me. Much of his Donegal twang has been replaced with something distinctively English.

'It's really good to see you,' I say.

Aisling and Dee hang behind me and I'm not sure how to introduce them. I haven't referred to Aisling as my girlfriend before and I don't want the first time to be in front of Dee.

'You remember Aisling Purcell,' I say.

Oisín stares at me blankly.

'Her mam runs the B&B.'

'Ah. Maureen's daughter.'

'Yes. Yes.'

'Hi,' Aisling says. 'It's nice to see you again.'

Oisín smiles and shifts his attention to Dee.

'And this is?'

'Dee,' I say, 'Deirdre McKenna.'

'Hi,' Dee says.

Oisín looks at her as if he's never seen anyone so perfect in his whole life. I know that look. It's exactly how I looked at her when I first saw her.

'Have we met before?' Oisín asks. 'I have the strangest feeling that I know you.'

'Erm...'

'Dee was a Gaeltacht student a few summers back. She stayed in Mam's house,' I say.

Oisín's smile twists into a cheeky grin and I know he instantly suspects something is going on between me and Dee.

'Right,' he says, standing up again. 'Who needs a drink? I know I do.'

I cast my eyes to the two empty pints already on the table. The girls take a seat and I go to the bar with my brother. It's cramped and loud and making conversation is difficult. I say something about his nice suit and he tells me longer hair suits me.

We return to the table and I can tell from Dee's face that conversation between her and Aisling has been equally strained. Oisín and I sit, we drink and slowly chat begins to flow. As the evening progresses Oisín spends less time talking to me and more time laughing with Dee.

'Who knew she was so funny, eh?' Aisling says.

'Um,' I say.

Aisling becomes tipsy quickly. She drapes her arms round me and I have to physically peel her off every so often. She kisses me and she taste like salted peanuts and vodka.

'Is she all right?' Oisín asks.

'Oh God, I think I'm going to be sick,' Aisling says.

'Get some air,' Oisín says, and he glares at me to get her out of here before she throws up all over the place.

I stand and help Aisling to her feet. She's floppy like a rag doll, and guiding her towards the door is hard work.

We make it outside just in time. Aisling bends in the middle and throws up on the footpath.

'That's bloody disgusting,' someone shouts at us from the far side of the street. 'Someone will walk in that.'

Aisling straightens and drags a shaky hand across her mouth.

'I'm sorry. I'm so sorry,' she says.

'It's okay.'

She tries to kiss me but I pull back.

'Let's get you some chewing gum or something,' I say.

I link her arm and I walk and she staggers to the nearest shop. I buy water and chewing gum and give them both to her. Aisling's dexterity is slow and uncoordinated. I try to ignore how much it frustrates me. I feel terrible for leaving Dee and Oisín alone, stuck making awkward conversation.

'C'mon. We need to get back,' I say, taking the bottle from Aisling and screwing the lid back on.

It takes even longer to walk back and there's a bouncer on the door now. He's as tall as John Paul and twice as wide.

'Is she all right?' he says.

'Yeah. Just excited. It's her first time in London.'

'You're Irish?' he says.

'We are.'

'Right, go on. Make sure she doesn't have any more.'

He steps aside so we can pass by. There are even more people inside now and I can't remember where our table was. Music is blaring. The floor vibrates.

'Oh, I love this song,' Aisling squeals, and she throws her arms above her head. 'Let's dance.'

I shake my head, and take her hand. Finally, I spot Dee. Oisín is leaning towards her and nothing about their conversation appears awkward. Dee laughs, and Oisín too, the way old friends do. I make my way through the crowd, taking care not to let Aisling's hand slip out of mine. We're just metres away from the table when I see Oisín cup Dee's face. She smiles. And then he kisses her.

FIFTY-TWO

FIONN

'Fionn, what are you doing? Oh my God,' Dee shouts and jumps to her feet.

I have Oisín by the collar. The lapel of his suit jacket is crumpled in my fists as I shake him. I glare at him, and he looks back, belligerent and defiant, as if I'm somehow the one out of line and not him. I want to punch him. He'll fight back. He's bigger and stronger than me. Still, I want to punch him.

'Please. Please stop this.' Dee's voice washes over me, as if I'm lost at sea and she's calling to me from the shoreline.

'What the fuck is wrong with you?' Oisín says.

He's calm; almost amused. I hate him. In this moment I cannot abide my brother.

'Let him go,' Dee shouts.

I hear the fear and the anger in her voice, even above the loud music.

Dee tries again. 'Fionn, let him go.'

Oisín doesn't budge. He doesn't try to pull away and he doesn't reach out to grab me in return. But his glare burns into me like a bird of prey, biding his time.

'You kissed her,' I say. 'What the hell did you do that for?'

My voice cracks as emotion gets the better of me. Now I want to punch myself.

'She's a nice girl,' Oisín says. 'I like her.'

His answer isn't good enough. My grip on his jacket tightens until my fists begin to tremble.

'Why do you care who kisses Dee? You have a girlfriend,' Oisín says.

He flicks his eyes onto Aisling, who has remained sitting.

For a moment I forgot she was there. I look at her. Her cheeks are pink and her eyes are glassy and lacking focus. She's sitting slouched and floppy, with her mouth slightly dropped on one side. And yet, in spite of her drunken state, all I see is hurt and confusion etched into every inch of her.

'What's going on, Fionn?' she says.

'Your boyfriend has lost his bloody mind,' Oisín says.

Finally, my fist collides with my brother's face. My knuckles smash against his cheekbone and his head turns to the side in response. He spits and I wince. I've never punched someone before. I had no idea it would hurt so much. I let Oisín go and I shake out my aching hand.

He staggers. I think he's going to fall, and for the first time I realise he's drunk. He's not as drunk as Aisling, despite drinking twice as much. But he's far from sober. He steadies himself.

'I deserved that,' he says. 'But don't pretend this is about her.'

Oisín points to Dee. Tears are rolling down her cheeks.

'Say what this is really about.'

He shifts from one foot to the other, edging forward.

'Admit you're jealous. You can't stand that I got the hell out of Cloch Bheag and you got stuck there.'

'Fuck you,' I shout. 'You have no fucking clue.'

'Enlighten me then, little brother.'

Oisín raises his fist for the first time. I take a step back and shove my hands into my pockets. My brother didn't kiss Dee tonight. A stranger did. I have no idea who this man standing in front of me, in a fancy suit, is. All I know is who he's not. Oisín's face is as I remember, albeit hairier. That is where the resemblance to the brother I once knew and loved ends. Even his accent is different now. Oisín is as dead as Seány. It's about time I accepted that.

Dee looks at me. Her eyes are full of questions. Questions I don't want to answer. I take Aisling by the hand and try to pull her to her feet. She's uncooperative and it embarrasses me.

'That's it, run away,' Oisín shouts.

I snort. 'Running away is your speciality, Ois. Or haven't you realised that yet?'

The punch comes as I'm walking away. It catches the side of my jaw and almost knocks me off my feet. I stagger, and fall against the table next to us. I knock over wine and the two women at the table look up, horrified. I'm about to apologise when Oisín grabs me and twists me to face him. The second punch is harder and the third makes me see stars.

'Stop it. Please, please stop it.'

The beat of a bass drum, laughter and chatter, and Dee crying rings in my ears. I'm in darkness. Perhaps I blacked out. Or perhaps I shut my eyes because the look on Oisín's face pains me more than his fists.

'Stop it. Oh my God, stop,' Dee cries, and I regain my sight to find her tugging on Oisín's arm. 'Look what you're doing to him.'

Oisín looks at her and staggers back. 'I'm sorry. I'm so sorry,' he says.

I flop onto the ground. My head is spinning.

Dee drops to her knees beside me. Her hands are on my face and I'm instantly comforted.

'Are you okay?' she sobs.

I watch Oisín as he flops into his chair and downs the last of his pint.

'Aisling, get some ice,' Dee says.

Hands are on me again. From behind. Not Dee's. Big, strong hands. They yank me to my feet.

'I knew you were trouble, Irish,' the bouncer from the door says.

He drags me past tables and chairs. And the bar. Dee hurries after us. And Aisling. Outside, the bouncer tosses me aside like old socks. My shoulder hits the footpath first. The cold cement chews past the layers of my clothes to bite my skin.

'Fionn. Oh my God, Fionn.'

Dee races towards me. She's breathless. She tries to help me up, but my legs are weak and I'm not ready to stand.

Aisling stands back and folds her arms. Her face is the colour of the concrete footpath.

Dee tries to help me again, but I shake my head.

'Fionn?' Aisling says.

My name is the only word Aisling utters. She doesn't need to say more. I already know all her questions.

Why are we here?

Do I need to be worried?

Do you care about me, the way I care about you?

And the most important question of all. The same question Oisín asked. The question I need to ask myself.

Why do I care who kisses Dee?

FIFTY-THREE

DEE

'Are you okay?' I say, placing my hand on Fionn's shoulder. My fingers are shaking. 'Do you think anything is broken?'

He trembles. I take off my coat and drape it round his shoulders. It's a terrible fit, and it can't be keeping him warm, but he looks at me and smiles. The relief of seeing him smile almost doubles me over. I think about all the times he has given me his coat over the years and my heart swells. I wonder if we're sharing that same thought. It certainly feels as if we are. My mind floods with memories. Cloch Bheag. A knock on my bedroom window, and his teenage face waiting there when I drew back the curtains. The taste of his lips on mine. The feel of his skin against me. Inside me. How much I love him. How much I always have. The feeling is overwhelming and I can't bear to see him like this. I want to take him in my arms and fix everything. I want to fix Fionn. I guess, I always have.

'Do we need to call an ambulance?' Aisling says.

Her voice slices into my thoughts as her words run into each other. It's hard to tell where one ends and the next begins.

Fionn bypasses my gaze and his eyes seek out Aisling. He looks at her with round, puppy-dog eyes. I think it's an apology.

She comes forward, at last. Her arms are wrapped round herself and she's slouching as if she's hurt. For a moment, I wonder if I should check, before I remember no one has laid a finger on her. But that doesn't mean she's not hurt, I realise.

Aisling squats at the far side of Fionn. He keeps his eyes on her. I stand up. I'm suddenly so aware that I am in their space. Fionn and Aisling have a space. A place where only the two of them belong. I'm crowding it. Intruding.

Aisling leans in and kisses Fionn's cheek. He winces and I have to look away.

'That bouncer was a prick,' she says. 'Did you see that?'

It takes me a moment to realise she's talking to me.

'Do you see how he pushed Fionn?'

I nod. I did.

'Bastard,' she says, raising her voice.

I turn round. Security has resumed position on the door. He stares straight ahead, with his shoulders back and his round belly pointing forward, as if he can't see the carnage on the foot-path next to him.

Fionn's eyes are locked on mine.

'Where does it hurt?' Aisling asks.

Fionn tries to take a deep breath, but the pain stops him.

'Everywhere,' I answer for him.

'Tell me what to do. Tell me how to help. I don't know what to do.' Aisling sobs. She sniffles and drags a shaky arm under her nose.

Fionn allows himself another look at me. His eyes are full of pain. But I know it's not the bruises or possible fractured bones that hurt. Fionn's heart is broken. And mine breaks for him. I keep my eyes on his. And without words I answer Aisling's questions.

I know what to do. I know how to help.

I reach into my pocket and pull out the keys to my flat. I

shove them into Aisling's hand. She's dazed and ditzy and I have to physically curl her fingers round them.

'Aisling,' I say. 'Ais.'

She's a sniffling, crying mess.

'Ais,' I shout now, and shake her a little.

She pulls herself together and stands. Then she opens her hand and looks at the keys.

'Fionn is freezing. It's probably shock,' I say. 'Get him back to my flat.'

'Aren't you coming?'

'Not right now.'

Panic flashes across Aisling's face. The responsibility is too great. But I'm not backing down. If she loves him, and I think she does, then she needs to step up and take care of him the way I would.

'The address is 34b Finsbury Royal.'

Aisling nods.

'34b Finsbury Royal,' I repeat.

Aisling nods again.

'Say it.'

'34b Finsbury Royal,' she says.

'Okay. Good. Don't forget it.'

'34b Finsbury Royal,' she whispers, over and over.

I reach into my other pocket and pull out some cash. I pass it over. Then I step into the street and wait for a taxi. Within seconds a distinctive black cab approaches and I wave my arms. The cab stops and I turn back to Fionn and Aisling.

Fionn is on his feet now with Aisling's arms tucked under his.

'Jesus, mate,' the taxi driver says as his window rolls down.

The driver turns his attention back to me and his hesitation to become tangled up in something radiates out.

'He fell,' I say.

'Into a fist,' the driver adds.

'He needs to get to 34b Finsbury Royal,' I say.

The driver remains unconvinced.

'It's my flat. I'm new in town and my friends are just visiting. Things got messy. Please.'

The driver nods and I repeat the address. I open the sliding back door, and Aisling and I help Fionn into the back seat. Aisling climbs in next to him and I close the door.

'Thanks,' I tell the driver, as I step backwards onto the footpath.

'He's lucky to have a friend like you. Enjoy the rest of your night,' the driver says, then he rolls up his window and drives away.

FIFTY-FOUR

DEE

I take a deep breath and re-approach the door of the Knight's Arms. I expect to be turned away by security but I'm prepared to beg to be let back in. To my surprise, the bouncer steps aside.

'They're trouble, those two,' he says as I pass by.

I stop walking and look up to find his head cocked to one side and genuine concern in his eyes.

'I saw the way you looked at him. But if you want my advice?'

I don't.

'Sack that tosser off before he ruins your life. He's her problem now, eh?'

Without responding, I lower my head once more and walk back inside. Oisín is speaking to the women at the table next to us. They're older ladies, in their seventies perhaps. They smile and nod and listen as Oisín speaks. They seem to enjoy him and I'm taken aback considering what just happened. Someone has cleaned up their spilt drinks, and they are sipping on two fresh glasses of white wine.

There is a pint of Guinness waiting on Oisín's table and a

vodka and Coke. He looks up, and smiles when he sees me. I sit down at the table and wait for him to join me.

'You bought more drinks,' I say.

Oisín raises his pint towards the ladies at the table beside us and mouths, 'Cheers'.

'I had to,' he says, turning back towards me. 'Fionn spilled their wine and—'

'I meant for us. For me.'

'I took a chance you'd come back.'

'Fionn's in a bad way,' I say. 'I don't think anything is broken but—'

'Good. That's good.'

Oisín takes a mouthful of his pint. I've lost count of how much he's drunk tonight. A lot.

'Don't you want to know why he's here?' I say.

'Isn't that obvious?'

I glare at him. His confidence, which seemed so alluring at the start of the night, is coming off as arrogant and cocky now.

'He's here because you're here,' he says.

I snort. 'It has nothing to do with me.'

'If you say so…'

'It hasn't.'

'Sure.'

Oisín shrugs. It's infuriating.

'He came here to tell you something important. And then you punched him,' I say.

'Eh. He punched me first, remember?'

I sigh. I can't argue with facts.

'Is that why you've come back?' Oisín says. 'To tell me what Fionn couldn't.'

'Yes.'

'Fair enough. I admire that. But at least have a drink first. From the look on your face, I think you need it.'

I glance at the glass of vodka and Coke but I don't touch it.

'Your mam is sick,' I say. 'I'm sorry to blurt it out like that but there really is no other way to say it.'

Oisín lowers his pint. And finally, I see a resemblance to Fionn that stretches past their chocolate eyes, high cheekbones and dark, curly hair. I see the imprint of a childhood growing up on Cloch Bheag.

'It's serious,' I say. 'I don't know how long she has but I know it's important to Fionn that you know.'

'I'm sorry to hear that,' he says.

His response is as cold as it is generic.

'Didn't you hear me? Your mam is dying. She might not be here next year.'

'And as I said, that's very sad news. I can only imagine how hard Fionn is taking it all.'

'He's been great, actually. He's coping better than I think most people would. But she's your mother as much as his. I'm sure this must all be very hard to hear.'

'No. Lorna stopped being my mother when she started being Seány's.'

I inhale audibly. It's not the time or the place to gasp, but I can't help it. I haven't heard Seány's name in so long it takes my breath away as my senses are flooded with memories of a special little boy.

'You shouldn't say stuff like that,' I say. 'Your mother loves you to bits. She has been broken-hearted all these years. She was devastated when you left.'

'She told you this, did she? Because I've never known my mother to wear her heart on her sleeve.'

'No. Not exactly. But I've talked to Fionn about it.'

Oisín snorts and throws his head back. 'That's a good one! Come back and lecture me when you know what really went on.'

'I know what happened.'

'No!' Angry saliva sprays from Oisín's lips. 'No you fucking don't. And neither does Fionn.'

'I know Seány was your son,' I say.

'And you think figuring the obvious out makes you some sort of genius. Give me a break.'

'Then tell me? Explain why you walked out of Fionn's life one day and you never came back.'

I feel myself cross a line. I have no right to ask Oisín such personal questions. Hours ago we were strangers. But I know so much about him and, yet, I know so little. I expect him to tell me to fuck off. Or maybe he'll get up and walk away. It catches me by surprise when he says, 'Marie and I loved each other.'

I believe him, and suddenly I feel crushingly sorry for him. Oisín and Marie could have been a beautiful love story and instead it's a devastating tragedy.

'We would have been good parents,' Oisín continues. 'We would have loved him. But no one gave us a chance. No one let us try. Marie's parents didn't want anything to do with the baby. They didn't want her to be a mother. They'd have kicked her out. They'd have disowned her.'

I can't keep the horror off my face. It's hard to imagine any woman being forced to give up her baby. I remind myself that she wasn't a woman. She was a child herself.

'Then my mam and dad got involved,' Oisín says.

There's so much pain and resentment in him. It's hard to listen.

'They said the child would have a better life if they raised him.'

I open my mouth but no sound comes out. No words feel good enough.

'Do you want to know the worst part? Do you want to know what was worse than all that?'

I hold my breath. I'm not sure I'm strong enough to hear it, but something tells me Oisín desperately needs to say it.

'I believed them. I fucking believed them all. I thought my

son would have a better life without me in it. But where is he now, huh? He's dead. My little boy is dead.'

The band finishes playing but silence doesn't follow. Drunken voices rush in to fill the void. My head hurts.

'It was an accident,' I say. 'Seány's death. And your dad. It was a terrible, terrible accident. No one is to blame.'

Oisín pushes the last of his pint away.

I reach for his hand, slowly in case I spook him, and he stops talking. But he lets me take it; he even offers me a half smile.

'I know how hard it is,' I say. 'Fionn told me once that, every morning, when he wakes up Seány is the first thought in his head, and he's the last thing he thinks about every night before he goes to sleep.'

'That's the difference,' Oisín says. 'Fionn sleeps!'

I swallow hard. 'I wish there was something I could say.'

I'm hyper-aware that I am out of my depth trying to comfort a man who has lost a child.

'Maybe if you talk to Fionn,' I say.

'There is nothing to say. Cloch Bheag is a place and a time I try very hard to forget. If I didn't, I don't think I could function.'

'But your mam.'

'My mam and Fionn are a distant memory too.'

'But that means forgetting Seány too. I don't believe that's what you want. Is it?'

The lights come on and Oisín swallows. I can almost see the lump work its way down. People begin to move. They pull coats on and layer on hats and gloves and scarves.

'It's late,' I say. 'I should get a taxi.'

'Do you want to walk for a while?' Oisín says.

I look at him, unsure.

'It's freezing. I think it might snow,' I say.

'I like snow,' he says.

I smile. I like snow too.

'I don't want to forget Seány,' he says. 'But the truth is, I didn't really know him.'

'He was wonderful,' I say, as we walk towards the door and onto the street.

'Maybe you could tell me about him sometime?'

A black cab comes into view but I let it pass by.

'You know what?' I say. 'A walk would be good.'

FIFTY-FIVE

DEE

It's freezing. The type of cold that works its way under your clothes and burrows into your bones until your teeth chatter and you can't feel the tip of your nose. Our breath dances in the air when we speak. And yet, I could happily walk for hours. Oisín and I stride side-by-side with our hands in our pockets to keep our fingers warm. My shoulder knocks against his arm every so often and he looks at me and smiles when it does.

Fresh air and conversation seem to have sobered Oisín up quickly. Quicker than me. He leads the way around city sights. Big Ben. The Thames. London Bridge. The Tower of London.

'That's where Ann Boleyn was executed,' he says, pointing to the commanding stone building across the Thames. 'Henry VIII's second wife.'

I nod. I knew. We learned about Henry and all his wives in school. But something about standing here, looking up at a place that is infamous in the pages of history books, sends a chill down my spine.

'Poor woman. I can't imagine.'

'Families, eh?' Oisín sighs. 'They do the strangest things.'

'They really do.'

I think of my parents in France. Drinking wine and eating cheese in a one-bedroomed apartment made only for two.

London is bright, despite a black sky. The warm, yellow glow of street lights is soothing, like countless fireflies buzzing to light our path. When I finally check my watch it's past 2 a.m. I'm not tired and neither is the city. I wonder if London ever sleeps. I doubt it. There aren't many others out walking, but there are some. Couples, linking arms and wrapped in winter layers to keep warm. Someone on a bicycle with a blinking front light. A man and his dog on a lead. By the time we reach Piccadilly Circus my feet are aching. The bright, electric bill-board on the corner takes my breath away. I've seen it in pictures and in movies but in real life it's even brighter and bigger and wower. Sony. Coca-Cola. Citroën. Big brands occupy prime advertising space. Underneath, a homeless man picks a half-eaten burger out of the bin and takes a bite. He's elderly, with wiry white hair and a long white beard. The contrast between the sparkly lights and the hardshipped old man pains me. It's an eye-opening reflection of the city. Nothing and no place is all light. Darkness is always there. But without darkness, how could we know to appreciate light?

'Do you like it here?' I ask.

'London?' Oisín says.

I nod. 'Yeah, London.'

He stops walking and climbs up a couple of steps of the fountain behind us and sits down. I join him.

'I do. I didn't at first. It scared the shite out of me to begin with. But I've been here a long time.'

'It scares me too,' I say.

Admitting it out loud is liberating and I want to go on. I look into Oisín's eyes. The red hue of the Coca-Cola billboard is casting a colour on his face. And I watch him for a moment. The way you would revere any beautiful thing.

'There would be something wrong if it didn't scare you,'

Oisín says. 'But if it doesn't work out, you can always go home. At least you have that.'

'I don't. I mean, I can't.'

Oisín's eyes narrow as if he's looking deep inside me, trying to find the words written on my soul. I know this look. Fionn looks at me this way sometimes. But he usually looks away, having read me like a book. Oisín can't quite seem to open the pages. So, I help him.

'My parents moved to France when I finished college.'

'And you didn't fancy France?'

'I wasn't invited.'

'Oh.'

I take a deep breath. 'Yeah.'

'Fuck. Wow. Okay.' He runs a shaky hand through his hair.

The action is too familiar. I have to look away.

'I can visit. Anytime. And my mam calls a lot. But...'

'But it is what it is,' he says.

'It is.'

I bring my eyes back to him and he's smiling at me sympathetically. He doesn't criticise my family that way so many others do. He simply says nothing at all and it's the best thing he could possibly say.

'Make this city work for you,' he says, getting to his feet. 'Make friends with it. Trust it. Let it fill you up and let it be enough. It works. It helps.'

He reaches his hand out and I take it. I'm on my feet and we're walking again. I could use a friend, I think. And I hope London is up for the job.

We get a taxi back to my flat and Oisín gets out with me. I balk. I wasn't prepared to invite him in.

'Can we do this again, some time?' he asks. 'I promise not to punch anyone next time.'

I smile. Maybe London won't be my only friend after all, I think.

'I'd really like that,' I say.

'This is a nice bloody area,' he says.

He looks up and down the street of three-storey, terraced houses, like Weetabix stacked side-by-side.

'You haven't won the lotto, have you?'

'The flat is compliments of my job. I only have it for a few weeks until I get settled and find something.'

'That's some perk. What's your job?'

'TV presenter.'

His eyes widen and I blush.

'It's kids' TV. The graveyard shift, so not as exciting as it seems.'

'Wow. Can I kiss you again?'

I gasp.

'It's just, someday you're going to be famous. It would be really great for my ego if I could tell people that I kissed you.'

'Eh...'

Snow begins to fall. I feel it land on the top of my head and I watch it catch in Oisín's hair. The curtain twitches in my flat window and I see Fionn, looking out at the snow. I'm about to wave when Aisling appears behind him. She slips her arms round his waist and kisses his neck. He drops his head back onto her shoulder. He lets the curtain go. It steadies, and they're out of sight.

I take a step forward and press my chest against Oisín's. I close my eyes and wait to feel his lips on mine.

PART FOUR

FIFTY-SIX

FIONN

Four Years Later – June 2009

Cloch Bheag is thronged with tourists. They seem to multiply every year. Their cameras ready and snapping before they're even off the ferry. Americans mostly. But some Europeans too. I can't place their accents or tell what language they're speaking. French, or maybe some Italian. John Paul and Lainey are among the influx from the mainland – visiting for the bank holiday weekend. John Paul stands out more like tourists than a local these days. With the tips of his hair bleached and designer runners on his feet. I've seen his new van driving around the island a couple of times this week. It's bigger than his old one and *Burke's Timber Flooring* is printed on the side in bold, easy-to-read print.

'He's doing very well for himself,' Mrs Leary told my mam last week, and then Mam told me.

Mam's favourite days are Wednesday and Saturday. That's when Mrs Leary comes to visit. Mam doesn't leave the house any more. Unless it's for a hospital appointment. And, at home, she rarely leaves her room. I've moved the television into her room and her team at the hospital in Letterkenny organised to have a special bed sent to us. A water bed. They said it would be more comfortable and stop Mam from getting bedsores. But she refuses to sleep in it. I don't argue. She prefers to sleep in the bed she shared with Dad for more than twenty years. I move her as much as possible and, so far, we're making it work.

'You're a good boy, Fionn,' she tells me often.

Every so often, usually just after she's taken her morning or evening medication, she calls me Oisín or Seány. I used to correct her, but I've stopped now. I think it's easier for us both if we pretend.

'You're meeting your friends tonight, isn't that right, Oisín?' Mam says, as I bring her breakfast.

It's porridge and orange juice. We both know she'll only manage a couple of spoonfuls and a little sip, but it's our routine every morning and it brings us both comfort.

'John Paul is doing very well for himself,' Mam says.

She repeats herself often lately and each time I react as if I'm hearing the news for the first time.

'That's great, Mam. I'm happy for him.'

'You're meeting your friends for drinks later, Oisín, aren't you?' she says.

I turn on the television. 'Look Mam, it's Dee,' I say, pointing.

'Oh Seány, this was your favourite when you were little. And look how pretty that nice lady is.'

My chest swells with pride. I wish Seány could see Dee now, presenting her own kids' show on prime-time Saturday morning TV. Her dark hair is in pigtails, tied up with colourful bows, and she's dressed in a bright yellow t-shirt and pink denim shorts. She almost looks the same as she did when she was seventeen. As she was when Seány knew her. I can't quite believe it's Seány's anniversary today; eight years without my little brother. Longer with him gone than with him here. I try not to think about that. It's too damn much to bear. He'd be fifteen now. He'd have outgrown Saturday morning kids' TV. His attention would be focused on knocking on the window of the mainland girls staying here for the summer. I thought I would never get used to teenage girls making our house their temporary home . But, now, when I see them on the island laughing and chatting in their groups the way teenagers do, it's strange knowing none of them are staying in our house. They haven't since Mam got sick. I've never asked Mam if she misses that life, but I know she does.

Mam giggles as she watches Dee interacting with talking puppets. Her laughter lifts me. And I find myself light and smiling as I take a moment to enjoy Dee's antics on screen too. Dee chats with a pink monkey about what's coming up later on today's show. It's not long before Mam drifts into a content sleep. I take away the barely touched porridge and juice and I wait for Mrs Leary's knock on the front door.

FIFTY-SEVEN

FIONN

Later That Day

John Paul joins me on the boat for old times' sake. It's nice to have company even if I'm not too sure what to talk to him about these days.

'Work is going well,' he tells me, as we sail west, leaving Cloch Bheag behind.

'That's good.'

'Yeah. We're putting down the floors in a new housing estate in Clondalkin at the moment. Lainey says it's just round the corner from where she grew up.'

'And where Dee grew up too,' I say.

John Paul doesn't reply.

'Does Lainey ever talk about Dee?' I ask.

John Paul shifts from one foot to the other and scrunches his nose. 'The odd time, I guess.'

'I saw Dee on TV this morning,' I say. 'It's weird watching

her. It almost feels as if I shouldn't, not when she can't see me back.'

'I haven't seen it. Lainey won't put it on,' John Paul says.

I make a face. 'It's been years. Is she still envious?'

A flash of irritation sparks in John Paul's eyes and it's obvious he doesn't appreciate my line of questioning.

'Lainey isn't envious of anyone. She's glad she got out of the showbiz game. She said she doesn't know how anyone sticks it, to be honest. I guess it takes a very specific type of person to suck up to the big bosses.'

It's my turn to feel annoyance. I resent the implication that Dee is anything less than a hard worker who deserves her success.

'Lainey is office manager for Burke's Flooring now,' John Paul says. 'We wouldn't be half as big an operation without her. We have three vans and ten lads on the team now.'

'My mam told me,' I say. 'That's great, JP. I'm really happy for you.'

'Thanks, man. That means a lot.'

I think about giving John Paul a hug, but I settle for a gentle smack on the back. He nods and smiles. Seagulls fly overhead, cawing and searching for their lunch. The engine chugs and the bow chews through waves, spitting them out. The sounds of the ocean never cease to take my breath away.

'I'm going to ask her to marry me,' John Paul says.

The hungry birds and breaking waves lose my focus as I turn towards my best friend and throw my arms round him.

'That's fantastic, JP. Fucking fantastic.'

'I'm shitting it,' John Paul says. 'What if she says no?'

'As if.'

'She's dropped a few hints,' he says, clearing his throat with a nervous cough. 'Valentine's Day and her birthday. But I thought this weekend would be the best time. The June bank holiday weekend is always a special time for us. Remember the time Lainey and Dee came to visit and we camped out on the beach?'

I swallow. I remember. It was Seány's first anniversary.

'I can't remember where you were,' John Paul says, and I can see him searching his brain.

I hope the answer doesn't come to him. Seány is a distant memory to most people now, and I'm comfortable with that.

'You were probably out here.' John Paul points, towards the dark water that stretches ahead endlessly.

'Probably,' I say.

'You really think she'll say yes?' he says.

'She loves you, JP. You're a lucky man, you know that.'

He smiles. He knows.

'And what about you and Aisling? Any sign of wedding bells there?'

'Fuck no. Jesus no. We're nowhere near that,' I say, raising my hands above my head as if John Paul's words have somehow threatened me.

'Fair enough,' he says, but he seems taken aback by my words. 'Just don't mess her about, eh?'

I grimace. I never thought I'd see the day I received relationship advice from John Paul Leary.

'You'll be my best man, won't you?' John Paul says.

'I'd be honoured.'

FIFTY-EIGHT

DEE

One Year Later – 7 June 2010

'Monday is a strange day for a wedding,' Sammie says, as we sit in our favourite coffee shop tucked on the corner of a side street near the BBC's head office.

'It's a bank holiday weekend,' I say, blowing on a mocha that's too hot to touch.

Sammie slurps an iced something-or-other with lots of whipped cream on top and I wish I'd ordered that instead. London is sweltering today. The guys in weather said it's the hottest June for almost twenty years. Lainey and John Paul are lucky with gorgeous sunshine for their big day.

'So let me get this straight,' Sammie says, between slurps. 'They're getting married on an island. Even though she's from Dublin and he's lived in Dublin for years.'

'Yes. But he's from Cloch Bheag originally.'

'Cloch Bheag,' Sammie says, and it sounds almost exotic in her London RP accent.

'It means "Little Stone" in English,' I explain.

'Aw. I like that.'

'It's a beautiful place,' I say. 'Especially on a day like today. I can only imagine how fab their photos will be.'

I look out the window at the sun shining between buildings, casting oddly shaped shadows on the footpath. People pass by in linen trousers and summer dresses.

'I still can't believe they didn't invite you,' Sammie says.

I take a mouthful of coffee. It's still too hot and I scorch the roof of my mouth. And yet it doesn't sting as much as knowing that Lainey is getting married today and I won't be there. I'm not wanted there.

'I wasn't expecting an invite,' I say, truthfully.

'Your ex-best mate marries the guy you set her up with, and they don't invite you.' Sammie tuts. 'It's rude. That's all I'm saying.'

'We haven't spoken in years. I wouldn't even know they were getting married if Lainey's mother hadn't told my mother.'

My parents are flying in from France for the wedding. I've invited them to London several times but my mam says big cities make her uncomfortable.

'We'll see you in Donegal, love,' Mam said when she called last month.

She was horrified to discover I wasn't going. She offered to talk to Mrs Burke about it.

'There must be some sort of misunderstanding. Elaine Burke practically grew up in our house.'

'We drifted apart. People do,' I said.

Mam said she'd take lots of photos on my Dad's new iPhone 4 and she'd email them to me.

'I'm getting very good with a computer these days,' she said.

She is. She regularly updates me with photos and emails detailing her and my dad's Mediterranean retirement.

'So, are you going to stalk Lainey and I-can't-remember-his-name's big day on Facebook?' Sammie says, dragging my thoughts back to the here and now.

I stare at her blankly. The roof of my mouth is pulsing and I wonder if I've done some proper damage.

'John Paul,' I say, and I add, 'No. I hadn't thought about it.'

'Liar,' Sammie says. 'Everyone thinks about things like that. You *are* friends with her on Facebook, right?'

'Yes.'

I accidently sent Lainey a friend request a couple of months ago when I was snooping on her profile. She was online at the time and accepted the request before I had a chance to retract it. I've liked some of her statuses since. The one about becoming office manager at Burke's Timber Flooring, for example. She posts photos often. Titbits of her and John Paul's happy life. I like them all. I don't think she has ever acknowledged any of my photos. Not that I post often, and never anything personal. The nearest I got to personal was a recent photo of my feet to promote shoes I was gifted by some up-and-coming designer. I never leave a comment on her stuff. I do, however, read all her comments from girls we went to college with and, of course, Aisling and Fionn. I've never sent her a direct message. Although, one night after a blazing fight with Oisín and a bottle of wine, I did think about messaging her. I called Sammie instead. Sammie is who I call now. Probably a little too often.

'Oh my God, is that her?' Sammie points to a blonde girl in a bathrobe, with curlers in her hair as she sips champagne.

The photo is captioned: *Thank you to @IslandKatiesbeauty for making me beautiful.*

'That's her,' I say, looking into Lainey's eyes that seem to sparkle with excitement.

Sammie orders another coffee and mine finally cools enough to drink and we sit and spy on people from my once-upon-a-time-life.

I click into John Paul's profile and there's a photo of him and Fionn in finely tailored navy suits.

'Holy shit, I thought that was Oisín for a moment,' Sammie says, as she points at Fionn.

'It's his brother,' I say.

I almost never talk about Fionn. Oisín can't bear to hear his name and I've never had reason to tell Sammie about him. Sammie is my best friend. We spend an inordinate amount of time together. We work together, socialise together, shop together, bitch together. I also like to think I am Sammie's best friend. Sometimes I think she knows me better than I know myself. She can pre-empt my worries or concerns before I voice them and her advice is always spot on.

'Your skirt is not too short, the people in wardrobe know what they're doing.'

'Ignore Twitter, it's full of envious bitches.'

'If you fart on camera, pretend it's your shoe.'

'Interview for the big job. I believe in you.'

She always has my back and I trust her completely. I also know that Sammie knows London Dee. She knows the person I have worked very hard to become. The person who interviews for the big job and actually gets it. The person who is moving from kids' TV to hosting her own talk show.

I am more than happy to become the new face of mid-morning television. A face that is a million miles away from a girl who played camogie and climbed out a bedroom window on a sleepy island. I have left that girl far behind. The girl who once loved a boy and his little brother so much her heart was full.

It took a long time but my heart is once again full. Full of ambition and drive and contentment. Or at least it was, until recently. Ever since I found out Lainey and John Paul were getting married, my full heart has been leaking a little. It's as if a shard of gossip from my old life has pierced the perfect bubble of my new life and, slowly, I am deflating. I haven't told anyone I feel this way. I keep waiting for the feeling to pass. I'm hoping that after today, after the wedding, it will.

'Oh my God, he's gorgeous,' Sammie says, still focused on Fionn. 'Do you know if he's single?'

'Afraid not,' I say. 'In a long-term relationship, as far as I know.'

'Bugger it. Why are the good ones always taken?' She laughs.

The good ones.

Sammie and I fritter away another hour, clicking from profile to profile to profile; piecing together Lainey and John Paul's wedding from uploads. We linger at length on each shot. Discussing dresses and hair and shoes. We relish those who upload countless snaps and curse those who don't upload any, or have their privacy settings activated. Until we stumble upon a photo that catches my breath. I look away.

'You okay?' Sammie says, noticing the sudden shift in my mood.

'Yeah. Yeah. Course.' I look into my empty coffee cup. 'Should we get going?' I say.

Sammie places her hand on my shoulder. 'What's wrong?'

'Nothing. Just the coffee shakes.'

I stand up and sling my handbag over my shoulder. Sammie does the same and we leave and walk back to work. I try to concentrate but for the rest of the day I can't get that last photo out of my head. The one of Fionn and Lorna, side-by-side in their finest clothes.

I lock myself in a bathroom cubicle and retrace my steps online to find the photo again. I find it on Aisling's profile and I realise she's the one who's taken the shot. I recognise Lorna's kitchen in the background – it hasn't changed in ten years. But she's not sitting at the table, as I always remember her. She's in a wheelchair, with a blanket over her knees. Skin clings to her cheekbones like papier mâché and her hair is thin and barely there. Her eyes still sparkle with kindness and warmth. She's wearing a purple dress, but only the top is visible as the blanket covers her legs. She's smiling, as is Fionn. Lorna looks happy, despite her frail frame. But behind Fionn's straight teeth and dapper good looks are heartbreak-heavy eyes. And all of a sudden, I'm transported back to the girl I once was, who loved a boy with the whole of her heart.

FIFTY-NINE

DEE

Six Weeks Later – July 2010

I'm standing in Euston station with a croissant in one hand and a takeaway coffee in the other when my mobile begins to ring.

'Fuck it, fuck it,' I mumble.

There's nowhere to set my coffee down and I settle for bending and placing it between my feet.

I press my mobile to my ear and say, 'Hello.'

'Hello,' Sammie says, far too cheery for this hour of the morning.

'Ugh. God, what?'

I wish I was a morning person. It would make my life so much easier.

'I see you,' Sammie says, in a sing-song voice that belongs in a horror film.

I spin on the spot, kicking my coffee over. 'Shite. I spilled my coffee.'

Sammie laughs.

The station is quiet, as it always is this early. I peer ahead as far as my eyes will allow me, and into corners, but I don't see Sammie.

'Where are you?'

'King's Cross,' she says. 'And with a full cup of coffee.'

'Ha. Then you don't see me. I'm in Euston.'

'I see you,' she sings again.

'Stop it. That's creepy. And no, you don't see me. Like I said, I'm in Euston. Anyway, I better go, I need to get another coffee.'

'I'm looking at you right now,' Sammie says.

'We're not in the same place.' My voice is an octave higher.

'Doesn't mean I'm not looking at you.'

'Oh God, it's too early for cryptic shite. What the actual hell are you talking about?'

'You. I see you. Or more specifically, I see a big giant-arse billboard with your face on it. It's right here in the centre of the station. You look a-mazing by the way.'

'Oh fuck off.'

'I'm going to hang up so I can send you a pic—'

'Sammie,' I say. 'Sammie wait, don't go.'

There's silence on my phone before it dings and a message from Sammie comes through. I open it and gasp when I see a photo of my face lighting up the main advertising space in King's Cross station.

On the Couch with Dee-Dee is written in swirly font, next to me sitting on a giant, red sofa. I remember the photo shoot. It's at least three years old and was taken when I had a horrible headache after partying with Oisín and his colleagues the night before. I thought the PR people planned to use the picture for some newspaper article that never saw the light of day. I never imagined hungover me would be towering over one of the busiest train stations in London.

I bump into myself countless times on the rest of the

journey to work. My face smiles back at me from the side of a bus, above a deli and on a street corner. By the time I reach my dressing room, colleagues are gathered at my door and clapping. Cindy, from make-up, has appeared with a cake. There are no candles to blow out, but there is rainbow icing and I hope we're not going to have to eat a slice at this hour of the day. Within minutes my tiny dressing room is thronged with people wishing to congratulate me, and, when my phone rings, I almost don't hear it. I excuse myself and step into the hall to answer it. I expect to see Oisín's name on my screen. He's probably spotted a billboard somewhere on his way to work. My heart races when, instead, it's Fionn's name flashing up.

I move further away from my dressing room door and the hyper commotion inside, and I press my phone to my ear.

'Hello,' I say.

'Dee?'

'Yes.'

'It's Fionn. I'm sorry to call out of the blue but it's my mam…'

My breath catches. I'm not ready.

'She's gone. She died this morning.'

SIXTY

DEE

Cindy lowers the cake as I walk back into my dressing room.

'Dee, you all right, girl? You look like you've seen a ghost,' she says.

She places the cake down on my dressing table and waves her hands to shush the clapping. People lower their hands by their sides and, sensing the sudden shift in the mood, they file out the door as quickly as they piled in.

'What do you reckon all that was about?' someone says on their way out.

'Someone probably found out she slept her way to the top. Wouldn't surprise me if she got fired for it,' someone else says.

I hear Sammie's voice on the corridor. It's raised and defensive; something about rumours and envy. There's an awkward apology from someone and then silence. It washes over me as if I am made of countless grains of sand.

'Sorry I'm late,' Sammie says, knocking on the ajar door. 'God, that looks good.' She points at the rainbow cake. 'Where is everyone?'

Cindy makes a face.

'Jeez, who died?' Sammie says. 'I thought this was supposed to be a party.'

'Oisín's mother passed away this morning,' I say.

Cindy's hand covers her mouth.

'Oh shit,' Sammie says. 'Me and my big mouth. I didn't mean—'

'I know,' I say, taking her hand and squeezing it gently. 'It *was* supposed to be a party. But I have to go. I have to go home.'

'Of course. Of course. Is there anything I can do?'

'Can you let production know? The funeral will be in Ireland, so I don't know how long I'll be gone.'

'Yeah, yeah, absolutely. I'll fill in for you myself, if I have to.'

I squeeze her hand again and smile. We both know Sammie would rather boil her head than step foot on my side of the camera.

Oisín hasn't left for work yet by the time I return home. He's sitting at the kitchen table, mindlessly spooning muesli into his mouth as he scrolls through his phone. He looks up when he hears me come in.

'You're home,' he says. 'Did you forget something?' He twists his wrist and glances at his watch. 'Aren't you on air in an hour?'

'Did Fionn call?' I ask, although the answer seems obvious.

Oisín lowers his spoon into his bowl and looks up at me. His eyes are glassy and full of pain already. He knows what comes next, and I hate myself for having to say it.

'She's gone, Ois.' I choke on the words as I try to push them out. 'Your mam passed away this morning. I'm so sorry.'

He stands up and scrapes the last of his cereal into the bin, then he places his bowl on the countertop and walks out of the kitchen. I wait a moment, gathering myself. The previous owners of our Georgian three-storey home have done a fabulous job of restoration. Oisín and I didn't change a thing when we bought it just before Christmas, but suddenly, everything about my home feels wrong.

I dab around my eyes with kitchen towel and follow him. I find him in the sitting room. His back is to me as he stares out the commanding bay window overlooking our quiet end of the cul-de-sac. I tiptoe towards him and stop next to the grand piano that neither of us can play. I choose my words carefully.

'At least she's not in pain anymore,' I say.

The doctors gave Lorna a year but she fought for five. Five years that could have been filled with visits and making memories. But they weren't. The weight of regret is instant and crushing. If it feels this way for me, I can only imagine how Oisín feels.

'Fionn said he'll let us know the details, date and time of the funeral and stuff,' I say, 'But maybe we should fly home today, if I can book something? I'm sure Fionn will need help organising everything.'

Oisín continues to stare out the window. His elbow bends every so often. It's not quite 8 a.m., but I can tell he's raising a glass of whiskey to his lips.

'Your mam is with your dad and Seány now,' I say.

Oisín spins round. A splash of fiery, burgundy whiskey sloshes over the edge of his glass and hits our walnut floor. He ignores the mess and drains the rest of the glass, then he slams it down on the lid of the piano with unnecessary force.

'I have to get to work,' he says. 'I'm late.'

I grab his hand and try to turn him back but he shakes me off and walks out the door.

SIXTY-ONE

FIONN

I stand in front of the mirror and fix my tie. Grey hair is creeping in above my temples. I am twenty-eight years old. I look older. I feel older. I promise myself that today will be the last time in my life I ever wear a suit.

Outside the house, old men shake my hand and tell me they are sorry for my troubles.

'She was a lovely woman,' they say. 'She'll be missed.'

I lead the procession behind the hearse, as Mam makes her final journey across Cloch Bheag. A road she has walked many times, with mine or Oisín's or Seány's hand in hers. Today, I walk alone, with no family either side of me. Behind me are John Paul and Lainey, and John Paul's family. Aisling walks with her family. And I spotted Dee somewhere among the many faces. I didn't look for Oisín. I know he's not to be found.

At the church, I listen to the priest talk about Mam's life. About the whole O'Connell family. He paints a beautiful picture of happy people. For a moment I remember that we once were. I sit alone in the front pew. I slide the silver foil out of my packet of twenty John Player Blue and I fashion a paper boat. It's not as good as the ones Dad used to make. The folds aren't as precise, but I try my best. I sit it on my knee and stare down at it once in a while, as if I'm waiting for it to set sail.

After the mass I find John Paul. He lets go of Lainey's hand when he sees me, and hurries over.

'Lovely mass,' he says, as if it's important to me to hear it. 'And the singing was lovely too. Very nice hymns.'

I didn't hear the hymns. My mind was far away. I was on a beach on a summer Sunday playing with my parents and my brothers.

'Can you do me a favour?' I ask.

John Paul nods. 'Sure.'

'Can you give this to Seány, please?'

I open my hand and show him the small paper boat I made. He looks at the boat and then at me.

'At the graveyard,' I say. 'Can you leave it there for him?'

John Paul takes the paper boat but I can tell he's confused.

'Wouldn't you rather leave it there yourself?'

I shake my head. And I walk away. I can't watch them lower Mam into the ground. I can't say goodbye.

I hear Lainey tell John Paul to follow me. I look over my shoulder every so often, but John Paul knows not to come after me. Not today.

I'm aware of the footsteps behind me. Ones that tread so gently that, even if I strain, I couldn't hear them above the seagulls and wind. It takes half an hour to reach the lighthouse on foot. I don't look back. Not even once. I stop when I reach the cliff edge and I stare at the horizon. There are no boats. Every fisherman in Cloch Bheag is at the graveyard today. Saying a final farewell to the wife of one of their own.

She doesn't speak, but when I feel her hand on my shoulder I crumple inside like an accordion. And when she says my name, my knees buckle. I finally turn round to find Dee behind me. She's been crying. Her cheeks are pink and blotchy. The wind blows her hair off her face and she squints as the sun shines in her eyes. She gathers me into her arms and I let myself fall against her. And for the first time since Mam died I begin to cry.

SIXTY-TWO

FIONN

I have never seen Dee look more beautiful. Her ivory skin is glowing and her eyes are smiling, despite her tears.

'Thank you,' I say, finally letting her go. 'Thank you for coming.'

'I really, really liked your mam,' she says.

I nod. I know. Everyone did. Even Oisín, once upon a time.

'He didn't come?' I say.

Dee takes a deep breath. 'No,' she says, letting it back out slowly. 'I'm sorry.'

I sit on the grass. I tuck my knees against my chest and wrap my arms round them. Dee lowers herself to sit next to me.

We stare out to sea, sitting in comfortable silence, for a long time. It's the most content I've been in longer than I can remember. I feel her thigh against mine, and her shoulder too.

'Where's Aisling?' she asks, eventually.

I shrug.

'I didn't see her.'

'She was there,' I say. 'Just not with me.'

'Oh.' Dee picks a blade of grass and runs it through her

fingers. 'I'm sorry,' she says. 'I thought you two were good together.'

'We weren't. She deserves better. John Paul told me that years ago. And he was right. But, nonetheless, I hurt her and I regret that.'

'You're a heartbreaker, Fionn O'Connell, do you know that?' Dee giggles and knocks her shoulder against mine.

I turn, to take in her beautiful face.

She tosses the blade of grass aside and her eyes meet mine.

'You broke my heart,' she says. 'Do you remember?'

I nod.

'After the ball,' I say.

'After the ball. You told me to go back to Trevor. Remember him?'

I snort. How could I forget?

'Anyway.' Dee shakes her head, giggling and smiling. 'It's all water under the bridge now. But, yes, for a long time I was broken-hearted after you.'

'I was too,' I say.

Dee makes a face. It's innocent and curious and I had forgotten how much simply being near her makes everything better.

I lean in and kiss her. My lips are on hers before my mind catches up with what I'm doing. It's perfect. But as quickly as it began it's over and Dee pulls away.

'I'm sorry,' I say, and I can feel heat creep into my cheeks. 'I shouldn't have done that. I was way out of line.'

Dee's mouth is gaping and I can literally see her mind racing to catch up with what just happened.

'It's just, I can't help myself when I'm around you,' I say, as if that's somehow a good enough reason.

'I'm pregnant,' she says, so suddenly and so softly I almost don't hear her above the familiar sounds of the shoreline.

But I do hear her. I hear the words the slice into my gut like a blade. *A baby. Oisín's baby.*

'Wow,' I manage after too long. 'Congratulations.'

'Oisín doesn't know,' she says.

I feel both honoured and concerned that she is telling me before him.

'He doesn't want kids,' she says.

'He said that?'

'No. But he won't talk about children. Won't look at them when we're out. If we're in a restaurant and there's a baby at the table next to us, he'll ask them to move us.'

'He used to spend Sundays taking Seány for walks in his pram,' I say. 'He loved that time with him. I know he did.'

I can't align the Oisín of my childhood with a man who doesn't want to be a father. We've grown apart, for sure. But surely no man can change that much.

'The timing is awful,' Dee says. 'I start my own show in three weeks. And a baby bump isn't exactly the look they're after.'

'Everyone is entitled to maternity leave,' I say.

'Sure. But six months is a long time in showbiz. If I'm off the air for as long as I was on, people will forget me.'

'You're not forgettable,' I say.

Dee blushes and, despite her success and fame, deep down she's still the same shy girl I met all those years ago.

'Anyway, listen to me. Worrying about my career when you've so much more on your plate. Are you okay?'

I've lost count of the number of people who have asked me that question in some guise or other over the past week.

Time helps, people say. Or, *she's in a better place. Are you okay? Will you be okay? You will be okay.*

Advice and questions are endless. They come from a good place, but they are hard to hear and even harder to answer. I lie when I reply. It's easier for everyone that way. I say, *I am okay*, and if they look as if they don't believe me I add the promise that I will be okay in time and then I change the subject or walk away.

It's different when Dee asks. I can't seem to lie to her. Not because she would see straight through me. She would. But because I don't want to.

'I don't know what to do now,' I say. The lump in my throat is so huge I think I might struggle to breathe soon. 'I knew this day was coming. I've known for a very long time. And somehow it seems to have sneaked up on me. And I don't know what to do now. I don't know what the fuck to do.'

'There is nothing to do,' she says. 'You just take it one day at a time.'

'Is that what you're going to do?' I ask.

Dee's expression changes and I wish I hadn't said that. Losing a parent and becoming one are two very different things.

'It's what I've been doing for a very long time,' she says.

She reaches for my hand, and I let her take it.

'You could come to London, you know?' she says. 'For a while at least. See if you like it. I know I'd really like it if you were there.'

'And how would Oisín feel about that?' I say.

She knocks her shoulder against mine. 'There's one way to find out.'

My instinct is to shake my head. But I don't. For the first time in my life I could go anywhere because I have no reason to be in Cloch Bheag anymore. I always thought this day would be liberating. But it's not. It's overwhelmingly devastating.

'Say you'll think about it,' she says. 'Even if that's all you ever do... only think about it.'

Dee and I sit, hand-in-hand without words, and watch as glorious sunshine dances across the top of the deep blue ocean.

SIXTY-THREE

FIONN

'I want a good send-off,' Mam told me when she knew her time was running out.

By a good send-off she meant a round of drinks for everyone in Reilly's after the graveyard, and some grub. Although, for the life of me, I'll never understand why people feel compelled to feed half the island when they pass away.

Mr Reilly suggested soup and sandwiches and Mrs Reilly said that's what Mam would want. I didn't ask what soup, or what sandwiches. I didn't care. I took a guess at numbers, and paid upfront. Reilly's is the last place I want to be today. Or maybe, ever again.

Dee and I fall asleep at some stage. I wake when my phone rings. We're lying tangled around one another on the grass. My left arm has gone numb under her head and I try to slide it out without waking her. The sun is beaming down on my face, and I've no doubt my cheeks are burnt.

'Hello,' I whisper, pressing my phone to my ear.

'Hey. It's JP.'

'Hi.'

'Where are you?'

'The lighthouse.'

'What are you doing up there? Are you okay?'

'Dee is with me.'

'Oh. Right.'

There's a pause while John Paul mulls over what to say next. He obviously expected me to be alone up here. I'm glad I'm not.

'Listen, it's getting messy here,' he says. 'Aisling hasn't a good word to say about you. She's been chewing the ear off Lainey all afternoon about your break-up. Then there's her mam.' I can almost hear John Paul roll his eyes. 'Mrs Purcell has been in the ladies' loo for the last half an hour crying her eyes out. If anyone should be bawling, it's my mam. She was Lorna's best friend. But she's out here making sure everyone's bellies are full and their drinks are topped up.'

'And that's why they were best friends,' I say.

'Don't come down here,' John Paul says. 'It's a shit show. Everyone is drunk and emotional. Get yourself home. I'll grab us a bottle of gin and some 7up and I'll meet you there.'

'Is Lainey coming with you?' I say.

'Nah, she'll probably hang on here. Calm Aisling down.'

'Could you ask her to come with you instead?' I say, glancing at Dee as she begins to rouse.

I think about the baby in her belly and how scared she seems.

'Suppose,' John Paul says. 'But why?'

'I know they haven't spoken in a while, but I really think Dee needs her best friend.'

'Erm. Okay. Meet you back at the house in an hour or so, okay?'

'Okay,' I say. 'Bye. Bye. Bye.'

I lower my phone and watch as Dee rubs her eyes.

'Oh God, did I fall asleep?' she says, stretching and yawning. 'I'm just so tired all the time.'

'You did. But so did I. Best nap I've had in ages, actually.'

Dee smiles. I'm not sure she believes me, but it's true. I can't remember the last time I woke feeling rested.

I tell Dee about my drunken, messy neighbours in Reilly's and she seems relieved when I suggest heading straight back to the house. I don't tell her John Paul and Lainey will be there. But when we arrive, and find John Paul out front smoking and Lainey in the kitchen making tea, Dee seems pleased.

Lainey is frostier than I hoped she'd be. She passes a snide comment about Dee's up-and-coming show and something else about Oisín not being with her. When Dee looks as if she might burst into tears, Lainey changes the subject and says something nice about Dee's shoes.

We have tea and biscuits and we sit round the table and talk.

'Lorna made the best apple tart,' Lainey says. 'Do you remember, Dee? We couldn't get enough in the evening after a good céilí.'

'How could I forget,' Dee says, her eyes dancing with memories of a simple time when we were all young and happy.

We continue down memory lane. Each of us sharing stories and memories of times with my mother.

Dee and Lainey laugh a lot as they recall their summer in the Gaeltacht and I suggest to John Paul that we head outside for a cigarette.

'It's good to hear her laugh,' he says, glancing over his shoulder and through the kitchen window at his wife. 'I can't remember the last time I heard her laugh.'

I take my lighter from my pocket and light John Paul's cigarette first and then my own. I puff, two, three, four times before I take it out of my mouth and say, 'What's going on? What's wrong?'

'We're fucked, Fionn,' John Paul says, and he seems shorter

than his usual self, as if the weight of his problems has whittled inches off him. 'We're broke.'

'But things are going so well for you up in Dublin. Your mam told my mam all about it.'

'They were going great. But this recession is a bastard. No one has any fucking money. And do you know what people don't want when they've no money? Fancy timber floors, that's what. They make do with the carpet they've had for twenty years.'

I don't know what to say. I thought John Paul and Lainey had the perfect life. I guess appearances can be deceiving.

John Paul's hand is shaking as he brings his cigarette to his lips and inhales until he seems as if he might burst.

'The vans are being repossessed. Guys are coming for them next week. Even the tools are being taken. Lainey's dad says he's going to retire. Makes sense, at his age, I suppose. But what the hell are Lainey and I supposed to do? When the company folds that's both our jobs gone.' John Paul clicks his fingers. 'Gone. Just like that.'

'Why didn't you say something?'

'I couldn't tell you. Not with your mam being so sick.'

'Does your mam know?' I say.

John Paul shakes his head. 'No. I'm not sure Lainey really understands how bad it is, to be honest.'

He tosses his cigarette butt on the grass and smashes it into the soil with a wiggle of his foot.

'I have a favour to ask?' he says.

'Sure.'

'Can I come fishing with you again?'

I swallow. That was the last thing I was expecting him to say.

'I want to come home, Fionn.' He glances out to sea. 'I miss it here. I miss it bad.'

SIXTY-FOUR

FIONN

Dee and Lainey are singing. Their voices carry outside. John Paul looks at me and jokingly covers his ears. I tilt my head towards the house and we head back inside. The girls have opened a bottle of red wine. The glass in front of Dee hasn't been touched. She passes it to me and I drink almost half before returning it to her.

Lainey is leading the chorus of 'Willie McBride' and I never knew she could hold a tune. John Paul and I pull out chairs, and we all sit around the table and sing. I wish Mam could see me now, content among the people I care most about in the world.

Dee excuses herself to use the bathroom. When she hasn't returned after twenty minutes I go to check on her. She's not in the bathroom. Instead, I find her sitting on Seány's bed with a paper boat in her hand.

Seány's room is exactly as it was the last night he slept in it. Mam never changed his Pokémon duvet. She said it smelt like him, and oftentimes she would come into his room and hold his pillow or the duvet under her nose and take a deep breath. I tried it once. It smelt of Play-Doh and fabric softener. I didn't come into his room again much after that.

'Will you show me how to make these?' Dee asks, raising the paper boat in her hand towards me.

'Sure,' I say.

Dee doesn't take her eyes of the tall chest of drawers with colourful stickers dotted on the front and paper boats resting on top. The paper boats are different sizes and colours. They're sprinkled in dust after sitting for years untouched.

'Did Oisín ever make a paper boat for Seány?' she asks.

I can't remember but I like to think he did.

I pick up one of the larger boats from the back and dust it off. It's yellow and red and blue and made from birthday wrapping paper.

'This one,' I say, passing it to Dee.

She moves over and I sit beside her.

'Do you think he'll make paper boats for our baby?' she says.

'I don't know,' I say. 'I hope so.'

Dee holds the paper boat against her chest and sways from side to side, as if she's on board sailing the wide ocean.

'But if he doesn't, I will,' I say.

Dee steadies and looks at me with serious eyes. 'Are you going to come to London?' she says.

'I can't.'

Her disappointment is tangible. I share it and it hurts. Like a physical pain.

'But that doesn't mean I won't be there for you, and for the baby. I can't wait to meet him or her.'

'I'm going to tell him all about his big brother,' she says. 'Seány was such a special kid, I want my baby to know that.'

'Him?' I say.

'I've a feeling it's a boy,' Dee says, then she drops her head on my shoulder and we sit together lost in our thoughts.

PART FIVE

SIXTY-FIVE

DEE

Five Years Later – September 2015

I can't believe it's Aoife's first day of school. I sit at the breakfast bar and watch her spoon Coco Pops into her mouth. It only feels like five minutes ago she was growing in my belly. She's a definite O'Connell, so like her father and, of course, Seány, with chocolate eyes and dark brown hair that falls on her shoulders in bouncy curls. I often wonder if there is any of me in her at all.

She tugs at her tie and protests that it's choky and she doesn't like it.

'You'll get used to it,' Oisín says, and then he points to his own tie.

'Will not,' Aoife says, jamming her hands on her hips.

She continues to complain, finding a problem with her skirt, her blouse, her blazer and her shoes.

'Everyone has to wear the same uniform, sweetie,' I say.

'It's not fair. It's not fair. It's not fair,' Aoife grumbles.

Oisín exhales and rolls his eyes. 'She's spoilt,' he says, as he tells me often.

I ignore him. As I do often.

'Come on,' I say, as I pick up my daughter's hot pink *Monster High* school bag and sling it over my shoulder. 'Go brush your teeth and let's go. We don't want to be late on your first day.'

'Okay, Mummy.' Aoife hops down from the table and hurries up the stairs.

'Aren't you forgetting something?' Oisín calls after her.

Aoife turns round to look at her father.

'Your bowl and spoon. Put them in the dishwasher.'

Oisín watches intently as Aoife returns to the table and picks up her bowl and her spoon. She hurries over to the dishwasher, sloshing the remaining milk in her bowl all over her blouse in the process.

'Great,' I say, dragging a hand round my face. 'Now we're definitely going to be late.'

'I'm sorry, Mummy,' Aoife says, tears swelling in the corners of her eyes. 'I didn't mean to make a mess.'

'I know you didn't,' I say, slipping her bag off my shoulder and setting it down next to the table. 'C'mon. Let's get you upstairs and get you cleaned up.'

'Not until she cleans up here first,' Oisín says, pointing to the puddle of milk on the ground in front of the dishwasher.

'I'll clean it later,' I say. 'We don't have time to do it now.'

'Aoife O'Connell, clean up your mess,' Oisín shouts.

His loud voice startles me and Aoife begins to cry.

'We are going to be late,' I say, firmly. 'I will clean it up later.'

'This is why she is a spoilt brat.' Oisín shakes his head. He's no longer shouting, but his voice is still much too loud and forceful for indoors. 'Because you never let her clean up her mess. When I was a kid I had to clean up after myself.'

'We will be late,' I repeat through gritted teeth.

'I don't care. I want this cleaned up.'

Oisín grabs Aoife by the arm and shoves her towards the spillage. She yelps and I'm certain that he's hurt her. I step forward and place myself between them both. When Aoife is safely behind me, I tell her, once more, to go upstairs.

'I'll be up in a minute, okay?' I say.

Without another word Aoife runs out of the kitchen and I listen for the pitter-patter of her small feet on the steps of the stairs.

'You're ruining her,' Oisín says. 'She thinks you'll do everything for her.'

'I'm her mother.'

Oisín rolls his eyes. 'She needs to learn to be independent. We all have to be.'

'She. Is. Five.'

I'm filled with so much anger and frustration I can barely speak. Oisín is never-yielding in his criticism of our daughter. Aoife is too loud. Too hyper. Too tired. Too giddy. Too much a child and too present.

Upstairs I pull off Aoife's wet blouse and help her into a clean one.

'Why is Daddy so cross?' she asks me in her adorable south London accent that melts me every time I hear it.

'Is he?'

'Yes. All of the time. He shouts all of the time. And he doesn't like my singing.'

'You are a lovely singer,' I tell her.

'Will I sing a song now?' she says.

I smile and Aoife sings a couple of lines of a Katy Perry song on repeat.

We return downstairs and I tell Aoife to wait in the hall while I fetch her school bag from the kitchen. She waits by the front door with her arms hanging by her sides. I hope that as she grows older this will not be the memory she keeps of her first day of school.

In the kitchen, Oisín sits at the table. His hands are cupping a cut glass tumbler and I know without checking that it's filled with neat whiskey. I've long stopped being troubled that Oisín drinks alcohol with breakfast. And lunch. And dinner. And countless times in between. The milk puddle is still next to the fridge and I also know it will remain there until I return.

'We're leaving now,' I say.

Oisín stirs and a small part of me panics that he might suggest coming with us.

'I'll be gone when you get back,' he says. 'I've back-to-back meetings all day.'

'Okay,' I say, relief making me light-headed. 'I'll see you later.'

In the car, Aoife continues to sing. I glance in the rear-view mirror every so often and smile at the little girl who is the best part of my life.

'I'm going to tell everyone in school that my mummy is the lady on the telly,' she says, proudly. 'And then I'm going to tell everyone that my daddy wears a tie just like mine.'

'That's nice, sweetie,' I say.

'And then I'm going to say my daddy is shouty and cross all of the time.'

SIXTY-SIX

FIONN

Instagram is the bane of my life. There are only so many sunrises and sunsets that I can share online. John Paul says we need to post at least one photo a day to remain visible, and Lainey is constantly on my case about hashtags and followers.

'Instagram is going to take off,' she says, almost daily. 'Trust me. O'Connell's Fish already has twenty-five thousand followers. That's twenty-five thousand people we're advertising to for free. Soon, if it's not O'Connell's Fish people won't want to buy it or eat it.'

I have to hand it to Lainey, she has a fantastic head for business. Her Instagram posts almost make fishing look exciting. Almost. She shares abstract photos of all of our boats. *The Two Seans* features most. But she posts snaps of *The Dee-Dee* and *The Little Aoife* too.

She also posts photos of our life on Cloch Bheag, which paint a wholly untrue facade of how interesting living on an island is. My favourite is a picture of us partying in Reilly's. Lainey, John Paul and I stand in front of the rear window with fancy cocktails in our hands and the Atlantic Ocean behind our backs. Lainey captioned the photo #besties and #ThatView and within an hour the post had thousands of likes and comments from all over the world. The only comment I liked and replied to came from a verified account with over three million followers. Dee's account.

OnTheCouchWithDeeDee *@OConnellFish* *Looking great. I wish I was there.*

OConnellFish *@OnTheCouchWithDeeDee* *We wish you were too* 😊

I spend most of my time wishing Dee was here. Or, that she had more time to visit. Her career is on fire and I couldn't be happier for her, but it never gets easier to miss her. *On the Couch with Dee-Dee* is the UK's most loved talk show. It's a hit here too. I watch every episode on my phone. It breaks up long days at sea. I tune in to today's episode a little late, and I miss the cooking segment and Dee's first guest, but I catch the second half of the show.

Dee's powder-blue dress brings out her eyes, but something about the way they glisten today worries me and I decide I'll text her later.

'Thanks for joining us, Pat,' she says, turning to the man sitting on the opposite end of the large red couch. He has a box full of colourful pieces of paper beside him.

'My pleasure, Dee-Dee,' he says.

I balk. I never quite get used to Dee's guests calling her that.

'Now folks,' Dee says, turning back to face the camera, 'Pat is an origami expert and he is going to teach me some simple steps today. But, I should probably confess upfront that I don't have an artistic bone in my body.'

Pat laughs as if Dee is the funniest person he's ever met in his life and then he passes her a piece of white paper.

'Thank you,' Dee says, taking the paper while maintaining a bright smile. 'What are we making today?'

'Well,' Pat says, pulling a piece of paper out of the box for himself also. 'I was going to suggest a swan.'

Dee nods.

'But since you're not an artist maybe we should start with something easier.'

Dee's smile wobbles and her eyes narrow. It's only for a split second, before she regains composure, but clearly Pat has deviated from what they rehearsed.

'A swan sounds great,' Dee says, trying to gently steer them back on course.

'No, no,' Pat says. 'I have a better idea. A paper boat will work much better.'

Dee's wobble becomes more noticeable and this time she doesn't regain composure instantly. Her cheeks flush and her eyes shift off screen as if she's searching for someone. A producer. Or director, perhaps.

'I'm sorry,' she says, suddenly. 'You're going to have to excuse me. I think I've got something in my eye.'

Dee stands up and walks off the screen, leaving Pat on the couch alone with his mouth gaping. It cuts to a music video and suddenly One Direction are singing and dancing on my screen. I click out of the video link and scroll through my contacts to find Dee's number. I hit call. She picks up on the third ring.

'Were you watching?' she whispers.

'I was.'

'It was a total car crash.'

'It wasn't.'

'A paper boat! Why did he have to suggest a paper boat?'

'Because they're cool,' I say.

Dee sniffles.

'He's never made her one, Fionn,' she says. 'Oisín has never made a paper boat for Aoife.'

'Maybe he can't. Maybe it's too hard for him,' I say.

'I think he can, he just won't try. Or he won't let himself try. His walls are sky high and Aoife doesn't stand a chance of climbing them. I just want him to love her, the way I know he loved Seány.'

I'm not sure when a folded piece of paper became a metaphor to measure love. Maybe it was when Aoife was born and Dee hoped Oisín would love her the way a father should love a daughter. But there was no paper boat. Maybe it was when Dee told me she was going to be a mother and I knew she loved that unborn baby more than anything else in the world. She loved the child growing in her belly, the way I loved her. Or maybe it goes right back to when Seány was little and Dad made paper boats with the foil from the inside of his cigarette box and Seány collected like them like precious things. It's all of it. And so much more. We all just want someone to make us a paper boat.

'You give Aoife one,' I say at last. 'Get back on that couch and let Pat the Origami King make the best paper boat in the world and bring it home to my niece.'

Dee takes a deep breath and I hear her sniffle back tears.

'What would I do without you?' she says.

'You never have to find out.'

'Bye,' she says.

'Bye.'

The line goes dead and I return to the show. I manage to log in just as One Direction finish running up a pier on a cloudy day. The music video ends and we return to Dee sitting collected and smiling on her couch.

'Sorry about that, folks,' she says, 'But any excuse for a little One Direction, am I right?'

Pat seems a little less confident than before, but as Dee slips gradually back into her poised and professional persona, he relaxes and they begin to fold paper.

Pat talks viewers through the process, fold by fold, and the concentration on Dee's face is priceless. When they finish fashioning cute boats, Dee, once again, turns towards the camera.

'Well, there you have it. Paper boats. I won't lie, they're trickier than they look, but they are worth all the effort.'

Dee holds up her boat and the camera zooms in on it as she continues speaking in the background.

'There is a little girl in my house who is going to be very happy when I bring this home,' she says. 'Thank you very much for coming on the show today, Pat.'

'Thanks for having me.'

Dee wraps the show up in the usual way. A quick round-up of all their guests and a shout-out to the show coming up next. The screen blurs, the theme tune starts and the credits roll.

I can only imagine that in Dee's line of work getting to bring home freebies is a pleasant perk. But I doubt she's ever brought home something as simple, or as precious, as a paper boat before.

SIXTY-SEVEN

FIONN

October 2015

Mam loved Halloween. When we were kids she would take Oisín and me to the mainland to buy black sacks and plastic masks and glitter and pipe cleaners and we would create the wildest, most colourful costumes. Monsters, always. Even when Oisín was too mature for dressing up, and he protested about escorting me trick-or-treating, our Halloween trip to the mainland was something I looked forward to for the whole month of October.

Now I almost forgot what month it is. But I saw some decorations in Dickie's this morning when I popped in for bread and milk and they jogged my memory. I bought a trinket plastic witch on a broom. I am going to the graveyard today and I plan to take the small, purple-haired toy with me.

In the five years since Mam passed away, I have been to the grave twice. Once a couple of years ago because John Paul's mother was bitching that I was a terrible son and my mother's heart would be broken if she knew how little I came to see her. John Paul begged me to leave flowers or something at the grave.

'Anything, please, man. Just something so my mam knows you still care. I can't listen to her go on and on anymore.'

A few days later, I bought flowers on the mainland. A super-sized bouquet of red roses tied up with a cream bow. I got off the ferry and walked straight from the port to the graveyard. I crouched next to the headstone, but instead of laying the beautiful flowers I threw them in the nearby bin. *What good are flowers to people six feet under?*

I haven't been back since, no matter how often Mrs Leary grumbles. Once, after a particularly long week at sea and a few pints in Reilly's, I nearly told her to fuck off. But I remembered just in time that she was my mother's best friend. Being polite to the people she cared about would mean so much more to Mam than a bunch of fancy roses.

The graveyard is in a beautiful spot, if such a thing can be said about a graveyard. It's on a hill overlooking the sea and on autumn days, like today, leaves have blown off the trees and decorated the graves for Halloween. Red, brown and yellow leaves gather in the corners of graves and next to headstones. And for a moment it feels as if I have stepped into a beautiful watercolour painting. I bounce on my hunkers and catch the headstone not to lose my balance. I place the witch next to small potted plant that someone has left. I only notice now that the witch cackles if you press her tummy. The sound carries around the still and otherwise silent space. Birds don't chirp here, wind doesn't howl, rain doesn't pitter-patter. But, today, a small toy laughs and laughs. It's inappropriate and somehow hilarious and I laugh louder and longer than the silly witch. I know Mam would laugh too. And Dad and Seány, of course. *My God, I miss them.* I miss them so much it's hard to breathe. I flop onto my bum on the damp grass and I sway back and forth as if I'm at sea and I wait for the feeling to pass. As I know it always does.

When my heart rate returns to normal and inhaling no longer hurts, I stand up.

'Hey Mam,' I say.

I wait, instinctively, as if I'll hear her answer. When silence replies, I shake my head and run my hand through my hair. I feel foolish and awkward. A couple of blackbirds fly overhead, judging me. I exhale sharply and keep going nonetheless.

'I miss you. I knew I would but it's worse than I thought it would be. The house is so damn quiet.'

The birds fly away and I'm lonelier than ever.

'There was storm last week. High winds, crashing waves, shaking trees. You know the type. There was no thunder and lightning, unfortunately. Still, though, it was noisy. The house rattled and groaned and it almost felt as if I wasn't there alone, you know?'

The toy witch falls over and tips her belly against a stone. She begins to cackle and vibrate again. It startles me and I jolt.

'Jesus Christ.'

It's only then I realise how close I am to tears. I choke them back and finish my conversation with Mam.

'Anyway,' I say. 'I've been thinking...'

I pause and chew over my words. Suddenly, I'm a schoolboy asking to stay out past his bedtime. Or a teenager trying to wriggle out of chores.

'I'm going to ask John Paul and Lainey to move into the house,' I say.

As soon as I say it, I'm lighter. As if just voicing the idea out loud cements it. Sets it in stone.

'And I'm going to move into the garage. I want to give them space to be a real family.'

John Paul and Lainey have lived with Mrs Leary for almost five years. And although neither of them complains, I can tell how much they miss their flat in Dublin. I'd be a liar if I said I didn't worry that they miss their old life in Dublin too. Thankfully, any time John Paul suggests moving back, Lainey is quick to remind him that Cloch Bheag is his home. Their home. And I can't man three boats alone.

'This is where we belong now, JP,' Lainey says, regularly. 'You're a fisherman and a businessman. You and Fionn.'

'They're going to have a baby,' I tell Mam. 'Soon hopefully. Lainey has lost three already. JP wasn't supposed to tell me that. But I could tell something was wrong. Maybe if they have their own space, trying will be easier. JP's little brothers and sisters are all getting big now. Some of them are in their twenties and the house is full. Mrs Leary says she can't hear herself think and she's broke from feeding an army.'

I remember what a full house feels like. I remember the noise and smells and laughter of a house full of Gaeltacht students all summer long. I used to count down the days until they left. Until that summer with Dee changed everything. I'd give anything to hear a house full of giggling and loud voices again.

I don't tell Mam that. I don't tell her that sometimes I lie in bed and listen to the nothingness until it consumes me. The old pipes in the attic creak when the heating has been on. Sometimes, in summer, I open the windows and turn the heat on for an hour or two just so there will be noise when I wake during the night. I wake every night.

'So, what do you think, Mam? Do you think JP and Lainey would be happy in our house the way we once were? I think so.'

I replay old Christmases. Big trees, wonky trees, skinny trees. I think about birthdays. Not milestone ones, just any birthdays that come into my head. Cake and colourful wrapping paper. Sunday roasts, and apple tarts. Long summers, and even longer winters. And all with my family around me.

'I'm going to come visit more often, Mam,' I say. 'It's been good talking. Thanks for listening.'

SIXTY-EIGHT

DEE

Three Years Later – October 2018

Sammie has asked me more than once what happened to my arm, or my shoulder, or my hip. She asks so often I've started arriving at work half an hour early just so I can be dressed before she comes anywhere near my changing room. Olga from wardrobe has noticed too; her eyes narrow every time she notices a new bruise and she makes a tutting sound when she shakes her head. And Cindy in make-up layers my foundation on extra thick sometimes, but always without a word.

I want to shout at them, that it's not what they think. Oisín has never hit me. And I'm certain he never would. But it doesn't mean the bruises aren't his fault. They are. He's heavy, and dragging his drunk arse off the couch and up to bed almost every night is exhausting, difficult and sometimes disastrous. Once, when I fell asleep and forgot to set an alarm to fetch him, Aoife found him in the downstairs toilet with his pants round his ankles and a puddle of his own pee under him. She was young enough then to believe the bullshit story I told her about Daddy spilling some water and falling over. There isn't a hope behaviour like that would make it past a suspicious seven-year-old now. So, I wrestle with my drunk husband every night, and every day I try to ignore how my colleagues look at me and my battered body.

'Why don't you leave him?' Sammie says, one random Tuesday after the show.

We've stopped into the local coffee shop for a quick chat before I have to be on my way to pick Aoife up from school. Ever since Aoife was born the station have been amazing with my schedule. I drop her to school every morning and drive across the city and straight to the studio. The show finishes, and we quickly chat through the schedule for the following day before I leave and drive back to the school. I'm usually cursing traffic and breaking speed limits, but it's a small price to pay.

'I'm serious, Dee. You're like the most bloody eligible bachelorette in London and he treats you like a toerag,' Sammie says, as she waves at the girl behind the counter and, seeing us, she smiles and nods.

We grab a table while she prepares our order.

'Only I'm not all that eligible, am I? I have a seven-year-old, remember?'

'The most fabulous seven-year-old on the planet. Aoife is a blessing. Any bloke would be lucky to be around her.'

'But that's just it, Sammie,' I say, honestly. 'I don't want any blokes around her, do I? I have to protect her.'

Sammie folds her arms and sighs. 'Don't you worry that the person you have to protect her from the most is Oisín?'

'No. Never.'

'Shit, Dee, I'm sorry,' Sammie says, plucking a sachet of sugar from the pot in the centre of the table to fidget with. 'I didn't mean to upset you.'

I shake my head and place my finger over my lip. 'Shh.'

I recognise the guy at the table behind us. He's wearing a bucket hat, indoors. And most of his face is obscured behind a newspaper. Nobody reads newspapers anymore. It's the majority of him that I don't see that tells me exactly who, or more accurately what, he is.

I tilt my head towards his table and wait for Sammie to catch on. She gets it almost immediately.

'Fucking paps,' she groans, and then she stands up and catches the attention of the barista.

Sammie returns to our table a few minutes later with a take-away cup of coffee in each hand.

'Got them to go,' she says. 'Let's walk.'

Sammie stretches one arm out to me and I take the paper cup and follow her towards the door. I stop at the photographer's table and approach him.

'Do you need a photo?' I ask.

He's startled at first, taking a while to lower his paper and reveal his camera.

'Would you mind. That would be great. I'm working freelance and I've got fuck all this week. Got one of Stephen Fry but someone else had a better one. If I don't come up with something good soon, I won't be able to pay this month's rent.'

'Gimme a sec,' I say.

I place the paper cup on the table next to me and pop off the lid. I press the lid, with coffee residue against my cream blazer, creating an instant stain. Then I take down my hair and ruffle it.

'There,' I say, turning back towards him. 'Ready.'

'What did you do that for?' he says, befuddled.

'Now you've a better shot. No one wants to see me all neat and tidy. People like things a little messy, don't they? You can sell it as *Day from Hell* or something. Should be worth a bit more than a shot of the back of my head walking out the door, eh?'

He raises his camera and I try to look perplexed. I don't have to try very hard.

'Thank you,' he says. 'You've no idea how much I appreciate that.'

I smile.

Sammie is waiting outside.

'What the fuck did you do that for?' she says, as I join her on the footpath. 'You know that's going straight into one of those trashy magazines. Or online. It'll be all over Facebook by teatime.'

'I certainly hope so,' I say.

'You're mad, you know that.'

Sammie links my arm and I almost spill my coffee for real before we start walking.

'Let people think the worst of my problems is a bad hair day,' I say, taking a sip of coffee. 'It'll stop them looking for the big stuff.'

Sammie glances over her shoulder to make sure the photographer is gone before she says, 'Like Oisín.'

'I can't leave him,' I say, realising that I forgot to put milk or sugar in my coffee. Its taste is as bitter as I feel.

'Do you really care about stuff like that being big news? C'mon, Dee. You knew when you signed up for this gig that privacy would go out the window.'

'I know. But Aoife never signed up for anything. I don't want all the kids at school talking about her parents splitting up.'

'Do kids even care about stuff like that?'

'Their parents do. And kids are like elephants, they hear everything.'

Sammie scrunches her nose. 'Do elephants have particularly good hearing?' she says, genuinely seeming curious.

'I'd say so. They have very big ears.'

We both laugh, drink our coffees and walk.

SIXTY-NINE

DEE

One Week Later

Oisín is sitting at the kitchen table nursing a cup of coffee that I can tell has gone cold as he scrolls through his phone. The box of paracetamol and the detox smoothie that I leave out for him every morning haven't been touched.

I open the fridge, take out a can of Red Bull and offer him that instead. He takes the can and sets it down on the table without opening it or looking at me.

'Have you seen this?' he says, as he points at his phone.

I gaze over his shoulder but the light shining in the huge kitchen window is reflecting off his screen and I can't make anything out.

'What is it?'

'You.'

Oisín slides his phone towards me and finally I see the photo of me in the coffee shop from last week. I begin to laugh. I actually look pretty good for someone trying so hard to be a mess. I think they photoshopped my nose because it definitely looks smaller.

'It's not fucking funny,' Oisín snaps.

'It's just a bad photo,' I say. 'I was trying to help the photographer out and—'

'It says you're drunk. Before the school run.'

'What?'

I spin the phone round to face me and tap the screen to scroll up to the headline.

On the Couch or On the Lash with Dee-Dee.

'Oh, you have got to be fucking kidding me. I can't believe this,' I say.

'Is this some sort of a joke?' Oisín says.

His eyes are bulging and bloodshot, as they are every morning. The grey bags underneath hang fuller than usual. His hangovers are becoming worse. He's not fending them off as well as he did when he was younger.

'Is it meant to be a dig at me?' he adds.

I pull my attention away from the phone and glare at him. I'm not sure which is making me more furious right now, the stupid tabloid article or his self-pitying face.

'How could this possibly be anything to do with you?'

'My drinking,' he says.

I snort. I don't want to have another conversation about alcohol. Not before school, when Aoife is in the house. Not ever, actually.

'Have you any idea how embarrassing this is for me? What the guys in work will say?' Oisín continues.

'I doubt anyone in your office will care. Besides, it's pretty obvious the photo has been taken out of context. It's clearly a coffee stain on my blazer and I'm in a fucking coffee shop.'

'And what about all the other articles?'

'Oh God, it is too early in the morning for this.'

I take the can of Red Bull, open it and slug a large mouthful. I will never get used to seeing myself on magazine stands or online. And not because they're almost always unflattering imagines. The time my boob tried to escape my bikini in the Maldives. Or the cellulite on my butt cheek on the same holiday. It was our first family holiday. Oisín, Aoife and me. Aoife was two and I thought I'd got my body back in pretty good shape. The papers thought otherwise and enjoyed pointing out all my flaws.

Oisín offered to join the gym with me after that. I declined. But I've regretted it sometimes since. I wonder if he would drink less if he was working out. Deep down I know the answer.

'Mummy, I can't find my broom,' Aoife shouts from upstairs.

'Try under your bed,' I call back.

Aoife has practically lived in her witch's costume since it arrived last week. We've had arguments and tears at bedtime because she didn't want to change into her pyjamas. An up-and-coming Irish designer sent it to us, and I photographed her complete with a hat and broom and shared it on Instagram. Fionn liked it straight away and said she was the cutest witch he'd ever seen. Oisín hasn't seen her all dressed up yet. She was in bed every night before he came home from work.

'What does she want a bloody broom for?' he says.

'It's dress-up day in school today.'

He looks at me.

'For Halloween. Half-term starts today. They've a half-day, remember? You're picking her up at twelve thirty?'

I try not to look worried as I realise he's forgotten.

'Right. Yeah.'

Oisín holds his head and I shove the Red Bull towards him, but he doesn't take it.

'It's not there,' Aoife shouts again.

'Okay, hang on,' I call back.

I place the Red Bull on the table and turn towards the door, but Oisín grabs my arm.

'Ouch.'

He doesn't let go.

'Ois. You're hurting me,' I say.

He still doesn't let go.

'Oisín, for fuck's sake, stop it.'

He releases me. He didn't hold me tight enough to leave a mark but, nonetheless, I rub my arm. He looks at me with teary round eyes like a lost puppy. He's still a sixteen-year-old kid, lost in a man's body. I wrap my arms round him as he begins to cry. I hold my breath and hope our daughter doesn't come down the stairs and I finally accept something I should have a long time ago. Our problems are much, much too big for me to fix.

Aoife can never fill the hole in him that losing Seány left. And Oisín can never fix my heart that Fionn broke all those years ago.

SEVENTY

DEE

March 2019

I miss Oisín. Or perhaps it would be more honest to say I miss having another adult in the house. Aoife is wonderful, but there are only so many Disney Princess printouts I can colour in before I lose the ability to see straight.

It's been five months and Oisín and I haven't spoken a word in person since he left. He texts sometimes but only to arrange taking Aoife out for the day. On Saturdays, mostly. I drop her to his flat. It's less than five kilometres from our house but I always drive so I can leave quickly. Oisín comes to the door and scoops Aoife into his arms, but he never says hello or goodbye to me.

This Saturday is Aoife's eighth birthday. I spend the morning in a soft play area with twenty excited children from her class in school. I make small talk with twenty sets of parents I vaguely know from the school gate. They seem to know quite a lot about me, which is inevitable, I suppose. I hand out twenty party bags and I agree to twenty play dates that I pray never come to fruition. Finally, I bundle an exhausted and somewhat cranky eight-year-old into the car and drive to her father's house.

Oisín answers the door wearing a luminous pink party hat and holding a large helium balloon in the shape of the number eight. He passes the balloon to Aoife and she shrieks with delight. She waves to me and hurries inside.

Oisín speaks to me for the first time in months. 'Can I keep her tonight?'

I'm bleary-eyed and the question catches me off guard. I've no doubt horror ripples across my face.

'I... I don't think that's a very good idea.'

'I'm not drinking, Dee,' he says, as he shifts his weight from one foot to the other as if he doesn't know how to stand comfortably in front of me.

His cheeks are less flushed and his usually bloodshot eyes seem rested.

'Please,' he says. 'It's her birthday. I want to make it special.'

'She had seven birthdays before this. You could have made any of those special.'

Oisín's hurt is palpable and I almost wish I could take my words back.

'Can she stay?' he asks again.

I shake my head and walk back to my car.

'I'm going to get this right, Dee,' he calls after me. 'I'm not going to be a shitty dad twice.'

I sit into my car and my hands are shaking as I start the engine and grip the wheel. I'm replaying the look on his face as I pull off his street and into traffic. The hurt in his eyes hurt my heart. I believed him when he said he wasn't drinking anymore. But instead of feeling happy, I felt crushed. *Why did he have to wait until it was too late to finally quit?*

SEVENTY-ONE
DEE

Summer 2019

My days are long and the routine is stagnant. Up, shower, school run, work, home, homework, cook, bed. I can't imagine the paparazzi wanting to snap my life these days, they'd be bitterly disappointed. I find myself calling my parents more than I ever have before. FaceTime makes everyone look awful, but I'm often shocked by how rapidly my parents seem to be aging now. Dad broke his hip last month and I offered to fly over, but Mam insisted she could manage. I can see how messy their apartment has become in the background and I'm worried that they need more help than they are prepared to admit. For the first time in a very, very long time, I hate how far away my parents live.

'So this is Elsa,' Aoife says, holding up her latest masterpiece.

'Oh, love, isn't that gorgeous,' Mam says, in the thick Dublin accent I'm so glad she never lost.

'She's my favourite,' Aoife says.

'And all inside the lines too,' Mam says.

'I *am* eight, Nanna,' Aoife says, almost dropping my iPad as she jams a hand on her hip, insulted by the implication that her colouring might be anything less than perfect.

'Can you put your mammy on, love?' Mam says.

'Mummy, Mummy, Nanna wants you.' Aoife climbs down from the table and runs with my iPad in her hands towards where I'm chopping carrots.

'What did I say about running in the house?' I say.

Aoife shrugs.

'Cheeky monkey.'

I roll my eyes, wipe my hands in my apron and take the iPad.

'Hello Mam,' I say.

'Oh Dee. Look how thin you are. Are you eating?'

'Yes, Mam.'

'Properly? Just because you're on the telly doesn't mean you have to starve yourself.'

'I know, Mam. We're having lasagne for dinner.'

I turn the iPad towards some chopped veg and mince browning on the pan.

'Good. Good. By the way, they're showing reruns of *On the Couch with Dee-Dee* over here,' Mam says. 'Your father and I watch them every day at three o'clock. Don't we, Dessie?'

I hear Dad's voice nearby say, 'We do, we do.'

'That's nice,' I say.

'I don't know why they don't show the live episodes over here,' Mam says. 'It would be much better than that French shite. Sure, I can't understand a word they're saying.'

'You are in France, Mam.'

'Nonsense, good telly is good telly.'

'Okay, I better go,' I say, smelling that the mince is starting to burn.

'Put Aoife back on,' Mam says. 'I want to see the rest of her colouring.'

Hearing her grandmother's request, Aoife hops down from the table once again and takes the iPad. Their conversation about Belle and Ariel and Jasmine resumes. I zone in and out of listening as I hum the new Ed Sheeran song. He was a guest on today's show and he played us out.

'Oh yeah, Aladdin would totally kick the Beast's arse in real life,' I suddenly hear my daughter say.

Horrified, I slam down the wooden spatula, turn off the cooker and march over to the table.

I whip the iPad out of Aoife's hand and say, 'I'll take that, thank you very much,' in the most clipped tone I can muster. 'Mam, I'm so sorry, she never usually says stuff like that.'

I turn the iPad round and gasp when I find Fionn's face on the screen. It explains the sudden shift in Aoife's conversation, and I roll my eyes, playfully disgusted, that her uncle is teaching her about fictional fights and who'd kick whose arse. Also, I'm disappointed that they think Aladdin would win. Beast is an animal. Literally.

'Hey Dee,' Fionn says.

His smile makes me smile.

'Is this a bad time?'

I suspect I have sauce on my cheek. I took my make-up off hours ago and my hair is scraped into a tight bun, which I only realise now has been causing my dull headache all afternoon. I hate that he should see me like this. But I hate more that, after all these years, I still want to look good in front of him.

'Can we turn the camera off?' I say. 'I've just spent the last hour on with my parents, and I'm wrecked and look like shit.'

'You never look like shit, but I can call back later if this is not a good time.'

I hear the TV come to life in the sitting room, and I look

across at the table to find Aoife has left paper and crayons all over the place before she turned her attention towards cartoons.

'No. No, don't go. It's great to talk.'

'Just no camera,' he says.

'Yes, please. No camera.'

We turn our cameras off and I prop the iPad against the bottle of red wine I'll open when Aoife goes to bed. We chat about mundane stuff, while the sound of *Alvin and the Chipmunks* carries from the sitting room.

He tells me about Laney and John Paul's remodelling of Lorna's house.

'The place looks amazing. Like a whole new house. JP is a fantastic carpenter. New floors, new kitchen, new shelving. He's done almost all the work himself.'

'Sounds great,' I say, layering pasta and mince and creamy sauce in a baking tray. I've made far too much food for Aoife and me, yet again, and not just because I have no appetite.

'You should come visit soon,' Fionn says.

'Yeah, that would be great. Ouch, shit.' I burn my finger on the side of the pan.

'You all right?'

'Yeah. I'm fine.' I pop my finger in my mouth and wait for the stinging to pass.

Giggles trickle from the sitting room and I almost begin to cry. Aoife doesn't laugh often since Oisín left. She didn't laugh or smile at all in the first few weeks. I think she blamed me. Sometimes, I think she still does. But she smiles more now, and I love to hear her laughing. Even if it's only at silly cartoons.

'Fionn,' I say.

'Um-hmm.'

'Is it strange that Lainey and JP have transformed your house?'

'No,' he says with conviction. 'It's good. I can go inside now and I don't see ghosts at every turn, you know.'

I nod and clear my throat so he doesn't hear my voice crack. I put the baking try in the oven and there's a lull in conversation.

I'm about to suggest hanging up, so I can join Aoife on the couch for a while before dinner, but Fionn snatches my breath away before I have a chance.

'Is it true what they're saying? Did he beat you?'

I swallow hard. Suddenly the TV isn't loud enough and I find myself worrying that Aoife will hear us. I pick up the iPad, pull back the heavy sliding door next to the kitchen table and walk into the garden. I flop into the egg chair on the patio and turn the camera back on.

'Turn your camera on,' I say.

Fionn's concerned face pops up instantly.

'Didn't you ever learn not believe everything you read online?' I say.

'Did he hurt you? Because if he did, I swear.'

'Oisín would never hurt me. Not ever.' I take a deep breath before I add, 'Not physically anyway.'

'Why did you break up with him, then?'

'Why does anyone break up? It wasn't working.'

'I don't believe you,' he says, and it shocks me.

'Then you don't know your brother. He. Wouldn't. Touch. Me.'

'There was an interview with your make-up girl. She said she had to hide bruises.'

I shrug. 'So. There were lots of stories when we broke up. Did you see the one that said he left me for the girl that does the weather?'

Fionn smirks, and I know he saw it and knew better than to believe that bullshit. I'm disappointed he fell for the other, equally concocted lies.

'But you never let me see your face. You never want to Face-

Time. I never thought much of it before, but then when I read that article I put two and two together,' Fionn says.

'You put two and two together and got twenty-seven. I spend all my work life with a camera in my face. I'd rather not spend my downtime the same way. It's bad enough that my mother has discovered video-calling.'

'Okay,' Fionn says, and his jaw twitches. 'If you say you're fine then I respect that.'

'Good.'

SEVENTY-TWO

FIONN

December 2019

'They're almost ready for you, Mr O'Connell,' the girl with a headset and clipboard says.

She has short brown hair and the reddest lips I have ever seen. She introduced herself as Sammie when I arrived at the studio. She showed me to the dressing room and said if there was anything I needed, she'd be happy to get it for me. That was an hour ago and she's returning for the first time now.

She knocked on the door I wasn't comfortable enough to close completely, and waited for me to answer before she popped her head in.

'You're on air in ten minutes, okay?' she says.

I look at three empty plastic bottles that I've lined up in front of the mirror and I regret drinking all the complimentary water.

'Do I have time to use the loo?' I say.

She glances at the bottles and smiles. 'Sure.'

There's an en suite attached to the dressing room and I'm not sure why I waited for permission to use it. I'm so damn nervous I'm not functioning properly. I fiddle with the button of my jeans and I'm genuinely concerned I'm going to piss myself before I get my fly open. The relief is almost like pleasure. I flush, wash my hands and return to sitting on the small couch in the dressing room. I still can't believe I let Dee convince me to come on her show. And I still think it's a bad idea.

'It's a great idea,' Lainey said, when I told her and John Paul about it over pints in Reilly's.

'It is, mate,' John Paul said. 'Think of the free advertising.'

John Paul sounded exactly like Lainey. They've become so similar over the years, it's hard to tell where one of them ends and the other begins.

'What if she asks me something I don't know the answer to?' I said.

'There's nothing you don't know about fish,' John Paul said, then he patted my back and walked up to the bar to order another round.

That is as much as I prepared. Dee and I were supposed to run through some mock questions last night over dinner, but my flight was delayed and I didn't arrive into London until nearly 10 p.m. Dee sent me step-by-step directions from the airport, through the tube and right up to her front door, but, somehow, it still seemed to take an unpleasantly long time to reach her house.

The awareness that I stuck out like a lost tourist and the self-loathing that followed were horrendous. I could feel myself on the edge of panic a couple of times on the tube. Once, when the lights flickered, I actually yelped. That was a low point, I admit. I try not to think about the faces staring at me when the lights came back. I try not to think about the people that will be staring at me in a few minutes on their TVs. Sitting on a couch beside the person I love most should be the most natural thing in the world. But not when cameras are pointed in my face.

I think about peeing again but Sammie with the red lips and clipboard returns. She smiles, revealing a mouth full of stunning veneers, and says, 'Ready?'

I nod and follow her out the door and down a brightly lit corridor. The walls, on both sides, are decorated with framed photos of Dee and the famous guests she's welcomed on her show over the years. I can see Dee evolve in the photos as we continue along the corridor. We travel from the beginning of her career closer to the present day. Dee's hair gradually fades from brunette to blonde, her teeth become whiter, her clothes are more expensive, and she's thinner. Maybe too thin. One thing has remained consistent, though: her bright blue eyes and how they sparkle with kindness and mischief, just as they did when she was sixteen years old.

At the end of the corridor, Sammie presses her back against a heavy door. She forces the handle with her elbow and pushes the door open. I gasp, audibly. The studio is bigger and much brighter than it seems on TV. Dee is sitting on the iconic red couch and all the lights point towards her. She stands up as soon as she sees me and totters over to me in spindly stilettos and a beautiful royal blue dress that brings out the colour of her eyes and reminds me of the ocean. She's a different person to my friend who left the house this morning in tracksuit bottoms, Uggs and her hair tied up in a swirly knot-type thing on the top of her head. She's effervescent and beautiful and it's as if I am meeting her for the first time. I think in many ways I am. I can't catch my breath.

'Are you okay?' she says, taking my hands in hers and squeezing them gently.

I nod. I am okay. As soon as she touches me, I am okay.

'You look great,' she says.

My blue jeans and white t-shirt are new and designer, but I seem noticeably underdressed compared to Dee.

'Just come as yourself,' Dee said last week, when I rang her to know what I should wear.

Lainey took me shopping on the mainland after that, and now I have come dressed as John Paul.

'Let's go sit,' Dee says.

I nod again. Now does not feel like the time for words.

Dee leads me by the hand to the couch. We sit at the same time and she asks me again if I'm okay. She seems worried that I'm not. A man with a white beard and glasses approaches us; he speaks to Dee but every so often he nods encouragingly at me. I think this must be the man Aoife talks about often. The man she says looks like Santa Claus.

'Father Christmas is Mummy's friend,' Aoife joyously informed me one Christmas when she was four or five.

She's realised since then that Chris, who is aptly named, is the producer of On the Couch with Dee-Dee and not in fact a man who descends chimneys once a year. But she still talks about him often, and I know he must be very present in their lives. I'd never assumed Dee and Chris might be romantically involved until this very moment, when I see how he looks at her.

'You ready?' Chris says, and I realise he's speaking to me at last.

I wonder if I look as startled as I feel.

'Just be yourself, mate. Dee will take care of the rest. You're in good hands with her. Don't worry.'

'I never worry when I'm around Dee,' I say.

I instantly want to gobble my words, but they hang in the air like a thick cloud you can see. Chris shoots Dee a concerned look that says, Should we worry about this guy?

She looks back, scrunching her nose and shaking her head.

Chris turns to me once more and says, 'Good luck.'

'Silence on set, please?' A voice comes out of nowhere.

Chris backs away slowly as he holds three fingers in the air. He lowers them one by one. When his fist closes, Dee says, 'Welcome back, everyone.'

SEVENTY-THREE

FIONN

When I was a kid my father said my mother was like his favourite wine; she grew ever sweeter with age. Back then, I didn't understand what he meant. Mam was just a mam to me. I saw her as a hug-giver, a cook, a cleaner, a problem-solver, a mother. I never saw what my father saw.

As I sit next to Dee on the big, red couch, I finally understand what my father meant. Dee is a celebrity. A chat show host. A role model. A big name. A household name. But the people at home, watching us on their TV, don't know she is a fine wine. She grows sweeter year after year. It's not because she's changed her image over time, as the photographs on the corridor highlight. Or because she's famous. Or important and powerful. It's in spite of those things. In spite of everything that life has thrown Deirdre McKenna's way, the good the bad and the bloody ugly, she has become all the better for it.

The interview is effortless. Not at first, of course. At first, I'm stiff, awkward and self-aware. But Dee eases me gradually into it. The questions are easy. They're mostly about Cloch Bheag and fishing, and after a while I forget that cameras are rolling.

'Can you translate Cloch Bheag into English for us?' Dee asks.

Dee's Irish was never fluent, or even all that good. Nonetheless, I know she could easily translate herself. I smile at her, and she grins back at me. I take great pride when I announce the name of the island as 'Little Stone'.

'Little Stone,' she says, and the nostalgia in her eyes melts me.

For a fleeting moment we are right back on Cloch Bheag, meeting for the first time. I wish we could rewind. I wish we could be a pair of carefree kids sitting on the beach again. I wish so hard my eyes almost tear up.

Dee looks away from me and into the camera and says, 'Believe me when I tell you, folks, that I think Little Stone might be my favourite place in the whole world.'

'You should come back more,' I say.

'I should.'

I remember the cameras, and I immediately regret taking us to a personal place. Heat circles the neck of my t-shirt and works its way up to my ears.

Dee stands up and turns her back to the camera. I've watched almost every single one of her shows and I've never seen her turn away from her audience at home like this before. Her eyes burn into mine and the damn heat in my neck intensifies.

'Do you know why I really invited you on today's show?' she says.

For a moment it feels as if she's forgotten that she's presenting. She's slipped out of her TV persona and fallen back into the familiar Dee I know. Something feels off. The heat creeps closer to my face. It's uncomfortable and I'm certain the cameras are picking up on it.

'Today is special,' she says. 'Do you know why it's special?'

I wince. I'm lost and confused. And I'd rather have this strange conversation somewhere else. Anywhere else.

'Today is the thirteenth of December,' she says. 'Friday the thirteenth, as it happens.'

She taps her ear. I can only imagine Chris is in her earpiece shouting at her to turn round. I wish she'd listen.

'Some people say Friday the thirteenth is unlucky. In fact, they made horror films about it. I haven't seen any. Horror films give me nightmares.'

I smile. I'd forgotten that about her. Lainey loves to tell the story of how Dee wet her pants when they snuck into the cinema, underage, to see *Scream 2*.

'But other people say luck is what you make it, don't they?'

I'm not sure if her question is directed at me or the people at home. I don't answer. Finally, Dee turns round and sits beside me again. So close her thigh brushes against mine, and I know for sure my face is as red as her couch by now.

'You really don't know why I brought you on the show, do you?' Dee says.

'To talk about fish,' I say, and as soon as I say it not only do I hate how pathetic it sounds, I also know it's the wrong answer.

'Well sort of,' she says. 'Ladies and gentlemen,' she goes on, shifting in her seat to face the camera head on. 'You won't know this, but Fionn here is an amazing person.'

I swallow hard. I don't know where this is going and I'm not sure I like it.

Dee places her hand on mine and I almost jump.

'Fionn lost his little brother and his father when he was just a teenager. But instead of falling to pieces, as many would, he got to work helping others.'

Dee looks at me with pride in her eyes. I snatch my hand back. Bile works its way up the back of my throat and my chest is tight and feels as if it might crush my heart. I can't believe she told everyone about Dad and Seány. I'm not stupid. I know sob stories make great TV, but I never thought Dee would use *my* story. I never dreamed she would ravage Seány's memory for ratings. I hate her for it.

I've seen Dee's segment on local heroes many times. Some poor sap has their story of woe shared with millions. Dee gives them a verbal pat on the back and tells them how marvellous they are for overcoming whatever shit was thrown their way. Friends and family rush in. There is hugging and cake and sometimes tears. Then the end credits roll, the theme tune plays and the ad break starts. The poor sap is never seen again.

I am clearly today's poor sap. I'm not sure which hurts more, the realisation that I fit the bill or that Dee thinks I do.

'Fionn became captain of his first boat on the thirteenth of December 2001. He was eighteen years old. Just a kid, really,' Dee says. 'Today marks eighteen years since that first sailing.'

She's beaming with pride. I stare at Chris in the distance. He seems equally pleased and I've no doubt my life is making good TV. I do the maths in my head; Seány would be twenty-four years old now. A man. *My God.*

'By the time Fionn was in his mid-twenties he had three boats and eight staff,' Dee continues. 'But he wasn't done there. He moved out of his home and passed it over to his best friend and his wife so they would have a place of their own after their wedding. I mean, folks, if only there were more people in the world like Fionn, am I right?'

As suspected, someone appears with a cake. There are candles on top and I assume I should blow them out. I do. Dee cheers and the crew all clap. John Paul and Lainey rush in from the sidelines and someone throws their arms round me.

'You couldn't deserve this more,' John Paul says.

'You're our hero,' Lainey adds.

People flood the floor. The studio that seemed large and bright earlier is crowded and cramped now.

I spy Katie. She hugs me stiffly and says, 'You deserve this, Fionn. We're all so happy for you.'

She's speaking for Cloch Bheag collectively, as a community, that much is obvious. But I barely know Katie any more. I see her from time to time behind the bar in Reilly's and she knows my usual is a pint of Guinness. We don't often make conversation past that.

Mrs Leary is next to gather me into her arms. She smells like apple pie and it reminds me of Mam. My heart hurts and I hold my breath until she lets me go.

'She'd be so proud of you, you know,' she says.

Aisling is here. And her mam. They both congratulate me, as if I've won some sort of a prize. Mrs Purcell shakes my hand and Aisling hugs me; she lingers longer than anyone else. In spite of our break-up I think we are friends.

'It's not our fault we love people who don't love us back,' she said one night in Reilly's when a few drinks too many loosened her tongue.

I didn't ask if she meant Dee. I didn't have to ask.

A handful of other acquaintances from Cloch Bheag embrace me or shake my hand and everyone tells me that my mother would be proud. I'm not sure what of, but I thank them regardless.

Finally someone announces that we're off air and my head fills with the theme tune as I imagine the credits rolling.

Chris wriggles his way through the Cloch Bheag residents and places his hand on Dee's back. It makes me squirm.

'That was brilliant,' he says. 'Absolutely brilliant. Dee, you handled that beautifully.'

Dee looks away and Chris leans forward and shakes my hand. 'Thanks for coming in, mate. And congratulations on all the boats. That's really cool.'

When Dee turns round, Chris says, 'Are you crying?'

Dee drags a shaky finger under her eye and shakes her head.

'Right, let's head upstairs and run through a few things for tomorrow's show.'

Dee nods.

'Thank you, everyone,' Chris says, raising his voice to command everyone's attention. 'Sammie will show you to the green room for some light refreshments.'

Sammie seems to appear out of thin air. She gathers my neighbours and herds them towards the door like sheep.

Dee looks at John Paul, Lainey and me with a gaze that tells us not to follow them. Then she cups Chris's elbow and says, 'I'll be upstairs in a minute.'

His smile is friendly but I can tell he's expecting Dee to wraps things up. She waits until he leaves and then, at last, she throws her arms round me.

'You were wonderful,' she says, 'I am so proud of you.'

'Is he your boyfriend?' I ask.

'Chris?' Dee snorts. 'Ha. No. He's nearly the same age as my dad. I've known him for ever. He's the one who got me this job, remember?'

I shake my head. 'You didn't tell him we knew each other.'

'He's friendly with Oisín,' she says, 'I didn't want to make things awkward.'

'More awkward than telling most of Britain about my dead brother.'

Dee's expression changes. She finally notices how distressed I am.

'Fionn, I thought this would be a surprise.'

I puff out. 'It was certainly a surprise.'

'I'm sorry. I'm so sorry if I upset you. It was never my intention.'

I don't reply.

'It was my idea,' John Paul says. 'I thought it would be a nice way to thank you for everything.'

I can't look at him. I can't look at anyone. I stare at the

ground, marked out in square, rubbery tiles. I suppose so no one slips on set. I count them. *One. Two. Three.*

'Fionn,' John Paul calls me, but I keep counting.

I know my friends meant well. Their excitement and joy radiates like heat from a furnace. It should warm me. But it doesn't. In fact, it leaves me colder than I have been in a long time. Dee said I didn't fall to pieces after the accident. It was meant as a compliment, I know. A measure of my strength in the face of unbearable loss. But it hurt. It hurt as if someone took a blade to my soul and carved me up. Because when Seány left he took a piece of me with him. Dad took a piece. And Mam. Oisín took his chisel to me too, more than once. And, although she doesn't know it, and maybe she never even meant to, Dee owns the greatest piece of me. I can never be whole. Not when pieces of me are scattered like grains of sand on the shore.

'I'm going for a walk,' I say, at last.

'Lunch. Please?' Dee says, reaching for my hand to coax me back. 'My treat.'

'Yeah. Maybe.'

Dee throws a thumb over her shoulder and towards the door. 'This won't take long and then we can go somewhere nice and talk. You'll join us, won't you, JP and Lainey?'

Lainey looks as if she'd rather stick pins in her eyes.

'Sure, Dee, that would be lovely,' John Paul says, nudging his elbow into Lainey's ribs.

SEVENTY-FOUR

FIONN

Lunch was nice. I had no idea what I was eating. The menu was entirely in French. I saw John Paul google a few things, so I just copied his order. The water came in still or sparkling but not from a tap. There was a lot of cutlery and Dee said to work our way from the outside in.

Lainey had lots of question about Dee's seemingly fabulous life.

'Do you have to buy your own clothes or does a clothing fairy hand-deliver them every morning?'

Dee blushes. 'I mean, I get some freebies for awards shows and that sort of thing. And anything I wear on set is covered by the studio. But day-to-day it's just regular clothes.'

The questions keep coming and soon John Paul and I are merely spectators as two old friends catch up.

Lastly, Lainey asks, 'Do you ever wonder what things would be like if you never left Dublin? If we were both still working in radio and eating fish and chips from a box on our lunch break in the park.'

'God, those chips were good,' Dee says.

'The best.'

'I do think about it, you know,' Dee says, suddenly becoming serious. 'I think about what my life might be like if I stayed at home. Every time there's a picture of me online with a nasty headline about my cellulite or the bags under my eyes or my bloody personal life, I think about how different it might all be if I had just stayed in Dublin with my friends.'

Lainey's mouth opens and air rushes out but no sound. I don't think she was prepared for an honest answer to her question.

'But then you wouldn't have Aoife,' I say.

Dee's face lights up just hearing her daughter's name.

'No. You're right. I wouldn't. And she really is the best part of me.'

The conversation is more rounded after that. There's reminiscing, some slagging of John Paul's receding hairline and some promises that we'll all make an effort to get together more. I listen, mostly. I hope they're serious about catching up regularly.

Dee pays for lunch.

'I insist,' she says, sliding the bill towards her before any of us can see how much it costs. I can only guess it's a lot. 'It's the least I can do after you travelled all this way.'

'We haven't come from outer space,' Lainey says, getting her back up again for no real reason. 'It's a fifty-minute flight.'

John Paul elbows her in the ribs again, and this time I think it hurts because she jerks away and tells him to fuck off.

It makes me sad. I realise the promises of regular catch-ups were just conversation filler. Time has let much too much water flow under the bridge.

Dee checks her watch and reaches for her bag. She apologises as she stands up. 'I have to pick Aoife up at three. But you guys should stay, move to the bar, have a few drinks.'

John Paul winces and I can tell the prices in a place like this worry him.

Dee passes me a credit card. 'Please, on me. I really am so sorry about earlier. I'm mortified, actually.'

'It was a nice gesture,' I say.

I mean it. I see that now. I hate that I've made her feel so bad. I take the card and pass it to John Paul.

'Get pissed, JP,' I say. 'You deserve it.'

'Aren't you staying?' Lainey asks.

I turn towards Dee. 'I thought I could go with you? Pick my niece up from school?'

Dee smiles. And Lainey smiles. But not at each other. I can't tell if Lainey is delighted at the prospect of free booze or insulted.

She stands up and tugs John Paul to his feet. 'Right,' she says, linking his arm. 'I bet the porn star martinis in here are a-maz-ing.'

'Thanks for today, Dee,' John Paul says. 'It really was the most amazing experience.'

'Yeah. Thanks,' Lainey says.

Before she leaves Dee walks round the table and hugs Lainey. Lainey is slow to let go of John Paul at first. But finally she wraps both her arms round Dee, and they sway on the spot for a moment.

'We really, really will catch up more,' Dee says.

'Yeah,' Lainey says, a little teary-sounding. 'I hope so.'

SEVENTY-FIVE

FIONN

There is security at the school gates. Private security. The type of guys you see escorting the royal family. I try not to smirk. Everyone drives and SUV of some sort. Range Rover, BMW, Mercedes. There are no Nissan Micras or Ford Fiestas in visible distance.

Dee parks her Range Rover Sport and clips the kerb. I tease her and she rolls her eyes.

'Wait here,' she says, hopping out. 'I'll just be a minute.'

I watch as she hurries towards the school gate like any regular mam running late. I wonder if all the other parents are famous. They're certainly rich.

Dee returns holding Aoife's hand. Aoife skips and jumps, jerking Dee's arm over and over. The back door of the car opens and Aoife climbs in. Dee secures her in her car seat and closes the door. It takes Aoife a moment to notice me in the front seat. But when she does, she throws her arms in the air and shrieks.

'O.M.G,' she says, sounding much too grown up for her eight years on this Earth. 'Uncle Fionn. I'm so, so, so happy you're here.'

She leans forward and offers me a lump of grey clay.

'It's an elephant,' she says, 'We made them in school but you can have it.'

'Where's his trunk?' Dee asks, hopping back into the driver's seat.

'Fell off.' Aoife shrugs, unfazed. 'Can we go to Donatellos? I'm starving.'

'What's Donatellos?' I ask.

'An Italian restaurant,' Dee says. 'It's Aoife's favourite. We go sometimes after school, it saves me cooking dinner later.'

'Wow. And here I was thinking every kid's favourite was McDonald's.'

Aoife doesn't say anything, but I see her make a horrified face in the mirror and poke her tongue out.

'How about we go to the park today instead?' Dee says.

Aoife makes the same face again and I don't blame her. It's close to freezing, and potentially snowing. The park does not sound appealing.

'Oh c'mon, you two. It'll be fun,' Dee says. 'Trust me.'

'Okay Mummy,' Aoife says.

'Okay,' I say, as Dee starts the engine and we drive away.

Dee turns on the radio, and we listen and don't talk as we make our way through barely moving traffic.

'She's asleep,' I say, after I follow the sound of gentle snoring and glance over my shoulder.

'It's the engine,' Dee says. 'She always falls asleep in the car. Do you remember when Seány would fall asleep in the back of your car?'

My heart skips.

'He would try so hard to stay awake, but he'd always drop off just before that last bend,' I say.

'Do you think Aoife looks like him?' Dee asks. She grips the wheel tighter as if she's nervous.

'I do,' I say. 'A lot.'

'Me too.'

We fall back into a natural silence and I stare out the window, taking in the sights of the city bursting with life and energy. Dee pulls up abruptly and asks me to stay in the car with Aoife as she hops out.

'Will just be a sec.'

I watch out the window as she buys some magazines from a stand on the street corner. She throws them onto the back seat next to where Aoife is sleeping and we continue our journey.

'Don't you want to know what the magazines are for?' she says, after a while.

'Reading?'

She laughs. 'Paper boats.'

My breath catches and for a moment I'm light-headed.

'There's a small lake at the park. I thought maybe we could make some paper boats and sail them. Aoife would love it. I would too, if I'm honest.'

I'm lost for words.

'Fionn?'

My mouth is open, but still nothing is coming out.

'Oh God, I haven't made this awkward again, have I? Shit, I'm sorry. I just... I saw the magazine stand and the idea sort of popped into my head. I thought it would be something really nice we could do together. But we don't have to.'

'It's a lovely idea. I'd like to make paper boats with Aoife.'

Dee sighs and I can sense her relief.

'I haven't made one in a very long time. So, God knows, they might be shite,' I say.

Dee's grip on the wheel relaxes, as does she. 'Don't worry,' she says. 'Aoife and I make them all the time. We can help you.'

I stare out the window again. Not because I want to view the city. But because I don't want Dee to see me cry.

SEVENTY-SIX

FIONN

Thankfully, Aoife is much better at making paper boats than clay elephants. At the park we rip pages from glossy magazines and fold and fiddle with the paper, creating multicoloured boat, after boat after boat. Aoife stumbles across an article about her mother in one of the magazines and stops to read it, grinning from ear to ear with pride. I take a photograph in my mind of a little girl's adoration for her famous mother and I hope I never lose the image.

Dee and Aoife are dressed more appropriately for the weather than me. They're wrapped in warm coats and hats and scarves. My leather jacket is doing a terrible job of keeping out the wind and my gloveless hands are blue. Dee offered me a pair of Oisín's gloves that were in her boot of her car, but I politely declined. Besides, I don't feel the cold when I'm with her.

Once we have a fleet as grand as the Spanish Armada, we agree it's time to set sail. It's trickier than we anticipated and most of our boats flop to one side or the other as soon as they hit the water. Aoife's are the noticeable champions and several of hers stay afloat.

'You have do it like this,' she tells me, taking one of my stash of boats. She crouches on her hunkers and lowers the boat in.

'See,' she says, when it obediently floats.

I kiss her forehead and she grins up at me.

'Keep trying, Uncle Fionn,' she says, 'You'll get good at it, if you keep trying.'

'Is that what your mam tells you?' I ask.

Aoife stands up. Her head is well above my elbow. She's tall for her age, just as Seány was.

'No. My daddy says so. He says you have to just try and try when things are hard.'

I close my eyes for a moment. I sometimes forget that Oisín is a part of Aoife, just as he was a part of Seány. Of course Aoife and Seány are so alike. Brothers and sisters often are. I wish she could have known Seány. I know she'd have liked him so very much. He made much better paper boats than me, for one thing.

'Your dad is very clever,' I say.

Aoife laughs, as if she doesn't agree with me at all. I laugh too.

'You're silly, Uncle Fionn,' she says, still giggling.

Dee has her camera pointed towards us.

'Are you recording?' I ask.

'Yes. I now have video evidence that you just said your brother is very clever.'

I roll my eyes playfully. 'Why do I get the feeling I'm going to regret that?'

Dee's eyes burn into me, heating me from the inside out.

'Aoife, sweetie, be careful,' she says, shifting her gaze from me to the water's edge.

I turn round to find one of Aoife's boats has flopped onto its side. She's hunkered down and trying to reach it with a twig. I scoop my arms round her waist and snatch her back from the edge of the lake so quickly and forcefully that I almost topple us both over.

'Get back. Get back,' I shout.

Aoife begins to cry.

'Don't you know water is dangerous. You could drown.'

'Fionn, you're scaring her,' Dee says. 'Put her down.'

'Water is dangerous,' I reiterate.

I'm shaking. Aoife is too. She wriggles and squirms against me.

'Mummy. Mummy. Mummy,' she calls out.

'Fionn,' Dee says firmly. 'Put her down.'

I snap out of it. The reality of my overreaction smacks hard.

'I'm sorry. I'm so sorry,' I say, as I ease her gently down. I let go when I feel her feet on the ground.

Dee opens her arms and Aoife runs straight into them, burying her face in her mother's chest and sobbing.

'I don't like Uncle Fionn any more,' she says.

'Shh. Shh,' Dee says.

'I'm sorry,' I repeat, my insides quivering as if I'm on some sort of rollercoaster that I can't get off. 'I didn't mean to scare her. I just... the water... and if she fell... I just... I got worried.'

Dee's eyes burn into me. She's upset. 'I think it's time to go home now,' she says.

'I want to go to Daddy's house,' Aoife says, still sobbing.

'Not today,' Dee says.

'I want Daddy.' Aoife cries harder.

'I know.' Dee sighs. 'I know.'

Dee takes Aoife by the hand and they walk back towards the car park. I follow like a scolded dog. Dee throws the remaining paper boats into the nearest bin. I think it will be a long time before Aoife wants to play with paper boats again, and for that I am truly sorry.

SEVENTY-SEVEN

DEE

Oisín was glad to get my call.

'I'll be home from work by seven. You can drop Aoife over then. Or I can pick her up?'

'No! No. Don't come here. I will drop her over. See you at seven.'

I had no plans to tell Oisín that Fionn was in town. Though after today, I realise that was a secret I was never going to be able to keep. I drop Aoife to the door of Oisín's flat, make uncomfortable small talk like never before and leave. I don't tell him about the incident in the park. But I've no doubt Aoife will. I almost asked her not to in the car on the way over, but I stopped myself just in time. Today was scary for her and she needs to talk about it. But today was scary for me too. I wasn't scared for Aoife. I knew Fionn was trying to protect her. He gave her a fright but she'll be fine. Today was scary because for the first time in a while I saw Fionn's old scars rise to the surface. I saw them when he sat next to me on the couch as we filmed. I saw them at lunch when he buttoned up and barely said two words. And I saw them when he bundled Aoife into his arms. I saw him the way I used to: vulnerable and exposed.

Fionn is still in the shower when I get home. I set about making dinner, although I'm a little rusty. I can't remember the last time I cooked a sauce that didn't have to be puréed to hide vegetables. I put some chunky chips in the oven, season two steaks and pop them on a hot pan, and I make pepper sauce from a packet that doesn't involve more effort than stirring in milk. I open a bottle of red wine and wait.

Fionn is out of the shower for a long time before he finally comes downstairs. He has dried his hair and it falls in soft curls around his face. There's quite a bit of grey running through it now. Almost a quarter, I'd say. It suits him.

'Wine,' I say, tilting my empty glass towards him.

'Sure.'

I pour him a large glass and pass it over, and I refill my glass.

We eat and drink and talk. It feels a lot like I'm interviewing him all over again. I ask questions and he answers. But he very rarely asks a question in return. I tell him about Oisín's battle with alcohol and how he's getting on at AA.

'It's like getting to know a new version of him,' I say. 'A really good version.'

Fionn smiles but he doesn't reply.

I tell him about work; upcoming projects and that sort of thing. And I tell him about Aoife's school and her friends and her hobbies.

Finally, when the wine has gone to my head, I stand up and say, 'Well, I better get this mess cleaned up before bed.'

Usually, I would load the dishwasher and be done in five minutes. But tonight I fill the sink and wash up by hand. Fionn stands up and I pass him a tea towel. I wash. He dries. We don't speak. The nostalgia is tangible and I've no doubt he feels it too. Washing up alongside Lainey and Lorna every evening that summer on Cloch Bheag is one of my most cherished memories. I hope he knows that.

All too soon I'm washing the last glass. I wipe the shelf and let the water out of the sink.

'Well, I better get to bed so...' I say, not feeling tired.

Fionn folds the tea towel and places it on the countertop. He doesn't speak.

'There's more wine there' – I point to the rack above the fridge – 'if you'd like to help yourself.'

Fionn glances to the top of the fridge and back to me, and, still, there are no words.

'Or TV. Feel free to watch whatever you like. There's some good stuff just out on Netflix.'

The silence is starting to consume us.

'Okay. Well. Goodnight, so.'

I turn, but before I can step away I feel Fionn's fingers curl round mine. I turn back. His eyes are round and glassy, and I know what he's going to say. I know he's waited all evening to say it.

'I'm sorry,' he says, 'I thought she was going to fall.'

'I know. I know.'

'I never meant to scare her.'

'I know that too.'

'I never meant to scare you.'

'I think you scared yourself the most,' I say, stepping closer to him. 'She was fine, she was standing well back and she had a stick.'

'Accidents happen in the blink of an eye, Dee.' He clicks his fingers. 'It would have just taken a split second for her to slip and...'

There's perspiration on his forehead and he's shaking slightly. I pour him a cup of water. He sips, and steadies. I wrap my arms round his shoulders and he doesn't budge. It feels as if he is made of glass, and I take care not to shatter him.

'She loves you, you know,' I say.

I can feel his heart racing. I keep talking. 'She talks about you all the time.'

It feels as if his heart might beat straight out of his chest.

'Have you ever thought about speaking to anyone? A counsellor, maybe.'

'Dee,' Fionn says, so quietly I almost didn't hear him.

'Um...'

'Can we not talk?'

'Erm.'

'Can we stay here. Just like this. And not say another word. For a while.'

I hold him a little tighter, and I don't open my mouth. I won't say another word. I'll hold him forever if he wants me to. And part of me hopes he does.

SEVENTY-EIGHT

FIONN

I press my lips on hers and close my eyes. Suddenly, I'm a nervous seventeen-year-old all over again. She tastes like wine and contentment. And then her lips are gone. I open my eyes and she's pulled away from me. She's looking at me with her mouth slightly open and her finger touches her mouth, where my lips just were.

'Fionn,' she says, shaking her head.

I can't find words. I can't tell her I'm sorry, because I'm not. I want to do it again. And more. I want all of her. I always have.

'It's the wine,' she says. 'We had too much wine.'

I look into her eyes. I look at how tiny flecks of green scatter through her blue irises as if someone took the time to dust her eyes with glitter.

'Fionn,' she says, again, but this time she's not shaking her head.

She steps closer. My breath hitches.

'Are you sure?' she says. 'After today...'

I cut her off with my mouth on hers. I feel her gasp. It rushes from her body and into mine and a shiver runs down my spine. I love her. I love her more than air, and sleep, and life itself.

Getting undressed is messy. It's awkward and embarrassing just as it was when we were teenagers. We lose pieces of clothing on the journey from the kitchen to the sitting room. Dee leads the way now. We stand at the edge of the couch for a long time. Kissing. Breathing. Savouring. I take my time. I press my body against hers and let the pleasure wash over me like the ocean lapping the shore. Every inch of me remembers her, like a sense I lost long ago that's finally returning. Her smell, her taste her touch; so familiar, so missed, so longed for.

Dee guides us onto the couch. She lies on her back and pulls me on top of her. When I finally push inside her I remember what it's like to be content. To feel genuine happiness. Nothing and no one else exists in this moment. It is Dee and me. The world is a separate thing and it can't touch us.

'Oh Fionn,' she says. 'Oh Fionn. Oh Fionn.'

SEVENTY-NINE

FIONN

There's a strange pattern in Dee's sitting room curtains. When the sun shines through it casts shadows on the carpet like waves, and I long for the freedom of the ocean. I didn't sleep. I didn't expect to. Dee offered me space in her bed last night, but I couldn't go there. Not to a bed she shared with Oisín. Instead, I lay awake all night in the spare room replaying the last twenty years. I focus on the details in the moments that brought us here.

The sun isn't up long when the doorbell rings. I wait to hear Dee stir and answer it. But the big, old house is silent expect for the odd creak or groan that gives away its age.

The doorbell rings again. And again. Finally, the knocker begins to rattle and an impatient little girl shouts. 'Mummy. Mummy, where are you?'

Dee's bedroom door opens and I hear her footsteps hurry down the stairs.

'I'm coming,' she calls out. 'I'm coming.'

There's panic in her voice. I sit up.

'What is it? What's wrong?' Dee says, and I imagine her opening the door.

I throw my legs over the side of the bed and pull on my clothes that I was sensible enough to gather up last night. I stop in my tracks and freeze when I hear a deep, male voice.

'Hey,' Oisín says.

'Hi,' Dee says, and I can hear her surprise to see him.

'Daddy said I can have the morning off school and we can go get pancakes instead,' Aoife says.

I try to stop listening. But their voices are loud and cumbersome. Something about Dee joining them. Aoife's favourite place nearby. And Oisín wanting raspberries and maple syrup.

I'm slipping on my shoes when there's a knock on the bedroom door. I open it to find Dee in a faded AC/DC t-shirt. Oisín was obsessed with AC/DC when I was a kid.

'Erm,' she says, as she pulls a bobbin off her wrist and ties up her hair. 'This is all a bit unexpected but Aoife and Oisín are here. They want to go for breakfast.'

I don't know what to say.

'Erm. You could join us?'

I shake my head. We both know nobody wants that.

'I think I need to go,' Dee says. 'I think it will be good for Aoife.'

'Okay.'

Dee tugs at the bobbin and lets her hair back down. She crosses her legs and crouches slightly so her t-shirt hangs a little longer. Her body language is stiff and awkward, and I can't tell if it's Oisín or me who has made her feel that way.

'You okay to hang on here by yourself? I won't be long. Aoife has school, so it's just a quick bite, really.'

'Go.' I nod. 'Enjoy breakfast with your family, Dee.'

Dee's face lights up.

'Thanks,' she says. 'Like I said, I won't be long and—'

'Go. Go,' I say. 'Hurry before all the best pancakes are gone.'

Dee relaxes and rolls onto her tiptoes; she slides her arms round my neck and whispers, 'Thank you.'

I'm frozen to the spot as I realise it was me, and not Oisín, making her uncomfortable. It. Was. Me.

I wait in my room until I hear the front door close. Then I pack my backpack and walk downstairs. In the kitchen, I look for a pen and some paper. Along the way I find bits and pieces that paint a picture of the life Dee and Oisín share. A family life. The electricity bill still in his name. Hairclips and cufflinks, side-by-side in a drawer, happily forgotten about after a night out together, no doubt. Some of Aoife's old artwork from when she was just a toddler. And a small paper boat fashioned out of shiny foil. Just like the ones Dad used to make from the inside of his cigarette box for Seány.

At last I find a pen and paper and I sit at the table to write.

Dear Dee-Dee,

I love you. I have loved you from the very first moment I saw you. Do you remember that day on the pier? You wore a red Nike jumper and navy tracksuit bottoms with poppers all down the sides. You were the most beautiful thing I had ever seen.
You are still the most beautiful thing. Inside and out. Aoife is so incredibly lucky to have a mother like you. I see so much of Seány in her. I can't tell you how happy it makes me to see some of his spirit back in the world. But I see so much of you in her too. What a lucky little girl.
You have a beautiful home, Dee. Thank you for allowing me to be a guest here. Thank you for being my friend for twenty years. Thank you for letting me love you. It has been a pleasure.
But you have a family now. And they have to come first. It's taken me a very long time to see that. Is that selfish? Probably.
I have a favour to ask, Dee-Dee. How dare I, right? I'm just some guy who keeps waltzing in and out of your life and I think I have the right to ask favours. But, please, if you do this one thing for me, I will never, ever, ever ask anything of you again.

Give Oisín another chance. He needs it, Dee. He's always needed someone to give him a chance. There is a great man in there, I promise. Get to know him sober. I know you'll like him. I did! I'm not asking you to do it for you. Or even for Aoife. I'm asking you to do it for him. Everyone deserves a family. As much as I love you, I can't be the man who comes between Oisín and his family. He won't come back from it a second time.

I love you, Dee-Dee. I always have and I always will.

Goodbye,

Fionn xx

I fold the paper, write Dee's name on the front and walk back upstairs. I place it on her pillow. I pause and take a deep breath. The smell of her perfume fills my lungs. Then I fetch my leather jacket from the back of the door in the spare room and I leave.

I don't belong in Dee's world. I think, perhaps, I never did. The time we had was special but it wasn't meant to be. It was some sort of strange fuck-up of the universe. The world spun off its axis and threw a couple of mismatched teenagers together. It's about time I grow up and cop the fuck on. Life is not a fairy tale. And, even if it was, I'm no prince. I wouldn't want to be. Dee is not a princess either. She is more than that. She is a mother, a daughter, a friend, a celebrity. A memory.

I will miss her. I will miss her more than air and more than the sea. I will miss her for eternity, but it's time to go home. The people I love are waiting for me. They have been for a long time. The wait is over now. It's all over now.

EIGHTY

FIONN

My phone rings. I don't answer when Dee's name appears. I don't answer the next call or the one after that. I spend the day moving from one coffee shop to another. I buy coffee or tea and I hold the cups to warm my hands, but I don't drink it. I meet John Paul and Lainey in the airport in the late evening. By then, I've fifteen missed calls and countless texts from Dee.

'Who's that?' John Paul asks, pointing at my phone. 'That bloody thing's been ringing all day.'

'It's nothing important,' I say.

'Where's Dee?' Lainey says. 'I thought she'd be with you to say goodbye. I still have her credit card.'

I expected to find John Paul and Lainey nursing hangovers, but they're both fresh-faced and better rested than I've seen them in quite some time. I doubt they used Dee's credit card at all. Lainey asks me to mind the card and give it to her the next time I see her.

I say, 'Yeah, okay.'

We go through security and Lainey buys a bottle of perfume in the duty free for John Paul's mother and some chocolates for Aisling. We're first in the queue to board the plane and we're first on.

'Did you enjoy the trip?' Lainey asks me, as we trundle down the runway.

I look out the window as we climb into the air. The lights of London below are beautifully breathtaking, and I've never been so glad to leave a place behind.

John Paul grips the edge of the seat. His knees twitch and his arms tremble.

'Fuck, I hate flying,' he says.

'How can you be so comfortable at sea but not in the air?' Lainey giggles.

'I can swim. I can't fly,' John Paul huffs. 'Back me up here, Fionn.'

I'm listening. I'm smiling. I'm drifting off to sleep.

'Fionn,' Lainey says.

'Um.'

'We have something to ask you?'

My eyes open. John Paul's twitching increases.

'Okay,' I say.

'You can say no,' Lainey says.

'Okay.'

'Because we don't want you to feel any pressure.'

'Okay.'

'But JP and I spent hours talking about it last night, and we really think it's a good idea.'

'Okay.'

'Jesus, Lainey,' John Paul says, steadying. 'Will you just spit it out, you're making Fionn as jumpy as me.'

'You *are* making me kind of nervous, Lainey,' I say.

Lainey giggles, awkwardly. 'Right,' she says, with a single clap of her hands. 'We want to open the house to Gaeltacht students again.'

'Okay,' I say.

'Okay,' Lainey repeats. 'That's it. Just okay?'

'Yes. That's it. Just okay.'

'So, you don't mind?' she says.

I shrug. 'Why would I mind?'

'Well, because... because of all the memories.'

'They're good memories, Lainey. I think it's a good idea.'

Lainey claps her hands again. 'Okay. Good. Great. Because if I can't have kids of my own, this is the next best thing, right? Maybe this is how it was supposed to be. It feels right, you know?'

I smile. I don't know. I can't honestly imagine what John Paul and Lainey have gone through over the years, trying and trying for a baby that never came. But if this makes them happy, then I am happy for them.

'I've one more favour to ask,' Lainey says, pulling her shoulders to her ears and holding them there as she looks at me sheepishly.

'Go on,' John Paul encourages her.

'Do you have the recipe for Lorna's apple tart?' Lainey says. 'It's just, Dee and I loved that apple tart so much when we stayed with your mam. And I'd like everything to be just as it was before.'

'I know the recipe,' I say.

I don't tell Lainey that no matter how hard she tries, no matter how delicious a tart she makes, nothing will ever be as it was before. And that's okay. Time changes everything and everyone. It's how it's supposed to be.

'God, Fionn. You're the best. You're going to make some woman very bloody happy someday, do you know that?'

Lainey leans in and kisses my cheek and I write the recipe on a napkin and pass it to her.

Her face lights up and she folds it and places it into her handbag. 'I can't wait for this summer,' she says. 'It's going to be great.'

'Yeah,' John Paul agrees, kissing his wife's cheek. 'I think so too.'

John Paul and Lainey's happiness reaches out to me and wraps its arms round me like a warm hug. I hope their summer is great. I hope it's the first of many, many great summers for two people I love so much.

EIGHTY-ONE

FIONN

It snows on Christmas Eve. Lainey spent all of December wishing for a white Christmas. I am happy her wish came true. The falling snow makes the roads slippery and I take it handy as I drive towards the port. The heater in the car stopped working about ten years ago and I've never had time to fix it. I wrap myself up in the old blanket from the boot and try to ignore how my fingers ache, gripping the freezing wheel.

I park it in the usual spot, where the mouth of the road is widest and there is plenty of room for cars to pass by. The sky is clear and the moon is huge. It tugs the waves with a heave-ho and I listen as they break on the shore before being dragged back. I take off my shoes and leave them in the car. I peel off Seány's blankets, fold them and place them back in the boot. Then I walk. Across the long grass at the edge of the road. Across the cold, damp sand. Across stones and shells. And finally, the water hits my toes. My knees. My waist. It's not cold. It's home. I am finally home.

EIGHTY-TWO

DEE

It's Christmas Day. Oisín and Aoife are in the sitting room. I'm in the kitchen peeling potatoes and singing along to my Michael Bublé playlist. My phone rings. I expect to see Mam's name flash up. My parents sent Aoife a purple unicorn that says *Je t'aime* when you press its tummy. Aoife is much too grown up for talking teddies, but she hugged him and said she loved his accent.

I'm surprised when I see Lainey's name on my phone. I let it ring for a moment, deciding whether or not to answer. I tilt my head and secure the phone between my ear and shoulder as I keep peeling the potatoes, and I chirp, 'Hello. Happy Christmas.'

'He's gone, Dee,' Lainey says. 'Fionn is gone. He died this morning.'

I cut myself, then. The peeler slices my thumb and blood trickles against a big, yellow spud. Michael Bublé sings about a white Christmas as it starts to snow outside.

'Dee,' Lainey says, and I can hear her tears. 'Dee, are you there?'

I exhale. It's all I can manage.

'I'm sorry,' Lainey says. 'I know how much you loved him. How much he loved you. I should have done more to help you be together but I was too busy being a jealous bitch.'

Maybe I should comfort Lainey. Maybe I should tell her that it's not her fault that we grew up. Grew apart. Life dealt us all different cards. And Fionn's hand was too much for him to bear anymore. Maybe I should say he's with Seány now, because it's what I'm thinking. Hoping. But instead the words, 'It's Christmas,' tumble out. As if no one should leave this world on Christmas Day.

I don't know if Lainey says goodbye or if I do, but my phone is face down on the countertop and Oisín is holding my hand.

'Oh God, what happened?' he says. 'This might need a stitch, Dee. It looks deep.'

I stare at him, and into the eyes he shares with his brother.

'Dee, are you okay? You're as pale as a ghost. Come. Sit.'

My Michael Bublé playlist comes to an end as we sit at the kitchen table. Aoife's unicorn repeats *Je t'aime* over and over and over as she plays with him in the next room. It's all so normal. So mundane. And yet, nothing will ever be normal again.

I can't say it out loud. Not at first. And when I finally manage to say, 'Fionn is dead,' each word cuts like a blade.

Oisín's mouth parts a little, and air rushes out. There is a moment where neither of us move. Or breathe. Or blink. A moment when life as we knew it ends.

Oisín cries. Loud, angry, salty tears stream down his cheeks. Aoife comes to investigate and Oisín breaks the news. Then she climbs into his arms and they rock back and forth and he tells her that he loves her. Aoife cries as I've never seen her cry before. No hugs, or treats or talking unicorns, can fix her pain this time.

I don't cry. I put potatoes in the oven, I check on the turkey and I make gravy. I don't cry. My parents call. At some point

Aoife chats to them about all the toys Santa brought, or Father Christmas, as the kids in her class call him. She thanks them for her French unicorn. I don't cry.

'You're very welcome, sweetheart,' Mam says. 'Now, can you put your mammy on please?'

'Mum, Nanna wants you,' Aoife says, in a sing-song voice as she passes me her iPad.

I tell my parents about Fionn. I don't cry.

'Oh Jaysus,' Dad says. 'Pass on our deepest condolences to Oisín, won't you?'

And Mam says, 'I didn't know Oisín had a brother.'

'You remember him, Bernie,' Dad tells her. 'The younger chap. Still lives on that island.'

'Oh, the boy with the boats,' Mam says, as if a lightning bolt jogs her memory.

The call ends and I whisper, '*The boy with the boats.*' And then, I cry and cry and cry.

It's late now; maybe not even Christmas Day anymore. It's too dark outside to see if it's still snowing but I like to think it is. Oisín put Aoife to bed hours ago. We hugged for a long time and then he went home. I haven't left the spot on the couch since. The space where I made love to Fionn a couple of weeks ago and thought everything would finally be different. I guess now it will.

My eyes sting, and sometimes I think I have no more tears. And yet, they come. I thought my heart broke when Seány died. And then again when my parents moved away. More recently when I thought I couldn't make my relationship with Oisín work. Or when Fionn walked away from loving me for a third time. But my heart was only bruised before. Battered and dented. Now, on Christmas Day, with Fionn no longer in this world it is finally shattered into a million pieces.

The boy with the boats has finally broken my heart.

EIGHTY-THREE

DEE

Three Years Later

'It's small and smoky. And what's all that brown stuff?' Aoife says as she points at the ferry and scrunches her nose, unimpressed.

'It's rust,' I say.

'Isn't that dangerous? Will we sink?'

'It hasn't sunk in the last twenty years. I think we'll be fine.'

'Do we really have to stay all summer?' Aoife jams her hands on her hips.

'All summer.'

'Ugh, Mum. I'm going to be sooooo bored. It's an island. What is there to even do there?'

'You'd be surprised.'

'All just because this Elaine lady is having a baby.' Aoife rolls her eyes.

'Lainey,' I say.

'Why can't she get someone else to help her with the Irish-language students?'

'Because she asked me. And I need the break.'

'You call this a break? Why couldn't we just go to the Maldives? Maddison is going to the Maldives.'

'Well, I'm not Maddison's mother now, am I?'

As soon as I hear my own mother pass my lips, I laugh.

'It's not funny,' Aoife moans. 'Why couldn't I have just stayed with Dad?'

I stop laughing. 'Because your father is drinking a bit too much at the moment.'

'Maddison says he's an alcoholic.'

'Maddison needs to mind her own business,' I say.

'This is going to be the worst summer ever,' Aoife says. 'There better be Wi-Fi. I will literally die if the Wi-Fi is crap.'

I pick up my small case, and she picks up her very large one, and we drag them behind us onto the ferry. A bunch of island kids are sitting on the wall when we arrive. I count them. Two boys and three girls. I catch Aoife's smile from the corner of my eye.

'Don't even think about it,' I say. 'Mainland girls do not mix with island boys.'

'What?'

'It's forbidden,' I say.

It's hard to keep a straight face, as I secretly hope Aoife makes wonderful friends here.

'I know, I know,' Aoife says. 'The boy with the boat broke your heart.'

'Yes. He did,' I say, 'and I wouldn't change a second of it.'

A LETTER FROM THE AUTHOR

Huge thanks for reading *The Promise of Forever*. I hope you were hooked on Dee's and Fionn's journeys. If you want to join other readers in hearing all about my new releases and bonus content, you can sign up for my newsletter!

www.stormpublishing.co/brooke-harris

If you enjoyed this book and could spare a few moments to leave a review, that would be hugely appreciated. Even a short review can make all the difference in encouraging a reader to discover my books for the first time. Thank you so much!

The summer I turned fourteen, my best friends and I headed to a small island off the coast of Donegal for three weeks. It was Irish college and our parents thought it would be good for us. The deal was, from the moment you set foot on the Irish-speaking island, and for the three weeks you were a student there, you couldn't speak a word of English or you'd be sent home. When your parents had forked out quite a few quid for you to be there, getting sent home was pretty much a sin. I was dreading it, I won't lie. Why would anyone want to spend their school holidays in school? And not just regular school, Irish-speaking school. My Irish was shockingly poor and I was fine with that.

Little did I know that as we sailed away from the coast of Donegal and towards Árainn Mhóir that I was about to make some of the best memories of my life. There was Céilís and long walks, cars without bonnets, swimming in the sea, making friends, kissing boys, perfecting dance routines in a time before TikTok (I could have been famous, I tell you).

I returned every summer throughout my teenage years. Back to the same house with the same wonderful Bean an Tí. My heart truly broke when I heard of her passing a few years ago. She took such wonderful care of us.

I even managed to pick up fluency in Irish over the summers (totally accidently, but my parents were delighted – money well spent, eh?).

Around about the same age, back in regular old English speaking school, I studied the poem 'Mid-Term Break' by Seamus Heaney. I'm painting myself as a very studious young lady here; unfortunately, much to my mother's disappointment I can confirm I was not. See paragraph above re boys 😏. However, this poem had a powerful and long-lasting impact on me. The poet shares his grief when his younger brother was knocked down by a car and passed away. I can still recite the entire poem line-by-line. The impact of the last line will never cease to hurt my heart. Google it, trust me.

I guess somewhere over the years, my love for the Gaeltacht and 'Mid-Term Break' came together to create this story. Fionn and Dee are purely figments of my imagination. But they could be any of the kids who flock to the Gaeltacht island every summer and fall in love with the crystal-blue waters, windy roads and a sleepy island that never seems to fully wake. I gave a piece of my heart to Árainn Mhóir when I was just a kid and I am so, so very glad I did.

Thanks again for being part of this amazing journey with me and I hope you'll stay in touch. Feel free to find me online. I love nothing more than chatting books with my readers!

Brooke x

 twitter.com/Janelle_Brooke

instagram.com/janelle.brooke.harris

ACKNOWLEDGMENTS

Writing is a strange business; you spend so much time alone with your characters and their story that when you find your way back to reality it can be slightly disorientating. In that way, I am a lot like Fionn. His friends helped steady his sea legs when he returned to shore. So too, my team help steady me after months of writing. And I am very lucky to have a wonderful team around me.

To my wonderful editor, Emily – for loving this book as much as I do. Thank you!

Thank you to my lovely agent, Hannah at Madeleine Milburn; a powerhouse behind the scenes.

Thank you, Emma O'Neill, for your eagle eye – you've some talent. Wine and coffee on me for a while. 🌝

To Padár O'Loughlain @BurtonBoats. Your vast knowledge and insight about all things boats and fishing was invaluable. I am so grateful, sir. Any errors or misrepresentation (and a little poetic licence) are entirely my doing.

Leona, Annette, Tara, Jo, Sheila and Donna, thank you for reading an early (and slightly messy) copy of this book, and for not hating it. Your support means so much.

To my fellow writer and dear friend Caroline Finnerty. Our walks and coffee chats are a saving grace. Thank you for being the sounding board I so badly need. Vino soon, yes?

To Susan Brennan and Laura McPartland – thank you so incredibly much for dragging me (somewhat reluctantly) to the Gaeltacht all those summers ago. Those summers will forever remain some of my most cherished memories. What fun we had, eh?

My family, I love you!

And lastly, dear reader, without you none of this is possible. I am so grateful that you bought this book and I hope, so very much, you enjoyed reading it as much as I enjoyed writing it. Thank you, thank you!

Made in the USA
Monee, IL
16 January 2024